TRUE

TRUE

RIIKKA PULKKINEN

Translated from the Finnish
by Lola M. Rogers

OTHER PRESS

New York

Production Editor: *Yvonne E. Cárdenas*
Text Designer: *Cassandra J. Pappas*
This book was set in 11.25 pt Sabon MT by Alpha Design &
Composition of Pittsfield, NH.

10 9 8 7 6 5 4 3 2 1

Library of Congress Cataloging-in-Publication Data

Pulkkinen, Riikka, 1980–
[Totta. English]
True / by Riikka Pulkkinen ; translated by Lola M. Rogers.
  p. cm.
ISBN 978-1-59051-500-6 (trade pbk.) — ISBN 978-1-59051-501-3
(ebook)
  1. Women—Family relationships—Fiction. 2. Cancer—
Patients—Fiction. 3. Family secrets—Fiction. 4. Domestic
fiction. I. Rogers, Lola. II. Title.
PH356.P85T6813 2012
894'.54134—dc22

2011047118

All sorrows can be borne if you can put them into a story
or tell a story about them.

—ISAK DINESEN (Karen Blixen)

Maybe I'm daydreaming.
She makes me think of music.
Her face . . .
We're living in the age of the double man.
We no longer need mirrors to talk to ourselves.
When Marianne says "It's a beautiful day," what is she
   thinking about?
All I have is that image of her saying "It's a beautiful day."
Nothing else. Is there any point in figuring this out?
We are made of dreams and dreams are made of us.
It's a beautiful day, my love—in dreams, in words, in death.
It's a beautiful day, my love—a beautiful day in life.

—JEAN-LUC GODARD, *Pierrot le Fou* (1965)

1

A WOMAN WAS RUNNING toward him.
Martti had had the same dream many times. The woman was just about to say something, and he was on the verge of comprehending. He never managed to hear what she was trying to say; he always woke up before comprehension came.

He woke up again. His eye fell on the clock on the night table.

01:20.

Elsa was sleeping beside him. Her breathing was slightly labored, but no more so than when she was healthy. Martti had been able to fall asleep, even though at bedtime he had felt like he didn't dare close his eyes.

This was Elsa's first night at home in more than two weeks.

At first he had opposed her coming home, not because he didn't want his wife beside him—on the contrary, Elsa belonged here. She had been here for more than fifty years. But he was afraid that he would wake up one morning and find her dead beside him, her feet gone cold.

I'm rotting, she had said to him a week ago in the hospice, like a call for help. Don't let me rot. I want to go home.

So in the end they arranged it.

IT HAD BEEN only six months since Elsa got sick. In December Martti remarked that she had dwindled to half her previous size. She weighed herself at the spa and made an appointment with the doctor.

It's nothing, she said. Nothing at all, Martti said. Elsa wiped the worry from his face with a kiss.

Everything happened quickly—the examination, the biopsy, the diagnosis.

Martti cried on the way home from the hospital after the hardest news. Elsa was quiet, squeezing his hand the whole way, even in the elevator.

They stood in the entryway for a long time, leaning against each other. A Christmas star in the window, afternoon dusk in the room.

Let's have a really good Christmas, Elsa said. Just in case.

Eleonoora came with her family on Christmas day. Elsa hadn't had the heart to tell her yet.

But Eleonoora guessed—it was the kind of thing a doctor notices. It started right away—her worry, which to the less observant could seem like bossiness. Elsa didn't take any notice of her instructions, she just said, as she had to Martti, Let's enjoy Christmas.

It was a happy Christmas, in spite of everything. On Christmas Eve they went skating, and on Boxing Day they skied. Elsa was surprised at her strength, ate half a chocolate bar and slid down the hills as sprightly as a girl.

The treatments started at the beginning of the year. They only gave her the cytostatins for a few weeks, a month. Then they used the phrase "palliative care." That meant hospice. This time Elsa cried.

Martti tried to be strong and keep up his hopes. He asked her what she wanted to do.

We could drive somewhere, she said. We could just drive off into the dusk, without any destination, listen to music like we always do on road trips.

They had gone driving every evening now, since the end of February. The spring was light pink and pale yellow, like every spring. Elsa often urged him to drive slower so that she could see the sky better. The clouds moved across the sky like big buildings. At the beginning of March, in a parking lot in Lauttasaari, they heard a blackbird singing.

They sat there for a long while, with the lights off, in the dark, listening to the blackbird.

It's surprising how little there is to fear, Elsa said.

No, there's nothing to be afraid of, Martti answered.

BUT THAT WAS a lie. Martti was afraid of the nights, those nights when he would wake up alone from a dream that he couldn't get hold of. He was afraid he would wake up beside her and she wouldn't be breathing anymore.

Maybe Eleonoora feared that, too, because she had firmly opposed Elsa coming home.

Believe me, I know what to expect, she had said, when they were left alone together for a moment after a treatment consultation. I can't do it alone, and neither can you. And we can't expect the girls to look after her. It's too much to ask. They're hardly more than children.

Eleonoora's worry was certainly different than Martti's. Her sadness would be different, too, when the time came. But still, he wondered at her attitude. It was impossible to know anything about her but what he could see: meticulousness, an almost expressionless determination on her face.

More and more Martti was seized with a thought that had troubled him ever since Eleonoora became an adult: this woman had stolen his daughter from him, she was hiding the pigtailed, smiling Ella somewhere deep within her pragmatism. If Martti could just find some magic word from her childhood years, and say it, Eleonoora would be Ella again, jumping up and down in the doorway, grinning at her own reflection in the mirror, and they would go and get some ice cream.

The final decision about home care was made when Eleonoora's daughters themselves offered to help. She questioned both of them, told them in unvarnished detail what it was like to take care of a dying person.

I'm not afraid, Maria said without hesitation. Although she was the younger of the two, she seemed more mature than Anna. Anna had a moodiness about her. Martti recognized it as his own: he had once been sensitive in the same way. But in spite of her uncertainty Anna nodded decisively when Eleonoora asked her about helping.

In the last few weeks, Elsa had been doing better. She had a new pain medication, stronger than the others. It worked, but the doctor had said that it could cause disorientation and immobility.

Martti had panicked at the possibility that she could be disoriented and asked the doctor outright: how much longer? How many weeks?

Don't focus on the weeks, the doctor answered. There will be good days and bad days. There's tremendous variation in these illnesses. She may be almost symptom free at times.

Martti contented himself with what the doctor had said. He watched Elsa, putting all his hope in those three words: almost symptom free.

THE HOSPITAL BED and other equipment had been brought the day before.

Two taciturn men rang the doorbell, brought the metal contraption in as if they were delivering a table or a sofa, and put it together in the bedroom. Then came the IV equipment—which had been ordered just in case—and diapers, lying coyly in the corner in a cardboard box. The medications were in packets on the dresser.

"Splendid," Elsa said from the bed. "More splendid than any hotel I've been in."

"Glad you like it."

"But," she said, lowering her voice as if she thought the movers were still outside the door listening and she didn't want to offend them, "I still intend to sleep with you."

"Yeah? If you want."

Elsa glanced disapprovingly at the box of diapers in the corner.

"I intend to take care of my own business, of course," she said briskly.

"They're just here in case we need them," he heard himself say.

The role of the infirm was difficult for Elsa. She was used to being the caregiver. She had always taken care of others, to the point of exhaustion. That was a psychologist's job. Martti remembered the time when Elsa changed irrevocably from a girl to a woman: during those years when she defended her doctoral thesis and was offered a position in an international research group.

MARTTI LAY IN bed without moving. Elsa didn't waken. 01:25.

The dream hovered above him. It was a dense quilt, woven from time.

He got up and went to the window.

Some nights when he woke up from this dream, the sorrow weighed on him like a lid. He was under the lid, couldn't breathe. I'm not going to make it through this, he thought. If I feel like this now, what will I feel when Elsa's really gone?

In the end he found a way to calm himself. He would go to the window, open it, look at the sky, listen to the blackbird.

The sadness came and he let it come, felt it, as if getting to know it. He found it in the position of his hand, half reaching out. He had to make room for the sadness, to take it in his arms. Otherwise it would come as a dread, sudden and unexpected, on the corner as he was crossing the street or in the store when he was picking out mandarins or potatoes.

At those moments it was sheer panic.

Now, as he held the sadness, Martti was almost happy. The swallows had come early this year, they'd been carrying on boisterously since springtime. Up and down, up and down they flew, their voices filling the air. He stood at the window for a minute, another, letting the languor spread. The sound of the swallows was not in the sky but within him; there was no clear line between himself and the world outside.

These were the first moments in many years that Martti had thought he might be able to paint: the sky, the swallows, the light floating in the room.

He'd never grieved the end of his working days. He had been happy even without working. His studio in the garret, the building's lone tower, was still there. It was like a museum. Now and then he went up there, sat in the armchair, watched the sunset, opened the window, smoked. Last year he had given an interview to the monthly supplement of *Helsingin Sanomat*. The photos had been backlit. *A visionary in a tireless search for the perfect scene.* Actually he had regretted the interview a little afterward. He had succumbed to pomposity and then tried to make up for his grandiloquence with self-deprecation, but the humor had been lost in the final version of the interview. What was left was the true statement: *Art evades its maker just as reality evades us all.*

When he thought about his career he often noticed that he considered his most esteemed works and his highest achievements banal. It was as if he had spent his whole life tinkering with a sand castle.

Maybe it was this childishness that had kept him from mixing colors or stretching canvases, or even sketching on paper, doing anything to get started working.

He went up to the attic once in a while, sat and watched the changing light, melting from minute to minute into the corners, the silence.

That was just how the need to paint used to come to him, when he had the feeling that he was pure perception. Some people called it inspiration, but it was something much plainer, much more natural than that.

He was often asked about it in interviews. Journalists and biographers and exhibit curators presented the question as if they were asking about the existence of God.

He remembered how once in the sixties, sitting at a table on a damp evening, he had told a curator, just to amuse himself, "There's nothing mystical about it. I give up myself, and get the world in return."

Now he had that feeling on those evenings when he sat at the window looking at the sky and the swallows. He was pure perception, pure gaze.

But the dream wouldn't let go of him, and that surprised him.

At first he had pushed the thought out of his mind. But when the dream kept coming back, he started to have doubts. The feeling was just a glimmer, something like a scent, as elusive as the mental image you have of a person when you've met them a few times and don't yet know them but you start to think about them unconsciously.

When he woke from these dreams it was as if he could hear a smile, the sound of it floating above him.

Now he let the thought come. The woman in the dream wasn't Elsa.

2

ELEONOORA WOKE UP and saw the edge of the night table.

She closed her eyes again, and again saw her mother, the way her mother had been when she was quite young. She was swinging. It was the middle of summer, they were at the Sampo playground, her mother had kicked off her shoes and was picking up speed. Eleonoora was six years old, amazed at her mother's rambunctiousness, laughing at it. Her mother's hair was long.

It was strange how long her hair was. It had really grown, in spite of the doses of cytostatins in January. Hair growth can be a sign of remission, she thought. She should mention it to the attending physician.

Eleonoora opened her eyes again. She might slip back into the dream by wishing it, or she could wake up, make her way along the outer contours of the bedroom, guided by the edge of the night table, the digital numbers on the clock. But she wanted to see her mother again, young and healthy. She closed her eyes.

The playground returned. The stickiness of strawberries she'd just eaten returned to her hands. She was wearing red sandals that chafed one ankle. They were spending the day on Suomenlinna Island. There was a basket full of sticky dishes and one warm, uneaten chocolate pudding. She needed to pee. Her mother's pumps lay on the ground. She was laughing. Eleonoora was a little worried. She thought: mothers shouldn't be allowed to swing fast.

Now her mother had shorter hair, darker. She slowed her speed and got up from the swing, smiling.

Were you afraid I'd take off? she asked. Eleonoora nodded. My little girl, her mother said, and smiled tenderly. Don't be afraid. I'm staying here. I'm not going anywhere, and she bent over to put on her shoes.

Eleonoora could see bruises on her back. Blue marks the size of plates, yellowing at the edges.

You shouldn't swing if you have bruises like that, Eleonoora scolded. Now that she was scolding, she was an adult. Her mother must be protected, she thought. In spite of everything, she's more fragile than she lets on. When she thought this, she was six again.

She woke up. The clock read 01:20. She lay for a moment without moving. Eero breathed beside her.

It was at moments like this that the terror came. Night was a well. It was the terror of childhood, the same terror that would wake her when she was twelve, struggling between childhood and adulthood. It had no name then, it was just a formless dread. Now its message was clear: I will soon be motherless. Orphaned.

The word bounced around the room. Eero's heavy breathing as he slept made it even harder to bear.

01:21

Eleonoora waited, breathed.

01:22

Eero rolled onto his side, still sleeping. She wouldn't get up yet. She was hungry, but it wasn't really hunger, more like a kind of absence—a hunger that had lasted for weeks.

She had started weighing herself to make sure she didn't get too thin. She was preparing for the grief, grieving ahead of time by forgetting to eat. Her mother's daily shrinking presence made her appetite disappear, too. Or maybe it was a way to protect those weeks, to seal this short period of time within boundaries, to pay with lack of sleep and lack of food for some of her mother's pain.

The living know nothing of death, but dying, its stealthy inevitability, comes into the lives of the living. Time slows, reality is given walls of grief within which the dying and those who accompany them perform their rituals of devotion.

Each of them developed their own role in caring for her. Eleonoora held everything together, handling communications with the doctor and home health-care workers and making sure that everyone ate, slept, and got out enough. Eero was a loyal helper when needed. Anna, for her part, watched everything from a distance as if she were writing down every feeling that hovered in the air. Eleonoora's father was sometimes crushed with sadness and sometimes overly jolly, as if they weren't even dealing with a death, but something more like a summer vacation.

Maria took care of everything fearlessly, asking frequently about her grandmother's condition.

Maria was a crisis person. She was in her first year of medical school. Sometimes Eleonoora thought Maria would be a better doctor than she was.

Eleonoora had never been more businesslike. She had always had too much worry in her. Faced with her mother's illness, she erupted in rules and instructions. When she was a child it had been a generalized feeling, in her early teens it made her look under her bed and check the stove in the kitchen again and again.

Anna, it seemed to Eleonoora, had learned to worry from her. It had been her predominant characteristic, especially in the last few years, along with her earnestness.

The previous May, Eleonoora had found Anna lying on the floor of her studio apartment. She still didn't know what exactly had happened. Had something been going on for years that no one had told her about?

Anna's friend Saara had called her, sounding worried, and Eleonoora had realized that she hadn't heard from Anna in more than a week. Anna lived in a small studio on Pengerkatu, led a busy student's life, and sometimes they wouldn't call each other for a week at a time. Eleonoora had thought that Anna was busy with tests, evening walks, glasses of wine.

She had sometimes said, out loud, that she didn't know what was happening in Anna's life.

I live a different kind of life than you do, Anna had said nonchalantly. I live in a different world. Eleonoora let the matter go and didn't ask her any more about it.

Saara's call in May and Anna's days of silence nevertheless alarmed her. She tried to call Anna again and again, but there was no answer. Finally she drove over to her building. She rang the doorbell for ten minutes. A series of sad, grisly possibilities flashed through her mind. She dug the spare key that Anna had given her out of her bag and pushed it into the lock.

The apartment door struck something soft on the floor; Anna sat up and looked at her in an indifferent daze. She looked like she'd been asleep. Her hair was unwashed and disheveled, her skin pale.

"What are you doing here?" Anna said.

"What's happened to you?" Eleonoora asked, transfixed.

Anna shrugged her shoulders, stood up, looked past her, out into the hallway.

Eleonoora looked over Anna's shoulder into the room. It looked empty. There were spaces on the bookshelf, photographs missing from the wall. Had someone been living there, someone who had taken their things away with them? Or had Anna simply rearranged? The same strange photo of Anna that looked from a distance like an oil painting, like Gallen-Kallela's Aino walking into the water, still hung between the shelf and the sofa. The photo had been taken by a man Anna was dating for a while. Eleonoora had never liked the picture; she didn't recognize the woman in the photo as her daughter. Pale, solemn, stepping into the water, a completely different person than the one she had raised, the one who had giggled over her morning porridge on dreamy Sunday mornings, the one she had soothed in the night after a bad dream.

A child is born, a mother learns to know the child, learns little by little, year by year. And then another person comes along and the child changes under their influence and turns into a stranger.

Eleonoora had never got to know the man who took the photograph. She had met him a few times, but she couldn't really say that she knew much about him. He had a child: Linda. Linda had sometimes spent time with Anna. Eleonoora remembered a summer day several years before. Anna and the little girl had been at her house. Ice cream, rhubarb pie, whooping it up in the wading pool. The child had bangs and earnest, trusting eyes. She had fallen asleep in Anna's arms, sunk into a deep sleep while a nightingale sang. Eleonoora could see her own feelings from decades before, when a child was sleeping in her arms, reflected in Anna's face—love so overwhelming that there was a touch of pain in it.

ON THAT DAY in May, Anna stood before her with a different look on her face—defeated, humbled.

Eleonoora asked a few baffled, clarifying questions.

"How long has it been since you went out?"

"I don't know. A week or two."

"Why didn't you call me?"

Anna shrugged her shoulders again. "I wasn't up to it. I couldn't get up." Then she looked at her mother and, as if marveling at her own train of thought, said, "I was lying on the floor."

She started to cry. It started with one tear and spread to the rest of her body. Eleonoora held her in her arms, not knowing what else to do. There they stood.

Eleonoora said the nursery rhyme for hurts, their own shared rhyme of consolation, the one that her mother had said to her when she was a child. Whenever Eleonoora hurt herself her mother would take her in her arms and say the rhyme in a low voice. The last time Eleonoora had whispered it in her daughter's ear was when she was less than ten years old. But still the words came, she still remembered them. Anna listened and finally relaxed a little.

"The bee rhyme. I had forgotten all about that."

AT FIRST ELEONOORA had been afraid that Anna's grief wouldn't pass. She had made a mental diagnosis of depression and gingerly encouraged Anna to seek help. In the end, she let the matter drop.

Now and then a young person's heart is made of lead. It accumulates weight from random experiences; anything can add to its density, slip it out of joint. But it can lighten again just as easily, forget its troubles.

And that's what happened. Anna had Matias now, with his worn-out T-shirts, his store of a hundred gentle expressions and only one angry one. She had moved in with him almost immediately, just a month after they met.

When she visited Anna and Matias's house, Eleonoora noticed a wistful tinge under the happiness. Where had the years gone? When had she become so old that her daughter had her own home with a lovely boyfriend, offered her a piece of apple pie on a plate that she herself had received as a wedding gift more than twenty years ago? She saw a hint of trying too hard in Anna's happiness, as if she wanted to impress her with its authenticity.

01:32

Eero rolled onto his side. Eleonoora got up. She felt dizzy, her legs felt shaky.

She took the scale out of the cabinet and weighed herself. Fifty-one kilos. She hadn't weighed that little since she was breastfeeding. She ordered herself to eat a chocolate pudding on top of her regular breakfast. She looked at Eero, wished he would wake up, see how pitiable she was, and take her in his arms.

She stood for a moment in the chilly darkness, her ribs sharp against the paleness of the night.

Eero had pulled his knees up toward his chest and put his hand between his thighs as he always did. Something about his sleeping, his trusting presence, gave Eleonoora an unbearable feeling. It felt like vexation mixed with love. When her mother died Eleonoora would still have this family for whom she must necessarily survive.

There would be evenings, nights like this one. Spring would come. Eero would be his old steadfast self. She would get through it. Gradually she would start to laugh again. That was what was unbearable. She didn't want to. She wanted to cry, she wanted to build a cradle and put the rest of her life in it to cry, orphaned.

Eleonoora put the scale back in the cabinet and wrapped her robe around herself again. Her head hurt, her back ached.

She closed the bedroom door behind her, tiptoed across the hall, stopped at the door to Maria's room, and listened for a moment. No sound. Suddenly she had to open the door, to see Maria, if only for a moment.

The predawn moment, the dream of her mother swinging, the dread—all of it made Eleonoora feel that childhood uncertainty about what is true.

Maria was, at least. She lay on her side with a pillow between her knees, her blanket kicked to the floor. Her thighs glowed in the dimness, her mouth was open, her hair bunched up around her face.

She made a smacking sound with her mouth in her sleep.

It seemed almost comical to Eleonoora that a couple of decades ago she had pushed Maria out into the world—this woman with her farmhand's arms and husky laugh that filled the space around her.

Last summer Maria and her grandma, Eleonoora's mother, had washed rugs at the seashore. Her mother had still been strong then, there was no sign of the illness. Maybe it was already wending its way through the corridors of her organs. But she hadn't known about it yet, had lifted the wet rugs onto the drying racks, turned the crank, laughed when the water splashed.

That fall she gave her annual series of lectures at the university. Although she'd been retired for years, she hadn't stopped working. She still had an office in the department. Year after year her lectures drew several hundred listeners. They all wanted to hear the esteemed psychological researcher, to share in her wisdom.

The titles of the lectures were variations on her best-known book, *Recognition and Self.* The book had been a tremendous success when it was published. People had tried to make her into a lap for the whole of society to sit on, a motherly emissary of love.

Eleonoora had gone to hear some of her lectures. Her favorite moments with her mother were when they drove home after a lecture, her mother laying her head against the window and sighing good-naturedly, but with a hint of exhaustion.

"The science doesn't interest anyone. People come to these things to hear tidings of joy."

She didn't say it with disappointment, just a bit of resignation, gently, like a weary queen.

"Don't underrate yourself. They are tidings of joy. You deliver us from evil. Mothers, fathers, children—you give them permission to be happy."

She smiled a little.

"Why do they always need someone else to say it?"

Eleonoora had always been proud of her mother's success. She remembered from her childhood the busy evenings before her mother's trips, and when her mother came home, her own tears, a kind of frantic desire to own her, to be part of her, such unconditional love and admiration that she felt the longing even when her mother was with her.

Last summer Elsa had thrown a seventieth-birthday party. Her research colleagues from over the years were there. An interview given at the party carried an apt headline: "Pioneer of Psychology Still Has Sharp Mind and Open Arms."

Now her arms were disappearing. She would never wash rugs again. She would never turn seventy-one.

Eleonoora went downstairs. There were marks on the hall door showing the girls' heights in years past: Anna, Maria,

Anna, Maria. Suddenly Eleonoora felt jealous, almost angry at her daughters for making her always be their mother.

She scolded herself: don't be childish.

She picked the newspaper up from the floor. It was the most comforting thing for her in the morning. She made an espresso, heated milk in a saucepan, and poured the milk and coffee into a large mug. She made toast and buttered it carefully, didn't skimp on the cheese slices.

She read the paper, ate, listened to a blackbird. Night might be a well, her shouts might echo at the bottom of the well, but there was still the blackbird.

In the morning she would go to work, take care of a few routine tasks, keep herself together. At lunchtime she would call her father and mother to make sure everything was all right. Anna was going to spend the afternoon there so Dad could get a little free time. Eleonoora would call Anna and listen for any uncertainty, check up on her.

No, Eleonoora chided herself. She would leave Anna in peace with her grandma and drive over after work. Or maybe she would call the home health care service, ask about a few more details.

Everything had been arranged for her mother's return home: the bed, the pain pump, other necessaries.

The whole family had been together at the apartment in Töölö; her mother had wanted to have a welcome home party for her return.

Eleonoora had watched her mother's hand as it cut another piece of cake. The hand trembled slightly as she pressed the cake knife into the frosting. Maybe it was because of the diapers lurking on the other side of the wall; she had to prove that she still belonged with the kind of people who choose for themselves what they want to eat, who praise the flavor of the cake.

"Have another piece. It's not good for you, but it's not exactly bad for you either."

As she sat there, Eleonoora remembered her mother's severe expression when she was a child and had behaved badly once when they were out. It was like a wall; she thought she'd lost her approval and affection for good. But in the tram on the way home her mother had taken her onto her lap, her soft, slightly sweaty thighs against Eleonoora's damp skin. She had felt such a great gratitude for her mother's affection that she burst into tears.

How recent those days seemed, when her mother was a queen whose approval she thirsted for. Now her mother whined, made demands like a child, acted stubborn, capricious. She never did it to Dad, only to Eleonoora.

Eleonoora never would have guessed that it would feel like this, stupefyingly lonely, the role of the one in control.

She went to sit on the living room sofa and looked at Anna across the room—her father's portrait of Anna was hanging on the wall. She'd always felt both tender and sad when she looked at the painting. Anna sitting on a small stool, thoughtful, with the world on her shoulders. There were oranges in the background, bright as the sun. He had accentuated the shadow on the left side of her face as if he wanted to particularly mark the difference between the areas where the oranges and the shadows were.

There was a companion picture, a darker, bleaker composition—he had planned it as some sort of diptych. Eleonoora didn't know where the other painting had gone. Yesterday she had seen all of these expressions in Anna, including this seriousness, and the childhood look of concealment. Mom had resisted their caregiving plan, wanted to treat hospice care as visits. *Just come when you want to come. We'll have coffee.* Anna had offered to take the first shift. Eleonoora searched Anna's face for signs of dread and Anna glanced at her quickly, recognized her expression, and nodded emphatically, defying her doubts. Eleonoora remembered how when Anna was five she had burst into tears when she was told to try to do a somersault in gymnastics class. Her trembling chin, her eyes searching the corners for a place to escape. That look was still in her, somewhere behind her look of assurance. Eleonoora knew all her fears, all her sorrows, from the smallest to the largest. I'll come tomorrow, Anna had said again.

Eleonoora looked at Anna's face glowing through the darkness. It seemed to be floating toward her.

She decided that Anna would be all right with her grandmother for an afternoon. She wouldn't worry about it.

She needed both hands to keep the panic at a distance.

3

ANNA IS STANDING in the hallway in front of the apartment door. It's like any other day at her grandma and grandpa's house. A summer day from the past, when she was six years old. Or even yesterday, when they ate too-sweet cake and she staved off her panic and promised to come today.

It's the only thing she knows how to do for her mother. Day after day Anna sees her mother's grief grow heavier, trembling behind her mask of efficiency. Sometimes she takes off her mask for a moment when she thinks no one can see her, and she looks completely helpless.

YESTERDAY ANNA'S MOTHER was clearing away the dishes, went into the kitchen to put the plates in the dishwasher, and let her expression drop. Suddenly it was as if Anna had no hands. She would have liked to take her mother in her arms.

She wants to comfort her mother all the time the way that you comfort a child after a bad dream, but she can't find the words. Maria has diligence, practical gestures, and

uncomplicated words. Anna is helpless in comforting, all she
has are her clumsy arms, outstretched, stopped halfway.

SHE'S WALKED HERE from her apartment on Albertin-
katu, stopped in at Stockmann's to buy a gift for Grandma.
It is a bright day. A hot dog wrapper on the corner, a seagull,
a yogurt container, the usual cars. The day is silver and there
is sunshine and the garbageman's shout across the street, the
wide expanse of May.

Anna rings the doorbell and hears footsteps. Grandpa.

"Well, if it isn't Anna. Nice of you to come. Just had our
coffee and now Grandma's resting a bit."

Grandpa uses these tossed-off sentences to cover the embarrassment of just the two of them in the entryway.

Anna is alert. There's a jitter of restlessness inside her.

"Resting? Any pain?"

"Maybe a little. A little fatigue."

"Is she asleep?"

"Sleeping, dozing, you know."

Grandpa is familiar. This man—this visionary, as one
magazine called him. To have all his success, honors, and
respect, to carry his affection, his humor and melancholy,
the shapeless wounds of boyhood, through the years to
this moment, to go through exhibition openings and restless years in Paris and prizes and nominations and come to
this, this doorway, saying hello to his daughter's daughter
and trying to think of something to say. The years have
layered over him, each stage of life, each spring. Anna can
see them all.

Suddenly she remembers one of his charmer's looks, which have always seemed strange to her but still firmly belonging to her grandfather. She was twelve years old, wearing a skirt and dress-up shoes to go see him receive one of his many awards. At the end of the ceremony he threw his bouquet into the audience, smiling at the idea just before he did it. A woman journalist caught it, and he winked at her. The woman blushed and gave a curtsy. He lifted his eyebrows as if to say, Why are you curtsying? That's a gesture of humility. You can do better than that! The woman raised her own eyebrows questioningly. What? What should I do? He spread his arms. Anything you can think of! And the woman did an almost perfect pirouette, like a dancer, and then took a bow. He was satisfied with that, and blew a kiss to her. And then the whole play was over as quickly as it had begun.

Relationships between people are like dense forests. Or maybe it's the people themselves who are forests, trail after trail opening up within them, trails that are kept hidden from others, opening only by chance to those who happen upon them.

Anna remembers days at the park, the days in the studio when her grandfather was painting her. The portrait may have been the result of her mother's persistent persuasion, but once he got going he was pleased with it. Well, then, he would say at the door, Shall we go? and he would reach out his hand and Anna would take hold of it with vague thoughts about men, happiness, virility, and maybe even love.

Her grandfather's hand was sinewy and strong with dark hair growing on it. He smelled of aftershave and oily rags and a hint of turpentine.

After some time painting, they would go to the park, and Anna got to choose her ice cream. They would watch newly-wed couples, guessing what their names might be. Seija and Mikko? Amalia and Juhana?

Were you a boy once? Anna asked.

Yes, her grandfather answered.

Before Grandma?

Before Grandma.

And when you met her, you became a man.

Yeah, pretty much. That's when I became a man.

You fell in love with Grandma.

Yes, I did.

Were there any others before her?

A few.

What about after?

That's a silly question.

Were there any?

There was one.

Who was it?

The most wonderful girl in the world. Her name was Anna. The kind of girl you take out for ice cream.

Hmph!

That's just a dream now. It ended when she grew breasts. That's what happens when grandchildren grow as big as their grandparents—nothing's left but well-meaning self-consciousness.

Her grandfather smiles.

"I'm going out to take some time off, as your mother calls it." He says it with a grin, laying stress on each syllable.

He makes taking time off sound like some new kind of

coercion, something invented by the most adept overseers of concentration camps.

They share a knowing smile. It helps them keep their pact of disobedience, keeps them out of reach of this methodical woman's influence. That's what they used to be like. They would go to the Fazer sweet shop and buy treats in secret, although Anna's mother had forbidden her to eat sweets before dinner. They were freethinkers, happy-go-lucky, riding around on the tram and making up lives for the people who passed by.

Anna still has that habit.

She picks someone out from a street corner or tram car and imagines that person's days, their joys and sorrows. It makes the weight of her own days easier to bear, the grief like an ink stain that sometimes trickles through her, Tuesday evenings when the hallway in her building is filled with the smell of fried fish, nothing ever changing.

It's easy to tell a stranger's story. It's harder to stay in your own.

"What's Matias up to?"

The same question he asked yesterday.

"He's at the library rendering an account of decades past. Same as yesterday."

She cherished Matias in her mind. They had their days, too. It was only five months ago that they carried the sofa over the threshold, and all their other things. Sheer madness, after knowing each other for one month! They ordered pizza on their first morning and played old vinyl records—Neil Young, the Beatles. They played "All You Need Is Love" over and over, neither one admitting that they needed reassurance of their happiness. After shifting their furniture distractedly from one corner to another they made love in the armchair, because they couldn't think of any place to put it.

They put the blown-up photograph—the Aino photograph—in the closet. It was still there.

Anna wanted to take it down to the trash bins.

"You can't throw this away," Matias said. "It's still you in the picture."

"The old me," Anna said. "It's not me anymore."

"Yes it is," Matias said in the way he had of seeming to understand the whole world, which sometimes pushed her to the brink of fury. "People carry all their former selves with them."

In the photo, Anna's legs are breaking the surface of the lake. She looks serious, more serious than she feels, like the kind of woman who carries her fate proudly, unbowed. Carries it into the water, the cool rooms of the water, and through those rooms into another world. Although the picture is grave, the day when it was taken had been a happy one. He hadn't turned his gaze away once.

SHE AND MATIAS had a blank spot on the wall. They thought about asking her grandfather for one of his prints— were they at the cabin at Tammilehto or were they here in Helsinki, in the attic of the apartment on Sammonkatu? But they hadn't yet asked him about it. They had a lot to do, their chores, their Tuesday nights, all the usual things.

Matias knew Anna, and Anna knew Matias. Anyone would have thought them happy, and maybe they were.

They had days, nights, morning after morning, camaraderie, meals prepared together, walks on the seashore when the moon was a pale fingerprint on the sky.

But still Anna secretly dreamed of picking up a colored pencil one day and writing her good-byes on the floor. She would only take a few things with her—one of Matias's socks as evidence that he had existed, one Moomintroll cup.

It's possible for a person to walk out of your life without saying good-bye, without explaining why. It's possible to walk out the door and leave other people crying, shouting, lying on the floor for days.

It's possible to say *See you tomorrow* even though you know you'll never see each other again.

ANNA REMEMBERED THE little girl's neck. She could almost see it, the memory was so strong: Linda stretching out to take hold of her hand before they crossed the street. It was the first time she'd met Linda, who had just turned two at the time. Linda stretched out her hand and Anna could see her neck, a gleaming white strip between the ends of her hair and her shirt collar. That kind of trust. Only someone who's never yet lost anything can trust so unhesitatingly. Only someone who's never been betrayed.

"WHAT ABOUT YOU?" her grandfather asks. "What have you been up to?"

He's trying to think of something to talk about. He was more natural yesterday, when there were other people here.

"I've got my thesis to write. It's not really getting any-where. I was in the spring graduate study group, but there's a bit of a hitch."

"What's the problem?"

"The theme. It's too complicated."

"And the theme is . . . ?"

Anna realizes she's giving vague answers, as she usually does when someone asks her about her research. "Emanci-pation, that sort of thing. Women's lib."

She obscures the vastness of her theme, the uncertainty it creates—so much to read!—in irony, flashing a smile, exag-gerating every syllable: "I'm trying to track down an ancient woman from the misty folds of days gone by while simulta-neously attempting to keep up with the new woman."

Her grandfather whistles. The sound is preposterously old-fashioned, but nevertheless charming. For a split second she can see him at fifteen.

"Impressive," he says. "All you have to do is take up the question of the existence of God and you'll be able to com-pletely explain the world."

"I promise I'll advance into the theological realm in my conclusion."

Her grandfather is quiet, waiting for her to continue. Anna lets the silence trickle down the walls. She misses their days together. They should go for a tram ride like they used to. They used to be close, speak the same language. Where has that connection gone?

They could go to Cafe Ursula again, laugh at the dolled-up women, order pastries, and hang around among the pass-ersby. It's easy for her to see her grandfather as a young man, with his boyish troubles to bear, cherishing his plans. But there's a chasm between them. Looking at him makes the ink stain start to spread inside her again. She remembers her own troubles and wishes she could turn away.

When is it that family members become mirrors, painful to look at?

Anna decides she'll be here for a few hours. She'll keep her grandmother company, and while she does, her grandfather can go where he pleases. Then she'll walk out the door, meet Saara downtown and still have time to hit the books in the evening. Emancipation is almost a dirty word for her now— the whole thing seems stupid to her at the moment. Why did she choose a feminist angle? Now she can't change it.

But she'll write for a few hours this evening.

And before night comes, she and Matias will go for a walk on the shore. He'll bring his guitar, they'll drink the rest of the box of wine left over from the party last week. They'll sit on the rocks, the evening will turn cool, she'll get a little drunk even though she has to work at the bookstore tomorrow. The ink stain will be just a well-defined area inside her; she'll draw a line around it and won't let it spread.

"Well," she says, gathering all her energy. "Nothing to do now but wait for Grandma to wake up."

4

SHE WAS RIGHT on time, rang the doorbell at one o'clock sharp, as arranged. Martti had a doctor's appointment. What else would he do? Wander on the beach, sit in a cafe, eat a doughnut? He didn't know. The thought flashed inside him, caused a pain in his chest. This was what his life would be when Elsa was gone. Irresolutely planning out his days.

She was smiling shyly. She looked so much like she did when she was five years old and came to visit.

The nursery had been their granddaughters' domain. After they were born he and Elsa had got the old toys out of the attic and decorated the room as it had been when Eleonoora was little. The bed, the dollhouse, the toy box, everything.

Their favorite doll was Eleonoora's old one-eyed Molla. It was worn from play, had been mended, dragged along behind a sled, fed ice cream and strawberries for many summers.

Once Anna had taken Molla home without asking. Elsa had asked her about it the following week.

She had lied about it without blinking, said she didn't know anything about it.

I called your mother, Elsa said. Molla's at your house. How do you think she got there?

I don't know, Anna said. Maybe she walked.

Dolls can't walk by themselves.

Maybe she can. She might be the kind of doll that can walk!

She convinced herself of her own lie so seamlessly that it made him and Elsa smile.

A child's reality is made of dreams and play. A lie can weave into the mix imperceptibly. Or maybe that was what reality was like for people in general. Dreams, play, lies.

He let the familiar thought—it sometimes felt like anguish—come to him: what else has my art been, after all?

Anna seemed to have given up play now—she was a woman all of a sudden. Martti had noticed the change last fall when the whole family went out for dinner. She had just come back from Paris, came hurrying around the corner in high-heeled shoes, smiling, tanned.

"Who are you?" he had said. "My granddaughter has disappeared and been replaced by a *parisienne*!"

Anna had found pleasure in Paris, he was sure of that. At the restaurant she ordered wine, and as she sipped from her glass he thought, It happens anew all the time. There's always some who are young and convince themselves that this has never happened to anyone before them. They believe that their lives, their own joys and sorrows, are extraordinary. That their own love is stronger than other people's. They believe it will never be their lot to feel the days weighing on them. And they may be right. The young have the

whole world, and they toss it away without a thought because they're impatient for other, ever newer worlds.

He would have liked to say to Anna: Make a home for
yourself in your carefree days. They're dreams, but you
don't have to wake up yet. Ten years and you'll start to wake
up, five more and you'll struggle against the awakening, ten
more years and you'll be content with what you have. It's not
a bad thing, far from a misfortune. In fact it's a new form
of happiness, and you'll cherish it like all your other happy
feelings. More and more you'll have moments when you feel
the world is offering itself to you like a gift. But it won't be
the same. You'll look at the world like a painting, and time
will have framed it, the experience of time, and you'll enjoy
it in a different way than you did before.

"I WASN'T ASLEEP."

Elsa was standing in the bedroom doorway. She'd heard
their conversation.

She smiled a little. "Honey," she said to Anna. "You came.
We can make some cardamom buns!"

"Don't overdo it," he said.

Elsa scrunched up her nose. "If you keep up that forbid-
ding tone I'll swim to Seurasaari."

"All right," he said. "Make cardamom buns. Make two
batches, if you like."

Anna didn't look worried anymore.

5

DID YOU BRING the wine?" Grandma asks hopefully as soon as he's closed the door.

She looks as if she's shrunken in just one day, dignified and nullified at the same time, like an absurd accessory that's gone out of style. Her eyes, deep in their sockets, like a starved animal—a raccoon, or a panda. Hair in a wisp.

She called just as Anna was leaving her apartment. She was whispering, and Anna could tell she was keeping the call secret from Grandpa. There's one more thing that I want, she said. Anna had imagined an escape to a carnival, a joy ride in the car, a train trip to Moscow. But she wanted some wine.

"Syrah—good choice," she says. "Let's have a shindig. Let's go out and sit on the swing."

"Mom wouldn't like it if she knew."

Grandma flutters a dismissive hand in the air.

"That's to be expected. Mothers become children to their daughters, and daughters turn maternal. When you get to a certain age, you end up doing things behind your children's backs. But you know what? I intend to drink a few glasses of wine, regardless of what your mother thinks."

She tilts her head back and lets out a little titter.

"It'll be a death sentence for me," Anna hears herself say. It makes her smile.

Grandma is unfazed. "Only if your mother finds out."

Anna puts her bag down. She can let go of her uneasiness, loosen up. Grandma doesn't seem tired.

"We can have a proper talk," Grandma says. "Woman to woman, you know? Like they do in movies. Talk it all out. Since we have so little time left."

She takes the bottle and disappears momentarily into the kitchen.

Anna looks at the living room and library, lingers for a moment at the door to her mother's old room.

Molla is in her cradle dreaming endless dreams with one eye closed. When did she lose that eye? Was it torn off?

The dollhouse is in its usual place. It was a stage for hopes and dreams when she was a child. The woman of the house is sitting in front of a teeny tiny piano as if she's about to play it. Somewhere, maybe in the cradle, out of sight, is a baby doll. The larger child is deep asleep in the nursery next to the doll piano room.

The familiar joy of childhood comes over Anna. She would close the door to the world and get down on her knees, imagining a whole new reality. Sometimes when she stayed at her grandma's house she would wake up at night and play with the dolls. Night bent the rules, broke the firm boundaries of day, and the dolls seemed alive.

Maria would be sleeping on the mattress, snuffling, Anna careful not to wake her, wanting to play by herself.

As long as the game was hers and no one knew about it, anything was possible. There was no time. There were no hours. No room, no bed. No rocking horse in the corner. Even she herself wasn't really there. She melted into the shadows of the miniature rooms and was nothing but will, molding itself to fit the life of the dolls. Sometimes she was the mother's voice, sometimes the child's, sometimes the father's.

The only thing that bothered her was that Molla was too big for this little world. But she still brought Molla along to play sometimes. She would look at the life of the little house through the windows with her one eye. The effect was more fearsome than benevolent—Anna understood that even as a child.

She takes Molla from her bed, rocks her in her arms. The doll smiles, an ancient scar on her lip—it got torn at some time during play and was sewn back together. Nevertheless, Molla is happy and trusting: *there's nothing to be afraid of!*

"REMEMBER WHEN YOU stole Molla?" Grandma asks.

Anna gives a start. She didn't hear her come to the door.

"I remember. I hid her for a week. I don't know why I was so attached to her."

"Who knows? Children get attached to the strangest things."

Anna realizes she's stroking Molla's head.

"I love this dollhouse. It's stayed the same all these years."

"You can have it. You can have the whole thing as your inheritance when I die. Your mother might make a fuss about it, so it'd be best to write a will. Let's do that right now, while we have a glass of wine."

"Don't say that. Don't say you're going to die."

Anna's voice portends tears, she can hear them before she tastes them in her throat. They stand quietly for a moment. Let's stay here, Anna thinks. Let's close the door and decide that the illness has been canceled. Let's close the door.

She smells her grandma's familiar fragrance, the same skin cream that Anna used to spread in a thick layer over her face after her bath to make her grandma laugh. There's a hint of something new in the scent, musty and dark. The smell of death.

The horse chestnut trees outside the window, calm and imposing with their brand-new torches of blossom, cast a quivering shadow on the wall. Anna feels a peace which may be an echo from her early childhood. Lying in her baby carriage in the shade taking a nap, that same leafy color drawn on the awning of the carriage. Light, shadow, light.

"Guess what I want to do?" her grandma suddenly says.

"What?"

"Play dress-up. Remember?"

It was one of Anna's favorite games. She was Bianca. She would put on a dress and they would make up a life for the character. Bianca was a fine lady from Italy. When Anna was Bianca, she knew things that she normally had no inkling of. She would find feelings within herself that she didn't know she had.

"Remember how when you were Bianca you liked olives, even though you usually hated them?" her grandma laughs.

"I ate them from a plate, with a knife and fork."

"And you clomped around in high heels that were too big for you, talking about stock prices and airports and perfume.

If you put on the Bianca dress I'll see if I can fit into one I haven't worn since the fifties. That's one good thing about this cancer. I've gotten as thin as I was when I was twenty. Find something that suits you and I'll make us some lunch."

A WALL OF dust motes floats dreamily across her grandmother's room. Anna stands in the doorway for a moment. The sun's rays stretch all the way across to the opposite wall. There is no time here.

The closet is full of old coats, dresses, a couple of men's shirts. The Bianca dress is black and white; it dangles from a hanger. She doesn't take it. She wants something different.

She looks through the dresses, runs her hand over each one—decades hung on hangers. She opens the other closet door. It creaks ponderously. The clothes look old, like they've been hanging here forever.

She takes out one she doesn't remember seeing before. A pale dress with a generous skirt, maybe from the 1950s. A wide waistband, a square neckline that shows the collarbones, the skirt abundant with rustling fabric.

It's easy to imagine the parties: the room buzzing with expectation. Smiles and small talk and an atmosphere that gradually changes from nervous to boisterous. Some people meeting for the first time, some seeing each other with new eyes, or maybe sharing secret and painful memories. A murmur of voices from the living room, but two people, a man and a woman, don't hear it, they're looking at each other, terror and excitement and tenderness knocking around inside them because they know something has begun, they know they can't go back.

She takes off her shirt and jeans; the dress slips on easily. It's a little tight in the bust.

She feels like someone else in this dress. Did her grandma wear it once or twice a year, to the theater with friends, drinking a pink cocktail in a bar after a play, different than she usually was for a little while, glancing at the door through the hazy curtain of smoke and walking home with long strides? Not because that was her nature, but because it was, in some mysterious way, *the nature of the dress?*

"Where'd you find that?"

Grandma is standing in the doorway.

"It was in this closet. This isn't your 1950s dress, is it?"

Grandma gives the dress a long look.

"Take it."

"What?"

"I don't need it. Take it with you. You can wear it to parties and things. What about the Bianca dress? Why didn't you put that one on? Grab that one instead."

"Is it all right if I wear this one?"

Grandma shrugs. "If you like," she says, as if she wanted to dissociate herself from the whole thing.

Then she goes to the closet and immediately finds what she's looking for. She takes off her skirt and blouse. For a moment she's standing in the middle of the room pale-skinned, looking slightly helpless. Anna looks at the path of her spine, clearly defined, and keeps her shock at arm's length. She's so thin! She helps with the zipper, gently, gently. The dress is ridiculously loose, at least two sizes too big. Anna considerately makes no mention of this.

Her grandma looks satisfied.

"Right, then. Everything's ready. I even have onion pie," she says proudly. "I baked it yesterday when I got tired of having cancer."

THEY PACK A basket with a baguette and brie and onion pie and two small bottles of mineral water, plus some grapes, fruit salad, and the olive focaccia that Anna brought. They take along a quilt and head out like parisiennes. Grandma ties a scarf over her wisp of hair and puts on her old Chanel sunglasses.

They sit in the swing under the chestnut tree. Anna pours the wine while her grandma opens wrappers.

"Always did like the sound of wine being poured. When I was young I was afraid that I might well become an alcoholic, I liked it so much. But then I realized that I was more fond of the anticipation of festivity than I was of the wine itself."

Her gaze takes in the fluffy clouds, the boundless May sky, the nightingale on a branch of the tree, on silent watch before spending its evening song.

"I wouldn't hold it against you if you got a little drunk," Grandma says, sipping from her glass.

Anna tastes her wine. Grandma pats her encouragingly on the leg.

"So. Woman to woman, as we planned. Tell me about Matias. He's a sharp boy—and pretty. But I can see that there's a rub. Is it sex? Is that the trouble? Shy balls? A stiff pelvis? Or is it that the choreography's clumsy? Sex is often better if you think of it as a dance. Men don't always understand that, although I never would have thought Matias had poor rhythm."

Anna gets some wine in her nose. "Shy balls?"

Grandma pops a grape in her mouth as if she's talking about a rise in the price of milk. "Why sugarcoat it? Sometimes sensitive men are dull in bed." She sighs as if this was an unfortunate fact. "Let's just say there are men who like to turn the light out before they get going. It's usually shy balls. It's often associated with a high level of education and problems of attachment in childhood."

"I hope this isn't one of the great insights of your career."

"What if it is?"

"Then I should call *Ilta Sanomat* and give them a headline."

Grandma laughs. Anna can see her pink tongue. A person's tongue is the same from childhood to old age, the same tongue fumbling for the breast and later on for other food, the same tongue forming words, professions of love, and commands and scientific debates and more professions of love and requests and thanks for the care and attention.

"I'm just teasing. Besides, I gave them a good one last year."

"Oh, yeah. The nuclear family. That was a good headline. 'Researcher Denounces the Nuclear Family'!"

Grandma laughs again.

"I didn't even say that. I just said that the ideal of the nuclear family should be looked at critically. Has the ideal strayed too far from reality, since people nowadays are faced with every imaginable family configuration and are forced to adjust to it, and live quite happily? The world always comes between people, in every kind of family, which is how it should be. No one can deny their origins, their circumstances. Everyone has to survive their childhood and change the circumstances into something else. It's the only way to get through it, to become happy."

She laughs, gentleness in her eyes, as if the world is a clumsy thing with flaws that she forgives out of sheer tenderheartedness.

The interview had been purposely confrontational. The photograph was an old one, with grandma looking proudly straight into the camera. The summary insert made her sound like a radical in her day, a trailblazer in the jungles of academia. She snorted after she read it: I wasn't a radical. They'll believe anything. I just wanted to do research and help people in the process and keep my wits about me. If they want to call practicality and love for humanity radicalism, then fine, I guess I fit the criteria.

The nightingale on the branch hears them but doesn't say anything. Its eye is a shining black point in the universe. The bird is watching over them, mute and knowing, waiting until evening to disclose its counsel in a clear song.

Grandma cuts a thick slice of brie and spreads it on a piece of bread.

Anna can't help but think about the growth lurking somewhere among her cells. It's devouring her whole life, the same life that gave birth to Anna's mother and, in a way, Anna, too. A ghoulishly rational and coherent thought pierces Anna: life gives birth to life and life gives birth to death.

Grandma doesn't know Anna's thoughts. Suddenly, without warning, she says, "I've been thinking about you. What's going on in your life? Or what was going on last year, the year before? We didn't see each other much. But your mother was worried."

Anna turns her head. It's easy to turn her head and look at the apple blossoms, the climbing rose on the side of the house. Soon it, too, will push out buds and everything will start at the beginning again.

Grandma doesn't give up. "What exactly happened? What was going on?"

Anna reaches for the cheese too quickly. The knife falls to the ground with a clink.

She's spilled wine on the dress. One drop runs between her thumb and forefinger as if it knows the way. The stain begins to spread over the dress. If she doesn't put salt on it quickly it will never come out. It will never leave, no matter how much you wash it. It's already growing.

"There was something going on for years, wasn't there?" Grandma asks.

"Now I've ruined this dress," Anna says, upset.

She's still holding her glass. The glass is shaking. Grandma is looking closely at her.

"What of it?" she says. "So what? It's just a dress."

"But it's yours, and I've gone and ruined it. Do you have any salt? Should I get some from upstairs?"

Grandma is thoughtful, as if she were looking right through her. She opens her mouth to say something, closes it again, gazing steadily until she finally makes up her mind to say what she's thinking.

"Actually, it's not mine."

"What do you mean?"

"It's Eeva's. I didn't know it had been hanging in that closet all these years. I was surprised when I saw you wearing it."

She says the name dispassionately, as if she were mentioning a person long forgotten, someone she'd once spent happy days with, sworn lifelong friendship to, until, for some reason, because of a random whim or unfortunate misunderstanding, their connection was broken.

"Whose?"

"Eeva's," she says again.

6

THE DAY WAS warm. The moment he stepped outside
the building the world flooded over him. There were
some young boys at the tram stop, swaggering fifteen-year-
olds. A girl stood a ways off in triumphantly careless contra-
posto, glancing in the direction of the coming tram: she was
obviously one of the boys' classmates.

Yet another drama where attention must be rationed out
to obtain a greater reward.

Which of the boys did she want? Maybe the bland one,
the one who looked like a good boy, who carried himself
with what he thought was serious-mindedness. That's what
Martti had been like as a boy. Secretly sensitive, an easy butt
of practical jokes, touchy, occasionally sinking into romantic gloom.

He once drew a picture of Helvi, who sat in the front row,
and gave it to her shyly at recess. Loudmouth Helvi, whom
he had fallen in love with on some sort of whim—maybe because someone like Helvi wouldn't even look at someone like
him, which ensured that he could love her in peace.

That's what this boy was like. Was the girl Helvi? No.
This girl was sweeter.

The tram to Meilahti wouldn't come for five more minutes. He would change trams at Kisahalli, go to his doctor's appointment, where they'd put an old man's mask on him with their tests and measurements.

Seventy and over. It had happened without him noticing.

A person just wakes up all of a sudden and realizes he's old. He gets on the tram and notices someone offering him their seat. I'm not crippled, he thinks. And then he realizes—no, but I am old.

The group of young people was getting restless. The rowdiest of the boys started to jump onto the rails, trying to get the girl's attention.

The boy made a strange dance move that reminded Martti of something he'd seen on TV—a slow-motion video of a bird's leaping mating dance. They were like the leaps of a dancer with years of training. Just as polished, just as exhilarated and self-assured.

The girl gave the boy the finger. The gesture was disarming in its obscenity. Why waste time on such a thing when she could go over and kiss him?

The tram came; the teenagers jostled in through the rear door.

There was a meek-looking family in the middle of the tram: a father, a mother, and two little boys. The father held one boy by the hand. The boys were touchingly faithful miniature versions of their father—a shock of blond hair, an all-encompassing gaze. Knock-knees. Chubby hands.

Martti thought, no matter what happens to us we carry where we came from with us.

Martti himself had his father's nose. His father had died in the Continuation War, in December of 1943. The doorbell had rung, and he had asked if it was Santa Claus. The familiar pastor and two soldiers were at the door. His mother collapsed in the entryway, the servant girl pushed him and his sister away so they wouldn't see the scene. He remembered the hesitant words of the young soldier and his mother's strange anger: Out. Get out of here.

He was never supposed to talk about that. Not about his father, or the pastor at the door, or his mother's collapse. No one ever forbade him to talk about it, but he always knew that the whole scene, the whole memory of the pain, should be kept silent. They started leaving blank spots in the conversation where they would have mentioned his father. Reality had gradually closed over the wound, silence had bound his father's memory like a bandage, encased it. Silence—it's a strange grave.

But even then, when his father was dead, Martti still had his nose. Even back then it seemed strange, almost incomprehensible.

Those were the years when he started drawing. The worst bombing of Helsinki came in February; his mother lay on the bedroom floor and refused to get up. He hid under the table, afraid, crying for his father.

When the bombing had stopped, he had nightmares. Their servant—Irja was the girl's name—bought him paper and a stick of charcoal on the black market and said, Draw them, maybe it will help. And he drew them.

———

THE FATHER OF the meek family took his wife's hand. The older boy held a Spider-Man doll tight against his chest, the littler one had the same kind of toy in his clumsy hand.

The girl who had been flirting at the tram stop affected a bored expression. Martti saw her glance at the sensitive boy. The boy looked away—clearly a crush.

Emotion came, unhindered.

All the aspirations people had, their unquenchable hope, their tenacious faith in the brightness watching over the resonance of the May evening, the diligence with which they wrote and published the daily free newspaper and distributed it in its plastic pockets on the trams and subways; all these things awakened a sudden overflowing tenderness in him.

This is where the world is, with all its strangeness and triviality. This isn't a painting; it's the world, naked, within even his reach.

THE HOSPITAL WAS a familiar entity, like an organism. He walked down the corridor, stepped soundlessly through the sliding doors, and checked in at reception. He became a heart, lungs, circulation, liver, psyche.

He sat in the waiting room. The others waiting there were detached from themselves, from their lives; a youngish mother with an obviously feverish but lively child, a bald, middle-aged woman, probably a cancer patient. And an old man, like him, with perhaps exactly the same worries.

He sketched their poses, out of habit.

The nurse came to tell them there was an hour wait.

"You can wait in the cafeteria if you like."

He got up, walked back down the corridor. He saw a few very sick people. A woman lying in bed with an IV, serpentine veins gleaming through her skin. The sight of her didn't upset him, although Elsa came to mind, what was coming. He made eye contact with the woman and nodded. There was still hope in her eyes.

People are willing to endure almost any agony merely to have a few more ordinary days. Maybe just a hundred. Or ten. Or two, if that's all they're going to get. One day when they can get up, walk out a door, make a note of the weather and plan their lunch or who they'll meet, or cherish the mere idea of a walk through town.

He went to the cafeteria, bought a coffee, sat at a table and looked at the people. The people at the next table were talking about a trip to the countryside. One of them was sick—which one? He looked at both of them. There was a baby in a bassinet. Maybe they were here because of the baby.

He found himself dreaming of taking Elsa one more time to Tammilehto. Maybe they would sleep in the sauna again, see the morning, make coffee, the way they used to.

"May I sit here?"

It was the bald woman from the waiting room. She smiled, pointing at the chair in front of her.

"I love the end of May," she said. "Don't you?"

Martti felt it silly to use such a strong word as "love" with a stranger. But it was true. Of course he loved these days, these spacious, green rooms shaped like expectation. He thought for a moment about whether to use the formal *te*, as she had. She was beautiful. Eyes like pools, arching lips. But obviously sick, you could see it in the sheen over her feverish eyes, her collarbones that showed beneath her skin like two conductor's batons.

He used *te*, because of her illness. Or maybe her beauty.

"You must wish you were outside, then. It's a beautiful day."

"I'm dying," she said. "Could you tell?"

She looked him in the eye calmly, stirring her coffee. This was a zone of true statements. For some reason, here, where a heart is a heart and a liver is a liver, and plans are plans, and titles are as weightless as rumors, you spoke only in sentences that were absolutely true.

"My wife is dying, too," he said, as if that were a reply.

Suddenly saying it was easy. He had feared the grief the sentence would cause, but now it sounded simply factual.

"How much time does she have?" the woman asked calmly.

"They won't tell us. But through midsummer, the end of July if all goes well."

The woman looked out the window. "Have the two of you been happy?"

He didn't have to hesitate with his answer. "Yes, we have. Lately I've felt that we've been very happy."

"You only realize it fully afterward," the woman said.

Her wrist bones were like two thin sticks. Her eyebrows were perhaps drawn on with a pencil. Her eyes were strongly delineated. Suddenly Martti felt like he was talking to a circus artist—a tightrope walker or a wise clown.

"So," she asked. "What's the hardest part?"

He thought for a moment.

"The hardest part is to see the other person change. To learn them again. And to see in them that you've changed, too."

The woman nodded, satisfied with his answer; it was eternal and true.

"What else?"

He heard himself say it. For some reason it wasn't hard to say at all: "It was hardest when I loved someone else."

The woman didn't look surprised; she just nodded.

"What was her name, this other one?"

"Eeva."

There it was. He'd said the name for the first time in decades. It brought a few memories closer. They were individual images. Eeva in the sauna washing her hair. Eeva tired, her eyes swollen with sleep. Eeva angry, pale and flushed at the same time. He let the memories come, although they were painful.

More words came. He talked, although it felt more like someone inside him was talking.

"I've never loved anyone so much, although nowadays it feels like it was all a dream. Or maybe I've loved my wife just as much, but in a different way. It's different when it's true."

"Don't say that," the woman said, suddenly ferocious, spilling her coffee on the table in her excitement. "Love is always true."

He found himself nodding, as if taking orders.

"My only regret is that I wasn't braver," the woman said. "I don't regret what I've done. Unless you've committed an actual crime, regretting what you've done is the same thing as regretting your life."

Martti stepped out of himself for a moment to take note of the oddness of the situation. But who else could he tell? No one he knew.

"But your wife still wants?" the woman asked.

"What do you mean?"

"What does she want?"

"She wants to look at the sea every day. Yesterday she talked about swimming, although I doubt she'd be able to. She wants to see mornings and evenings. Maybe she wants to drive to our summer cabin one more time."

"Then you should take her to look at the sea, let her swim in spite of the risk, show her mornings and evenings. You should take her to the summer cabin. It will be enough." She smiled.

"And you? What do you want to do?"

She didn't pause in her answer.

"I want to make crepes with my daughter at our lake cabin in Saimaa. Over the fire. I want to eat one with sugar and jam. Then I want to sit there and knit and look at the lake."

"Maybe you will, then. Go there and make crepes. Knit."

"Yes," the woman said. "I will when I'm done with this."

They got up as if by common agreement, looked at each other like people who had by some caprice revealed everything to one another. The woman's smile asked for forgiveness, solidarity, confidentiality. Martti answered the smile.

THE DOCTOR PRONOUNCED him healthy, told him he had the circulatory system of a man of sixty. The doctor asked about Elsa. Martti had already poured his heart out in the cafeteria, he didn't want to do it again.

He let peace flow through his ardor, and peace came.

He had promised to be away all afternoon. Should he go to Restaurant Torni, drink a cognac, look at the view? Should he go to the airport and watch the planes, their exhilarating speed at takeoff?

He hadn't been thinking of Tammilehto. The cabin had been left unused all winter. Normally they would have made a ski trip over the lake as early as March, skied to the island if the ice would hold them, spent the night in a lean-to, taken a sauna in April, then got out the garden tools. But this spring they'd left it. Maybe it was the change in Elsa's condition, or maybe the idea of going to Tammilehto had been too emotional.

But now he suddenly wanted to go there. He wanted to drive, stop at the rest stop, chat with Seljavaara, the man who took care of the house while they were away. He wanted the quiet of the shed, the rustle of the woods behind the cabin, the view of the lake from the sauna porch.

Maybe it was because of Eeva. Saying Eeva's name out loud.

He wanted to be somewhere where he could think his thoughts through to the end. He couldn't do it in the city, he was too attached to life, to Elsa.

THE ROUTE WAS familiar. He stopped at the rest stop, as he always did. He sped up to two hundred kilometers an hour, happiness rising in him as it always did when he drove the car.

He let the happiness radiate from him the same way it had once when he was fifteen and had gone to the Ateneum after school to look at the paintings and felt himself swoon in the presence of their beauty and precision, then stepped into the bright air outside and felt the world beating within him. A moment of clarity: he decided he would study art, be good at it, brilliant. He decided he would move to Paris. The cars had honked their horns, he had run across the street and been able to feel his every seething, fervent cell, an inexplicable peculiarity, a shift in all his cells at once, under his delicate skin. He fell in love with every woman he passed, celebrated every ragged drunk and every scrap of paper clinging to the pavement. When he got home, he stood breathless in the living room doorway. His mother looked at him with her eyebrows raised.

"Have you fallen in love?"

He thought about Helvi and about the artists Schjerfbeck and Edelfelt and Simberg and the woman who had just smiled at him on the street. He brought back a mental image of Helena, a girl in the class above his, her pitiless lips, which he had always seen, but never had the courage or the skill or the vision to draw. Now he would.

No, he said. I've decided what I want to do. I want to be an artist. I'm going to move to Paris.

Oho, his mother said. You better hurry into the kitchen, then. Hilja left a plate of dinner for you. An artist can't go to Paris hungry.

He was still that boy. A thought flashed into his mind: only Elsa saw him that way, as the same boy he used to be. Eeva had seen him that way, but he had let go of Eeva. Now there was only Elsa. Maybe after Elsa there would be no one else. He took in the hopeful meadow and blue sky outside the car window, sketched it in his mind. It brought him comfort.

WHEN HE GOT to Tammilehto, the house lay dozing in the light, the leaves still sparse in the trees.

He took off his shoes, although the ground was still cool. He opened the door of the shed. Everything was as it should be, everything in its place. He felt a pleasant weariness in the presence of all these things, a melancholy cousin to his past hopes and enthusiasms. So much of it. Worthless attempted paintings, sketches, old tennis rackets. All kinds of junk.

He headed for the sauna. He had to put his shoulder into opening the door—it had swollen tight in its jamb over the winter. Finally it opened with a crack. The familiar smell of soap and birch flooded over him in the washroom. He took out a bench he had built some time back and put it on the porch. He noticed that the porch floorboards were sagging. They were rotting near the wall. If the damp had spread as far as the wall they'd have to tear it out.

He couldn't be bothered with that now. He was going to have a peaceful day, a peaceful lake, a peaceful May.

Finally peace came to him. He let thoughts that had been floating near him for days approach.

Eeva at the door, the way he'd seen her the first time— smiling, a little hesitant.

Had love begun immediately?

When it had all been going on for a while he had learned that for Eeva love was devotion, stepping outside herself.

Maybe that was her flaw—an inability to preserve herself on her journey toward another. Or it could just as well have been his flaw—something he couldn't receive. *You're impossible. How can I love you when you lose yourself in the strength of your own love!* Eeva had answered calmly, almost coldly: *Don't ever demand that I love you in moderation. You might as well demand that I turn to stone.*

Maybe it was this collision between them that had led to disaster.

He went over Eeva's features in his mind. He hadn't done that in years, although he had sometimes thought of her. Now he built her bit by bit.

Lips small but full. Bashful, girlish knees. The kind of thighs you might call spindly. He had loved those spindly legs, the unaccountable whiteness of those thighs. Restless hands, careless arms—she often dangled her wrists when she was thinking. Her breasts had been almost astonishing little buds, at least in the beginning, in the first few years, when she was only twenty-two or twenty-three.

His cell phone rang. He had to come back to the present. He did it by taking in the spruces on the island with his eyes. They'd had those branches back then, too, when he and Eeva had spent time here.

It was Eleonoora calling.

"Where are you?"

"Tammilehto."

"By yourself? Why? How did you get there?"

"I drove."

"You can't go there by yourself."

"The last time I looked, this cabin was in my name. The last time I looked, I was your father, and you weren't my mother. So I very well can take the car and come here all by myself."

"Just don't start painting. I heard from Mom that you've been planning to start up again. But don't start opening bottles of turpentine up there."

"Just as an aside, may I remind you that I have done all my painting alone? But since you mention it, I'd rather do some building."

"What?"

"Or rather demolition. Of the porch. The porch on the sauna is rotten. It needs to be replaced. We might have to tear out the wall."

"Don't start demolishing anything. We can look at it together and decide what needs to be done. How's Mom?"

"When I left, they were going on a picnic."

He could hear Eleonoora sigh.

"Right," she said resignedly. "Hospice is just one long damned picnic for Mom."

7

ANNA CROSSES THE street. She told Saara she would meet her at Esplanadi Park. She's already late.

She's carrying her jeans and shirt in a shopping bag. The hem of the dress flaps against her calves. The wine stain is invisible among the pleats. She feels a little hot, or perhaps agitated, her mouth dry from the wine. One question keeps racing through her mind: does Mom know? Does she remember Eeva at all? She always remembers everything. She wouldn't forget something like that. She might push it out of her mind, but she wouldn't forget. There's a difference.

Saara is sitting on the grass eating ice cream.

She has a turquoise silk ribbon tied in her hair. Maybe the color means something. Maybe it announces some new idea that Anna won't learn about until the fall. Saara's lip gloss is fuchsia. That, Anna knows, just means that summer can now arrive.

In high school Saara never wore any makeup, but once she got into the university she decided that her face was the same as the next person's—practical and modifiable, a certain kind of weapon.

"New dress," Saara says. "Pretty."

Anna would like to tell her right away what she's just learned. She doesn't tell her. She talks about ice cream. What flavor to buy—blueberry, caramel nut, or that new one with marshmallows in it?

"Look how bright the blossoms are," Saara says and nods her head gracefully toward the cherry trees, licking her ice cream cone. Saara is not opposed to cherry trees. There are quite a few things Saara's not opposed to.

"How bright," Anna repeats, trying not to say anything about Eeva right away.

She walks over to the cafe kiosk, the gravel crunching under her feet, her dress rustling. She is someone slightly different than herself. A different city opens up under her feet as she walks. It overlaps the spaces of this city and she can't quite make it out clearly. She orders old-fashioned vanilla from the vendor, who seems to have been made to sell ice cream cones—sunny and smiling, strong wrists, a carefree brow. Almost no seriousness in her movements. Nothing in her gaze but the coming days of summer. Anna's a little surprised at herself. When did she start ordering vanilla?

THERE'S A FEELING of expectation in the air. The seagulls have already arrived, the other woman who works at the kiosk shoos them off the tables.

A man in a suit goes by, wrapped up in his busyness, on his way somewhere from an office on Pohjoisesplanadi. It's ridiculous to swing a briefcase on a day like today, to pretend to be important, with a telephone to your ear. He's like a bright five-year-old playing at being a banker.

Saara talks lazily about her summer plans, waiting for the grade on an essay, a book she's just read.

"I just know something's going to happen this summer," she says. "Something has to happen," she adds emphatically, so that one might be misled into thinking her certainty was in fact desperation.

"This summer the old world will be demolished and a new one built in its place," Anna says.

And it's right for her to say so, although she actually fears the kinds of changes that Saara thirsts for. She would just as soon have continued those evenings when they were sixteen and stayed over at each other's houses. They were free of adults' demands, bought pastries and popcorn and frozen pizzas and bags of candy, watched *Dirty Dancing* twice, dancing along with Johnny and Baby, feeling the steps like a river flowing over a fallen log. The dancing was in fact a sort of churning after all they'd eaten, and they ended up lying on the floor giggling.

"What's new?" Saara asks now. "How's the thesis going? Have you read *The Feminine Mystique* yet?"

"Yeah, but I still need to find more source material. I should tie the subject to other historical events, not just second-wave feminism. I should read more. But I don't feel like it."

Anna thinks about Eeva. She didn't plan to tell Saara about Eeva. But Eeva won't let her go. Eeva's here already, close by.

No, not close by—Eeva is inside her. She put on the dress, and now she can't shake her.

Saara lies back and closes her eyes. She looks amazingly young. She's still the girl who came to talk to her in the hallway her first week at school, handed her one of her iPod earpieces and said *Listen to this* in a cooing voice that for some reason stirred Anna's womb, although she'd never thought she liked girls.

Oh don't be shy, let's cause a scene,
like lovers do on silver screens,
let's make it, yeah, we'll cause a scene.

After that they went everywhere together and shared the feelings a fresh friendship creates, the dazzled gratitude, a certainty that reality was exactly what they wanted it to be.

The next year they marched with defiant certainty in a protest against the Iraq war and believed they were changing the world.

What more do you need to change it but friendship, shameless faith, and trust?

Anna feels simultaneously like it happened only yesterday, and like it all happened years and years ago.

Before she moved to Pengerkatu, Anna lived with Saara for a year on Liisankatu. They had evenings that never ended, music, discussions over the kitchen table, an open door for guests. Their breakfasts stretched out, turned into debates. They played records and didn't care if the neighbors stared at them in the hallway.

Another friend of Saara's lives on Liisankatu now.

Saara smiles, still not opening her eyes. From above she looks a bit like one of Picasso's women, disassembled, fragmented, searching for a shape.

Sometimes Anna feels out of date around Saara, awkward, old-fashioned, always a step behind. Saara has the same fantasies she has, but not the same fears about getting there. Saara lives life in a way that Anna can't because she's too afraid.

ANNA'S THOUGHTS RETURN to Eeva. What does she know about her?

She only has a few facts. Eeva was from Kuhmo, and moved to the city to study French language and literature.

Anna conjures up a picture in her mind.

Eeva furrowed her brow when she was reading, which made her look a little worried. She had small hands, caught colds in the winter. Some kind of vague seriousness lodged in her eyebrows. When she buttered her bread or washed the dishes or brushed her hair, she would lose herself for a moment in the motions, look dreamy, relaxed and happy, like women in turn-of-the-century paintings. Like Schjerfbeck's women.

When she was about to laugh she first looked startled for a moment. A hundredth of a second later you could see horror in her face. Then the laughter would come bursting out.

Anna has this picture in her mind, and the beginning of a story on her lips: a man, a child, the child's astonishingly white neck, her trust.

The man had been one of the most admired of his day. Not at the forefront of change, not a provocateur, but certainly the most promising and indisputably the most handsome. A charmer, one of those men you sit down with in a restaurant and you don't get up for the rest of the evening, the kind of man you want to ask for directions to reality, to have him look across the table and tell you what it's really all about. Everyone wanted a piece of him. His attention was accepted like a gift. When he looked at you, it felt like you had never really had a shape until that moment.

Artists are like that—they have the power to see, they carry all the weightiest, best-shaped ideas, they make things real that would otherwise remain lurking at the threshold, at the bus stop, around the corner, in parentheses.

Anna still needs Eeva's voice.

The tree holds its blossoms above them as if it invented itself only yesterday. This has happened before, the exact same thing, but it has never been so fresh and so complete as now.

Eeva had days like these. Even this restlessness, this impatience to be somewhere else, someplace where life offered itself fully.

And there was more: Eeva had love, just like Anna. To give her all and get the whole world, that's what she believed in. That's what she was doing with the little girl, just as much as with the man.

Anna didn't intend to tell Saara about Eeva, but Eeva's here now, demanding that the story be told.

Anna's voice is a little different—softer, fuller—as she begins.

1964

THIS IS HOW it all begins.

Here I am. I'm standing at the door, about to ring the doorbell.

When it all begins, the new slogans haven't been invented yet, but the pill has already made its first appearance. People are already asking what's really happening, but skirt lengths are still of a sober length and cows still low in their barns.

When it all begins, I'm twenty-two years old. I'm halfway through my studies in spite of late nights in restaurants and occasionally tough bouts of homesickness for Kuhmo, where my mother and father keep ten cows and six bulls, in a farmyard painted with red clay. Where I come from milk is drunk warm from the milking, poured into glasses straight from the pail. It leaves a thick coating in your mouth.

When it all begins, I'm living between two worlds. I have Helsinki, glasses of wine bought with the last of my money, smiles that I toss across the room without thinking of the consequences, boys that I kiss in arched entryways, defying my mother's horror. I have cheap shoes and share an apartment with Kerttu on Liisankatu.

And I have Kuhmo, the meadow and the lake and the path through the woods that remembers me. I have a longing for home, nights when I lay awake in bed with the ceiling light on and cry from missing it, dream of the meadow, of swimming across the lake at night, bread cheese, starched sheets, and being nine years old, spending dreamy days at my desk at school.

But in 1964, the real one of the two is Helsinki. This is where I live, go to classes, walk down the street, meet people, most of them people Kerttu knows because she knows all the young people in this city, all of the ones that have ever had any opinions.

I have a tedious job at the hat counter in a department store and many different plans, not one of which has come true. Not that there's any hurry. In those years I'm still walking around in a dream that can drain away with waiting if you're not careful, those days when you feel that you have eternity before you.

All through the fall and winter I've listened to Vieno at the hat counter giving me orders, wanting to make a lady of me. Vieno uses words like waistline and bodice, discretion, chastity. I don't want a waistline or any of those other old words. I want to make up myself myself.

That's why I'm standing here at the door. It's May, the trees are still a thicket of bare limbs, although the weather's warmed already. I've just walked two blocks. There are beads of sweat on my neck from walking. I'm nervous. The flier I saw in the university lobby was simple: *Family seeks affectionate nanny who knows how to cook. Interested parties may contact us evenings.*

I ring the bell at exactly six o'clock because I believe the advertisement is meant for me. I certainly am affectionate. I often feel affection so abundant that it seems to flow from the tips of my fingers like nectar. My cooking skills are respectable. I know how to make bread cheese and how to fold potato-berry tarts, and my meat stew is thick and flavorful. I don't need board—I have a good arrangement with Kerttu on Liisankatu. We live in two rooms and a kitchen left to Kerttu by a great aunt.

I sleep in the second room, Kerttu stays in the living room, except for the weeks when her German boyfriend—or the other one, from Stockholm—is in town. Then it's best that I sleep on the sofa.

But now I'm standing at a door ringing the bell.

I realize later that my life, a completely new life, begins at this moment. Maybe the end of it is in sight, too, there at the door. But this is the beginning, and beginnings don't like to hear about endings.

Elsa opens the door. Then I see the little girl and the man. There he is, standing in the doorway. The girl comes from behind him, walks to her mother with a rag doll in her arms and holds on to the hem of her mother's skirt, looking at me.

I don't know what to think of her, other than that she's new, fresh. This is the moment that will always continue, later on, when everything else is over.

Me at the door, Elsa greeting me with a smile on her lips—because I haven't yet done anything to wipe the smile away—and the little girl beside her.

The only thing I notice about the man in that first moment is something comfortable in his eyes, a beauty which doesn't make a big impression at first.

We sit on the sofa. There's something horselike about the man, maybe it's his legs, maybe his hair. There's also something familiar about him which I can't put my finger on, something that keeps drawing my gaze back to him, his arms, his slightly wandering eye.

Elsa smiles, and I think she's pretty. The man shakes my hand, introduces himself.

"And this is Ella," Elsa says, putting the girl on her lap. The doll falls to the floor, the girl reaches her hand toward me, and I have no idea that reach will extend through all the years to come, reaching toward me, no matter where I go.

"Hello, Ella," I say.

Elsa tells me about their previous nanny, Hilma, who had to quit due to illness.

"That's too bad."

The man laughs.

"Hilma was a little too strict with Ella."

Elsa is a gracious person—she doesn't want to talk ill of anyone. She lays her hand on his thigh. They have that kind of affection between them. She lays her hand patiently on his thigh when he speaks too hastily.

He gets worked up easily—I learn that later. I learn to love the quick temper that in boyhood got him into man-sized trouble on the soccer fields and stone courtyards of his neighborhood. Elsa loves it, too. She loves it in exactly the same way that I do.

"Now," she says placatingly, her hand still resting on the man's thigh. "My husband," she says to me, "had certain differences of opinion with Hilma. Hilma was old-fashioned. I can tell you that our child-rearing methods are more liberal."

"What does that mean?" I ask curiously.

I'm accustomed to learning my lessons at the end of a switch. My father, who only survived the war by virtue of a Bible he kept in his breast pocket, thrashed my back with a birch switch whenever I forgot to say please or thank you. He's dear to me, but strict.

The man looks at his wife tenderly. "Elsa has principles. It's part of her job, you might say."

"We want our servants to be like members of the family."

I tell them about my mother and about the family I lived with my first year as a student, taking care of their children. I tell them about my job at the department store hat counter. I don't mention Vieno or that I'm applying for this job to get away from her. I tell them about Kerttu.

I don't tell them about our nights, our parties that sometimes last until morning. I don't tell them about the evenings when we have people over to visit. Evenings when we open up bottles of cheap Hungarian beer and Bordeaux Blanc, which we call Porvoo Plank. We talk about everything, make plans, though we're not sure about what. We read poetry. Often someone plays the guitar, and sometimes somebody will interrupt the song by opening all the bay windows and yelling something into the street, but a girl in the kitchen doesn't mind the noise, she only hears the music and lets down her hair and dances in front of the old wood stove until hairpins fall on the floor like dazed grasshoppers.

I don't mention any of that, so the man and the woman won't think I'm frivolous.

They wouldn't have minded. They, too, open wine bottles, and gather in the living room to talk. But I don't know anything about that yet.

"At home in Kuhmo I took care of the neighbors' twins when I was only fifteen and everyone was out haying. And I made meat stew for the whole village."

Elsa nods. Suddenly I feel as if I've said something wrong.

"You'll hardly need to do any heavy catering around here. My husband comes and goes, and you're free to go where you like in your free time."

I don't let my doubt show. When did stew go out of style?

I glance surreptitiously at the man. Do I know him from somewhere? I realize that I've seen him in the newspaper. With a little effort I remember strolling through an exhibition of his incomprehensible paintings, which were too modern for me. I like old things, clear lines and faces that stay where they belong without breaking into pieces.

Elsa drinks the rest of her coffee. I'm already infatuated with her. It was Elsa who I fell in love with in the beginning.

She has thick brown hair and eyebrows that look like little fuzzy caterpillars. Her smile is funny, like she's constantly, tirelessly looking for someone to play with, like she might say, without thinking, to anyone she was talking to, come on, let's go in the kitchen and get ourselves a big slice of Bundt cake and have a fairy coffee party.

I immediately think she's the kind of person you have just one more cup of coffee with, bake an enormous batch of rolls with on a rainy evening, or sit and cool down with on the porch of a lakeshore sauna. She would suggest one more swim, challenge you to a race across the bay. After swimming she would comb her hair in the candlelight, reflected in the cracked cabin mirror, and give you both French braids. But in those years Elsa has disguised herself in objectivity. She is making a career, standing on a dais in a lecture hall presenting her theories, writing reports and staying up late composing articles for international journals.

In those years, Elsa isn't extravagant. She's more assertive, adult, impenetrable. She thinks that a woman has to hide certain things about herself to be believed. Later she'll get her playfulness back. When she turns forty, she'll dance on the table. At her fiftieth birthday party she'll make a Freud and a Jung out of cardboard and sit them down at the dinner table. At her sixtieth, she'll end the night lying on the floor giggling.

But in those years she is businesslike. She's a scholar above all, then a mother, then a wife. Deep inside, at some level in the negative numbers, she's hiding a young woman who swims across lakes, a girl who at the age of fourteen celebrated winning a ski race by pouring blueberry soup on her head. I can see that woman in spite of her zealous attempts to conceal her, and I fall in love with her immediately.

THERE'S ONE THING I don't yet know as I sit here across from Elsa and her husband. As summer makes its entrance outside the window and my spoon clinks in my coffee cup, I don't know that I'm becoming a person Elsa will hate. Or if not hate, then at least disdain.

But now she's about to decide that I am the person she'll choose. She's slightly hesitant, wants to discuss the matter with her husband, deliberates between me and the well-wrinkled former nanny of five they interviewed earlier. I'm less experienced but she likes me better, she can't deny it. The wrinkly one made her think of a matron in an old movie with a rolling pin in her hand. She'd like to give me the job.

To confirm her decision she puts the little girl on my lap. The girl looks bedazzled and curious and gawky, as anyone does when they're first tossed fresh into the world.

She's warm, heavy, and slightly damp. She smells like milk.

She stretches her hand out toward me and takes hold of my nose without a moment's hesitation, looking at me in amazement. She shifts her gaze to the plate of cookies and bends over them, squirming a little so that the back seam of my dress starts to tighten. Cookie, she says. I could give her back to her mother—I'm hot and sweat is dripping down my sides. Soon she calms down in my lap. It feels as if she were about to fall asleep. She leans against me, breathing evenly.

Her tummy is round and warm, rising and falling feverishly.

"You seem to like her," Elsa says.

I nod. I'm afraid that my uncertainty shows. I exaggerated my child care experience a little. I want to get away from Vieno's sarcastic remarks, want to be in these rooms, in this friendly, self-assured woman's sphere of influence.

Elsa tells me about her research group, her traveling. Here is Elsa, proud, permissive, and sure of herself, explaining her extraordinary plans as simply and modestly as other people talk about an evening bowl of oatmeal.

I realize immediately that she is one of those people who will have it all, people compared to which others are wallowing in shiftlessness.

Elsa asks her husband to help her in the kitchen for a minute. I know that a discussion of whether to hire me is going on in hushed voices.

I don't know that it's the man who's not sure. He later tells me about it when we're lying silently side by side. He had an inkling of this and suggested the wrinkly one, but went along with Elsa's wishes.

I sit on the sofa with the little girl in my lap trying to hear a conversation about me. The little girl covers the sounds with chatter. I look around. A chest of drawers, books on a shelf. Careless housekeeping, modern furnishings. There's a television in the corner. I don't know if I know what to do with it.

On the wall are paintings, some of which, I later learn, are painted by the man, others by friends. The little girl climbs off my lap to the floor and runs to her mother and father in the kitchen. She's still shy of me.

I go and look at a painting leaned upside down against the wall. Something sloshes inside me. It's a Schjerfbeck. I've only seen them in museums.

Elsa steps into the living room, straightens her back.

"Why is this here in the corner?" I ask.

Elsa flutters a hand in the air and laughs. She bends toward me and lowers her voice like she's sharing a secret: "It's old-fashioned. My husband wants to take all the old pictures off the walls. Do you like it?"

The man is looking at me, smiling. I look away, then back again.

Elsa says with eagerness in her voice, "We'd like to hire you. If the position interests you."

The little girl turns her head and looks at me, her eyebrows raised. I do the same, and she bursts into bright laughter.

"I GOT A job," I tell Kerttu that evening.

She's sitting at the table eating. Her expression of surprise changes in a moment to enthusiasm.

My Kerttu: dark, thick hair, eyes black as lumps of coal. Kerttu's family is well-to-do. People still call her grandfather by his Swedish name, Brännare, although he changed it to Palovaara, believing that the country deserved people who said their names in their own language. Kerttu's home is a place where fervent pronouncements are made with big words like religion and fatherland, but Kerttu hides a whole great world in her dreams, unknown countries like exotic jewels.

I met her in the registration line for German class.

Don't you feel like we ought to cause some kind of scandal? she whispered to me, smiling. Take off our shirts, run across the lobby? I'll give you one mark, all my coffee breaks at the university, and my heart, if you'll do it with me.

We didn't take off our shirts, or even our socks, but we did spend all our coffee breaks together after that.

We've lived together in these rooms for two years and I've acquired Kerttu's habits and beliefs. She sleeps till noon one day and gets up at six the next. Sometimes she'll live for a week on risotto. Sometimes she eats in restaurants on a gentleman's tab, flashing her stocking seams on the way to the ladies' room. Afterward she tells me derisive stories about these men. It's all part of her secret plan, she says.

In these first years, Kerttu changes her style from seamed stockings and short skirts to jeans and black turtlenecks. Later she'll find new styles—she's a chameleon. At the end of the decade she'll be wearing a headband, halter tops, and white peasant blouses that lace up the front.

In the summers she goes wherever she wants to, works as an au pair for some people she knows in America, stays in Copenhagen with a girl named Ingrid who lets her sleep on the sofa. She'll come back from these trips with books and compacts and hats and words that I've never heard of, 45s that she plays in the living room so loudly that the paint shakes off the ceiling in the apartment downstairs. We'll listen sometimes to a hoarse-voiced woman, sometimes to blaring music with a name that's just been invented, the kind my mother calls pounding. Not yet time for Indian ragas— that comes a few years later. Kerttu hasn't yet tossed her halter tops in the corner, though by the end of the next decade she'll proudly wear nothing but a T-shirt and jeans, her breasts under her shirt like defiant apples.

But in 1964 everything is just beginning. Kerttu still wears her hair up in a beehive sometimes and coats it with hairspray from an aerosol can—a habit she will later come to disdain.

Kerttu is looking for something, she doesn't know what. She's restless and moody and overflowing and happy and she's decided that I belong with her in everything she does.

She takes exams on five books at a time in political science, history, philosophy—sometimes books with ancient covers. She swears that one day she'll shake the dust of this country off her feet and head out into the wide world.

But now, in May of 1964, she has sprayed hair and coal-black eyes, here on Liisankatu, and she's looking at me eagerly.

"You'll finally get away from Vieno. What kind of job did you get? Journalist? Interpreter? Or are you going to be a secretary somewhere? It's not the best job, but secretaries have good opportunities for promotions."

"No," I say. "I'm going to be a nanny for a family."

Kerttu's expression freezes, disappointment creeping into her face. She had imagined something else.

"You don't even like to cook."

"I'm learning to like it."

"Why?" Kerttu asks. "Why in the world would you?"

I hear my explanation: "Be serious. You know I need the money. You know I hate working at the hat counter."

I haven't asked my parents for money once since I moved to Helsinki. They wouldn't have had it anyway. In fact they've got used to getting letters once a week with a couple of bills in them from my wages.

"It's just a job," I say. "I'm going to take care of the child while the wife is traveling for work."

"Are you going to do the cleaning and the shopping?"

"Yes, I'll do the cleaning and shopping."

"See?" Kerttu says knowingly, popping a piece of bread in her mouth as if the gesture severs her from the conformity of this world. "You're going to be a maid."

"No. This is a real thing. It's a family. They said they wanted me to be like a member of the family."

Kerttu laughs bitterly. Defiance rises in me.

"They said I could have a room to use."

"Are you going to move?" Her eyes darken.

I soften, go to her and hug her. "No. No, I'm not. I'll just be spending the night there when she's traveling. It's easier that way."

"What does she do?"

"She's a psychologist. A doctor. She studies children."

Kerttu's expression brightens a bit. "What about her husband?"

"Actually," I say slowly, "I think he's a little bit famous. He's an artist."

I tell her his name. She's silent for a moment.

"Good," she says. "I know him. He's chummy with poets and people like that. He might be a man of substance. Good company, I mean. Or he might be a louse."

"He didn't seem like a louse."

Kerttu sighs, smiles. "All right. You have my permission. As long as you don't end up being a servant for the rest of your life."

I STILL HAVE to call my mother and father. My mother doesn't say she's disappointed, although I can hear that she is. She'd hoped for better for her daughter. Instead she talks about the television my father's bought. He got excited about the idea of a television when Mäntyranta won the gold medal in skiing. Before that he was against the contraption.

"What are you watching?"

"The test pattern," my mother says. "Isn't that exciting?" She's quiet for a moment. "So you probably won't be coming home for the summer."

"We'll see."

My father says what I was afraid he'd say: "You could have done that."

"Done what?"

He snarls the rest of the sentence out: "You could have done that here. Cook, boil porridge, watch the neighbors' kids."

I don't care what he says, because I want to build my own world, by myself.

IN JUNE, A day before Elsa's trip, I carry two suitcases over the threshold. Elsa is alone, the man has taken the little girl to the park.

She shows me my room. It's small but pretty. There's a view of the yard from the window—I can see a horse chestnut tree, already withering in the summer days, and two young apple trees. It's a lucky beginning. There's some kind of luck in it, though I don't yet know what kind.

Elsa packs her things in her room, taking clothes out of the closet, folding dresses and jackets into a large suitcase.

She pats me approvingly as she passes. She's giving me permission. I'm not a servant here, I can come into her bedroom.

"What are you going to do while you're there?" I ask, emboldened by her familiarity. "What do you study?"

She says simply: "We study children. We're developing a new form of therapy, a kind of play therapy."

While she's away she's going to spend her days at a clinic where the air is filled with cries for help, hurt feelings, requests to be picked up, rages freshly created. But above all the clinic's air will be filled with hope—Elsa's sure of this—the inexhaustible hope that every child carries inside. Room after room of children playing in a circle, children taking naps, sitting in the laps of mothers at a loss for what to do. Some children happily absorbed in dolls and puzzles, others gazing glumly at the brick walls of the building. Elsa will pick up a crying child, rock the child for a while, write down observations. She can't bear to leave a child unconsoled. There's no demand for explanations from Elsa's lap— it's broad, accepting, unquestioning.

"Look," Elsa says suddenly, grabbing a dress that's hanging in the closet. "I've been trying to think who this would fit. It's gotten too tight for me." She lifts the dress, examines it critically, peers at me. "Do you want to try it on?"

The dress is a pretty one, ordered from a seamstress. It's a little old-fashioned, but grown-up, the kind of dress that you need wisdom and experience to wear. I want to try it on. I want its gentleness, its dignity.

Elsa watches me undress. There's still a sisterly quality between us, a mutual approval, perhaps a hint of guidance.

She zips me up, opens the closet door to show me the mirror. The dress is a little too big—the bust is an empty dome.

"Look, it almost fits you," Elsa says smiling. "It's just a little loose. You can take it to a seamstress, have the seams taken in a few centimeters."

IN THE EVENING I try on the dress again in my room. I put it on carefully, stepping into it like a mold. It's a little too big, I don't completely fill it.

I look at myself in the narrow closet mirror.

I look like a copy, a slightly absurd imitation. Something needs to be done. I'd have to be something more, but I don't know how. The horse chestnut tree in the yard looks sinister in the dark as the lights go out. I lie awake for a long time and try to listen for noises. If the man and his wife are doing anything—and why shouldn't they, this is their night to say good-bye—they're doing it silently.

"SO," ELSA SAYS.

She drinks her coffee standing up. Then she gives me a look as if to say, are you ready? It's seven o'clock, bright sunrise.

We ricochet around the kitchen awkwardly, uncertain as rolled dice. The little girl gets worked up. She knows that something new is about to happen. She runs from one room to the next, climbs from my lap to Elsa's, from Elsa's to her father's.

He's quiet, avoiding my gaze. Later I learn that it's a habit he picked up as a boy when there was more than one woman present, a habit he hasn't shaken. When his mother would invite friends over, he would sit at the table with the women, see their bosoms heaving, those breathtaking mounds, and turn his face to the window.

A stolen glimpse, as if through the crack of a door: light flooding through the window, covering everything in a bright haze, but the women continue their murmuring talk, the light dances in their hair and on the pearl buttons of their sweaters. Their breasts are sublime and their smiles hold unspoken secrets.

He decides to go to his friend Lauri's house tonight. Maybe he'll call up his whole gang of buddies and they can go out somewhere for the evening. He doesn't intend to spend silent hours in these rooms with me. He'll give the child a good night kiss and walk out the door. That's what they're paying me for. To sleep in these rooms, so he can go where he wants.

When the front door is opened, the little girl bursts into tears. She knows that her mother is leaving. She runs to the living room and hides under the coffee table.

"Oh, little one," Elsa says, standing in the doorway. She goes into the living room with her coat on, shoes on her feet, takes the girl in her arms one more time, rocks her quietly, and whispers something in her ear not meant for anyone else to hear.

I wonder how I'll ever be able to bend like that, to give the kind of consolation that Elsa knows how to give. Uncertainty squeezes me as small as a fist.

The girl finally agrees to come out from under the table. She has her rag doll with her. She walks to the door, humble, with the doll, which is as big as she is, in her arms.

Elsa embraces the little girl for a long time in the street, in front of the car, as the suitcases are put in the trunk. She's not sure for a moment whether to hug me or shake my hand. She decides on the hug.

"You can take my daughter," she says.

I take the little girl in my arms, she presses her head against my shoulder, squeezing the doll under her arm, no longer looking at her mother.

The man glances at me. I nod. They can go. Elsa smiles a little before opening the car door. When they've left, the girl asks me to put her down. I strike a mild-mannered pose. I'm on my own now.

"So." The word echoes through the street, making me feel again like an imitation. "What would you like to do? We can do anything you like."

"Let's go to the park," the girl says.

That doesn't sound hard. We can go to the park and look at the fountain. Or maybe I'll take her to the seashore, show her the ships. We can buy some ice cream, ride the tram. We can name the trees that we see, dig in the ground with a stick, maybe see a worm, give it a name, too—Pekka, perhaps—and hope out loud that it finds whatever happiness can befall a worm.

"Molla's coming, too," she says.

"Good," I say. "Molla's coming."

Only now do I really look at the girl. It's been a long time since I looked at a child so closely. Pure is the word that first comes to mind, but not in the sense of being free of dirt—it's something else, something fresh. Her eyelashes are surprisingly long, her eyelids plump, her nose looks soft, rising from her face like a ripe berry. She already has distinctive expressions, but sorrow hasn't yet found its way onto her face, I can see that. Seeing it is unlike any other seeing—seeing something that doesn't yet exist, but that you know is coming.

I'll be the one to draw sorrow on the little girl's face. I don't know this yet, and I don't yet know that she'll survive. I won't survive as well. She's the one who will draw sorrow on me. She's the one whose disappearance from my life will leave me limp, so that I lie on the floor for days without moving, unable to get up.

WE WALK TO a busier street and I'm flooded with a whole
slew of threats. Maybe she'll get scared on the tram and start
to yell. Maybe we'll be run over by a street sweeper or a car.
Maybe she'll get lost and I'll end up shouting her name till
I'm hoarse.

Suddenly she's mute.

I can't look at her, don't speak to her. How does it feel to
have her see me whole?

She doesn't see me. She's two and a half years old—she
doesn't see anything about me except that I'm an adult, a
virtual stranger, a woman whose uncertainty is growing second by second.

I want to protect her from every possible loss. I notice myself thinking that we can never cross this intersection, that
it would be better to run to the arch of a building entrance
or a bomb shelter, to hunker there for the rest of our lives or
at least until her father comes home, thinking that I have no
intention of putting the little girl in any danger, of shattering
her face into unrecognizability.

The girl interrupts my growing dread by taking hold of
my hand.

Her hand is amazingly soft, it feels springy and plump.
Her grasp is light. I had already forgotten this trust, which
all children share, because they don't know any different,
the belief they have from birth that everything will be all
right. At some point in their lives it's lost in a moment, inevitably. If they're lucky, it comes back again. Someone comes
and takes them in their arms, wrapped in a blanket, in a

bedroom, or reaches an arm under a table, and they relearn what was inevitably lost when they lost their childhood.

But the little girl hasn't lost anything yet. She's saying to me, with her whole being, that I can protect her. She's not afraid of the trams clattering by, or the cars or the people or seagulls or falling trees or death, because she believes that I know how to protect her.

And as the seconds stretch out and the cars drive by and she doesn't let go of my hand, I begin to believe her. It's so simple. Her faith gives me faith. I squeeze her hand and don't intend to let go. I won't.

"Mommy says to look both ways when you cross the street."

"Aha. Well, Mommy is right."

I see a glimpse of her soft neck, pale, white, a bare spot between her coat and the downy fringe of her hair. I want to put my hand over it, to protect it. It's saying in all its dim luster that nothing bad can happen as long as it's not afraid to be so naked and vulnerable.

"You can buy me some ice cream," the little girl says.

"Maybe I will," I answer, and now I'm not afraid of anything, either.

8

SHALL WE GO to Seurasaari?" Elsa said suddenly.
They were on their way back from their usual drive.

"I don't want to go inside yet, I really don't," she said
coaxingly. "Maybe I could go for a swim."

"A swim? You're not serious. I won't let you go for a
swim."

"Why not?"

"You'll freeze to death."

Elsa gave him a meaningful look, her eyebrows raised. He
realized his slip and they both burst out laughing.

"All right," he agreed. "We can have one more outing."

"Let's pick up some tea from home," Elsa mused. "And a
blanket."

They brewed the tea in the thermos. Elsa packed two
large swim towels, wearing an impish grin. It was already
late, past ten, only a few joggers passing by. The sea borrowed its color from the sky. The power plant loomed in the
distance, flaming orange in the last rays of the setting sun.

It had been a warm day, but it had rained in the afternoon. Now, as the sun sacrificed itself slowly to the night,
everything seemed to float in a pink mist.

There was a swimming cove at the first curve in the road—
a boulder beach, with sand closer to the water's edge. A pair
of swans nodded to the rocks at the shore's edge. They were
like water lilies, floating silent and still.

There were no chicks to be seen. You could hear some
geese farther south, in the middle of the island's bay, thrash-
ing around in the water, the birds' annual pageant.

The sun was a ball of orange enmeshed in graffiti gray.

"What kind of sky is this?" Elsa asked.

This was a habit of theirs. He noticed the colors. Elsa
would ask for them, for the light, the sky's identifying features, and he would tell her.

"Carefree clouds," he said. "Like they've forgotten that
there ever was anything serious."

"And the moon?" Elsa asked, pointing at the sky, where
the moon was just resolving into a faded crescent.

"The moon is shy," he said.

"You know, I love how romantic you are, even if it has
gone out of style."

Elsa stopped, looked at the sun, looked at the rippling
water.

"I think I'll go in."

"Really? You mean to do it, then?"

"Who's going to stop me?" Elsa said, looking at him defiantly. "What if this is my last chance to swim? I suppose you
want to deny me that pleasure?" She said this with a smile.

"I guess not," he said.

She walked to the shore, using a cone-covered pine for support on her way to the water. She took off her clothes—coat,
shoes, pants, shirt, finally her underwear—without any shyness.

Martti glanced around instinctively. There was no one to be seen. He felt joy and terror at the same time. This seemingly muddle-headed, skeletal woman, in whom I can still see the outlines of my love, intends to go swimming, because the idea grabs her. I won't stop her—I'll go after her if it looks like she can't make it. But I won't try to stop her.

Elsa glanced back at him once more at the water's edge, as if seeking encouragement for her waywardness in his gaze. Then she stepped into the water.

A pleasurable little whimper escaped her lips: the water was cold.

All of a sudden he remembered being in exactly the same situation before: Eeva taking off her clothes, stepping into the water, glancing at him, wading out deeper, then bending over to swim. Calm strokes in supreme silence. The water was cold but Eeva didn't scream, didn't make a sound. As if she needed to prove her valor.

When she got out of the water, Eeva had come to where he was, and he had wrapped her in a towel, in his arms. That's how they laid claim to their intimacy, without words. It was justified by her swim in too cold water.

Elsa stepped calmly into the water, bent over to swim, two strokes, three. Then she stood up and came back to the beach.

"Done already?" he asked, and held out a towel spread open.

Elsa pressed into his arms with a smile.

"Lovely."

"If you die here, I'll never forgive myself," he heard himself say.

Elsa shivered, putting her clothes on slowly. He helped her. He insisted she put on an extra sweater under her coat.

"Now let's have a little tea," she said.

They walked up the hill. Elsa struggled up the slope on her own strength. They walked slowly past the fenced-off nude beach, looked at the bay opening out to their right. The water was divided by the familiar dock that extended from the foot of the stone stairs, benches at its tip for admiring the sunset.

"That way," Elsa said.

They laid the blanket on a bench, poured some tea from the thermos into their mugs. Elsa opened a package of Ballerina cookies and ate one with relish.

"Are you cold?"

"A little."

He took off his coat and wrapped it around her. She let her gaze drift to the horizon.

"I've been thinking we could drive out to Tammilehto," Martti said. "Do you think you'd be up to it? The sauna floor needs to be replaced anyway—Eero and Matias could help us with it. You could keep your eye on it, act as supervisor."

"Supervisor, eh? I can hardly turn that down, provided the pay is commensurate with my qualifications."

"What pay are you asking?"

"How about two cookies? Any less than that and my professional pride would be offended."

"How about three? What if I offered you three?"

"For three cookies I'd tear up the whole floor and dance the polka on it."

"You're hired."

Elsa put her hand on his thigh and looked at the clouds for a moment.

"I don't want to die."

She said it so suddenly that he was shaken.

"Are you afraid?"

"No. I'm not afraid. But I don't want to do it. I'm not ready yet."

Elsa closed her eyes. An image of her from the 1970s, when they'd spent a month in Dubrovnik, came into his mind. Elsa in a lounge chair, in a yellow bikini on the shore of the Adriatic, languid and mellow as she was now.

"Anna found the dress," Elsa said, her eyes still closed.

"What dress?"

"Eeva's dress."

"She did?" he managed to say. "Why do we have it? Why wasn't it given away?"

"It's been in the closet all these years."

"And?"

Elsa was quiet for a moment. She clicked her tongue. "I told her," she said.

"Why?"

"I want to tell about my life. I've started to think I should. If I don't tell it, it won't be told."

Would Anna tell her mother? Would they discuss it? Did Eleonoora already know anyway? It was certain that Eleonoora knew something, remembered some of it, or maybe all of it. They'd just never talked about it.

"Shouldn't you have talked with Eleonoora about it first?"

"Maybe," Elsa answered.

She looked at him, slightly at a loss. He could see she was afraid, maybe regretful.

"Maybe we should have told her from the beginning," she said. "We should have talked about it somehow."

"You thought differently back then."

"Back then I had seen so many suffering children, children who knew too much about the affairs of adults. I thought that a child had a right to live in a child's world, in play and fantasy."

"She's happy. Isn't she? Maybe she became a happy person."

"Maybe," Elsa said. "I do intend to bring it up. I'll tell her when the time is right. I'll wait for the right moment."

He didn't say it but he thought, the right moment will never come.

They sat there for a good while longer. They were waiting for the sky to turn orange, then rose, before it was finally blue. On the way back Elsa got tired and asked him to go get the car.

9

ANNA DOESN'T FEEL like standing in the bookstore in the murmuring afternoon. Two more hours. She and her mother have planned to meet at the door to Stockmann's deli. What luck to get to do the shopping for a trip to the countryside, walk down the fruit aisles and the greens counter, pick up some cheese or marshmallows or zucchini, expensive cloudberry yogurt or anything that comes to mind!

She's looking forward to the trip to Tammilehto, although she fears it may be difficult. You never know whether there's going to be laughter and banter or a strained atmosphere that could turn into an argument at any moment. Sometimes they just kid around, make food, giggle like sisters. At those times her mother is playful and as wild as a fifteen-year-old. Sometimes Anna can tell as soon as she sees her mother that it's one of those other times, when she lets drop complicated, sarcastic sentences or tries to dig up information about her with questions cloaked in empathy.

The bookstore is quiet, the air dry. Anna can hear the finicky sounds of the espresso machine from the cafe upstairs. Light collects in the skylights, books doze on the shelves. She gathers the books left on the counter into a basket.

Taking them back to their own sections is the single pleasure of her workday. She gets to go to the foreign paperback section, then up the escalator to the second floor—politics and economics—and maybe even to the third floor—art and travel books.

Anna invites a familiar thought that she often savors. How many beginnings of love are in the books sold here?

Almost every novel has a love story, a description of love beginning. And there's something the same about all of these stories—so much the same that their particular details are almost superfluous. But still, each one has its own secrets.

When you let go of yourself and are filled with joy and dread at the same time. When you understand that there's no turning back, that everything has fundamentally changed. When you realize that you're not at the place you thought you were at, you're already on your way toward the other person.

Anna walks to the escalator with the basket on her arm and goes up to the second floor.

Grandma and Grandpa met at a university party. Grandpa couldn't take his eyes off Grandma, who was just a dimpled, round-faced college girl majoring in psychology. Anna can easily imagine Grandpa. The kind of young man who's more likely to be called pretty than handsome. Elsa fell in love with his hot temper when provoked, his big plans for how he would make his living.

Anna's parents were sixteen years old when their love began, working on a group physics project that neither of them wanted to do. A Wednesday evening in his room, in the friendly shade of bold-patterned Marimekko curtains and a clumsy floor lamp.

The physics project was about gravity. Mom had argued with everything he said, although she had noticed his smile. Dad claimed he could eat an orange while standing on his head. No, you can't, she said. There's no way. Just watch me, he said.

And he swung into a headstand on the bed, leaned his legs against the wall, and took one bite after another from an orange. Mom's love started right at that moment, as he stood on his head with his skinny legs up against a Led Zeppelin poster, calm and focused, and ate the whole orange. He lowered himself and said with a smile, "Now you see that there are other forces besides gravity."

"Like what?" she said. "What kinds of forces do you mean?"

"Like trust, for instance," he said.

"What should I trust?" said Mom, who wasn't yet a mom but just a girl named Ella.

"How about what I tell you, for starters," the orange boy said with a smile.

Anna is envious of these stories. She'd like to have similar stories of her own.

She remembers Marc, last fall. She went to Paris four months after the breakup. A stupid idea, actually. She bought a cheap ticket. Alone in Paris! At home, the idea had seemed romantic and crazy, a symbol of freedom: her love had ended, she would shake off Helsinki and experience life as a different woman, by traveling alone in the city of love. When she got there she felt like an orphan. She wandered around, met a boy in a museum—Marc. They went to a cafe and shared a bottle of wine and their childhood fears. Marc kissed her on the banks of the Seine and suddenly asked, without any fuss, if she would move to Paris. He decided that they would fall in love and live happily ever after. But I don't even know you, Anna said. Just throw yourself into it, Marc answered.

And so she did: she threw herself into it in his apartment in the Marais. And it was over as quickly as it began. In the morning she gathered her things and slipped out without waking him. She never found out whether his promised love could have grown into something real or whether it was just a door to a brief and somewhat vague pleasure under a portrait of Che Guevara (how tasteless to hang a murderer's portrait on the wall!) in Marc's cozy but messy apartment. Maybe Marc was an impostor. Or maybe he was her great love story, and she passed it by. She'll never know.

OF COURSE SHE had that life, the one that ended on the floor by the front door. She would have liked to make that life completely real through love: to give her all and get the world.

She saw black for a moment. She knocked a book from the shelf as she walked by, bent to pick it up, and straightened up again. She smiled blindly at her coworkers. The world took shape again, she picked the basket up off the floor and continued to the back of the store.

WHEN SHE MET Matias, she didn't feel anything special. One smile across the room at a party, a somewhat pointless

conversation at a sticky kitchen table when all she was thinking was: that kind of boy.

Matias asked her out, she agreed, since there was no one
else. She noticed that she liked his smile. They drank cocoa
at Succés on Korkeavuorenkatu, shared a cinnamon roll. In
two weeks' time she was thinking that maybe the easiness
and comfort that was her overriding feeling with Matias was
the beginning of love.

In five weeks' time they carried the sofa through the door.

ANNA GOES TO the philosophy section, puts a book in
its correct spot on the shelf. On an impulse she checks to
see if any of her grandmother's books are in the psychology
section.

There's one copy of her most popular book, *Recognition
and Self*. Anna was in high school when she finally read it
for the first time, for a presentation on attachment theory for
her developmental psychology class, and as she read it she
felt a mixture of embarrassment and pride.

Her teacher said, "Is Elsa Ahlqvist really your grandmother? Imagine. Would you give her my regards?"

There was a picture of a child psychiatry clinic from the
1960s in their textbook. There were researchers in the picture who later had hypotheses and charts of emotional development named for them. And Grandma. Seeing her in a
picture in her second-year psychology textbook, she felt like
she was looking at a different person.

Anna opens her grandmother's book. The introduction
has always moved her. The case study of Luna, a girl found

lying in a cardboard box at a railway station who rebuilt her trust in the world little by little, has haunted her. She returns again and again to these words:

> *A risk to the self is always an unreasonable one, from a child's point of view. This is the conclusion I came to after observing Luna's weeks of painful development in the clinic. That moment when a child experiences the reality of self for the first time is the primordial moment of loneliness. It also offers the first opportunity for happiness. Every person's existence is a certified opportunity for great loneliness and great happiness. They are both within a child's reach at the moment she realizes her separateness from her parents. At that moment, the child is also a stranger to herself. It is only in the continuous recognition of the self in the safe, caring gaze of an adult that a child can become recognizable to herself. Recognition consists of experiences of both participation and separation. The beginnings of the self are in that rift, in that tension between blessed participation and rending separation. The event would perhaps hold nothing but tragedy if it didn't also bring the beginning of hope that is part of the solitary human condition.*
>
> *Imagine Luna, a girl found by a stranger, living in a cardboard box, a child who had experienced unheard-of sorrows. Imagine her groping attempts to reach out. She spent her first week of treatment rocking in a corner, apathetic, refusing to look anyone*

in the eye. In the following weeks she clung to her caregivers with a vise grip that seemed a cry for help. Little by little her trust grew. Imagine her first smile, from across the room, her first bold laugh in the playpen. Human life in its bare essentials is about nothing so much as trust. It's about the love that every person, even the maimed and oppressed of the world, bears toward others.

Anna remembers a childhood moment at the lake sauna, Grandma's strong arms and big soft breasts as she bent to turn on the hot water tap.

Maria was five, still shamelessly honest as small children always are, and she marveled at Grandma's breasts.

You're big up there, Maria said, pointing.

Yes, I guess I am, Grandma said with a smile.

Will those grow on me, too? Maria asked.

They might, Grandma said.

Then I'll be a mother, too, Maria said sagely.

You can't become a mother right off, Anna said. For that you need a man.

She was eight, and knew a few facts.

Yes, you can, Maria said. You never know. Some people might just turn into mothers.

Only in fairy tales, Anna said, taking to her role as the instructive, wiser older sister with satisfaction.

That Grandma, with the big breasts, is gone now. But there's still the Grandma that thought those thoughts, wrote those words in the book.

The book will be sold here after she's dead, too. People will thumb through it, read the introduction and think Elsa Ahlqvist must have been a wise woman, a good mother, a good grandmother.

Anna walks to the escalator. She again has the thought that she was toying with earlier. An unbelievable number of beginnings slept between the covers of all these books.

1964

LOVE BEGINS UNINTENTIONALLY. We're unguarded and we take no notice of the signs we may see weeks or even months before anything actually happens.

At first we avoid each other, exchange nervous courtesies and remarks about the weather. He sits at the kitchen table, preoccupied. He butters his bread, opens the newspaper, scratches his neck. What an abundance of private gestures, what a spectrum of fine gradations. I turn away; I don't want to know all this about him.

I wander from room to room as if I've found myself in a movie.

The man invites friends over for two evenings and closes the door on me. I hear a storm of laughter through the door, turn on the television. The newscaster on television looks worried. I didn't know that facts have to be told with a furrowed brow—I've only heard about the state of the world on the radio.

On the third evening he paints. Also the fourth and fifth. Night after night I hear him come clumping down the stairs as the dimness phases into morning. Maybe he's been drinking. I lie awake, listening, hearing every thud, the even sound of his breathing—it's strange and I'm afraid that he'll come into my room. What have I got myself into? What if he gets delirious, if he's one of those men who drinks a whole bottle with one swing of his arm?

He's not drunk. He can't see in the dark, loses track of the bounds of his body and bumps into things. I still don't know this. I've only just learned his morning sleepiness, his distracted gaze as he reads the paper. There are still a thousand things I don't know about him, and a thousand more after that. And another thousand and another, endlessly.

I hear him open the door. I lie there without breathing and listen. Nothing. I get up, creep across the kitchen into the hall and see him in the little girl's doorway.

"What are you doing?"

"Shhh."

He has an expression on his face I've never seen before.

"I'm watching her sleep," he says, as if embarrassed by his own tenderness. "I have to see that she's safe before I can go to sleep."

His affection for her is so genuine, but his art is pompous. He's full of himself, that's what I think. Some artist. A big deal famous artist. I think he hides himself in his work the way a bashful child hides in his play.

ON THE FOURTH day I call Kerttu.

"The husband paints every night," I say. "He barely says hello."

"It sounds excruciating."

"He's a snob. I don't know what to do with him."

"Go knock on his door. Tell him the kitchen's on fire, there's a flood in the bathroom and the walls are falling in, the little girl's taking a bath in the kitchen sink, and you're leaving the country. That'll get him downstairs."

"I doubt it."

I WORK UP my indignation as I go up the stairs. The attic absorbs the sound of my steps and smells like a sauna. I stop for a moment to listen to the creak, remember July evenings in childhood, at home in Kuhmo, in the darkness of the attic. I go to the door, lift my chin and knock. The man looks stern when I open the door without waiting for an answer.

"What?"

"I just wanted to know how much longer."

He looks at me like he doesn't understand the question, like I'm a strange, talking doll.

"I don't know—what do you mean?"

"The little girl's asleep."

"So?"

"What am I supposed to do?"

"How should I know? You can decide for yourself—you have the whole evening free. You could go for a walk or something."

"I can't, I have a hole in my shoe."

"Invite a friend over."

"They're all at a party, or engaged, or on their way to the justice of the peace."

He looks at me critically.

"Come here," he says, pulling me inside. He takes me by the shoulders and leads me to his painting. "Look."

He's eager, strangely bold—it comes from the hours of working, the surge of self-confidence. He's never touched me before.

"What do you think?"

The painting is ridiculous. I don't understand it at all, and I let him know it. "Lines and circles," I say simply. "I see lines and circles."

I exaggerate my nonchalance a bit, maybe I feel I should choose a side and stick to it.

"Maybe you don't care for art," he sneers.

I pounce on his dismissive tone with sarcasm, like Kerttu in her more self-important moments: "Certainly not this kind. What is this supposed to be a picture of?"

"Nothing," he says. "Art doesn't necessarily have to depict any specific thing. That's the old kind of art."

"I know what you're driving at. I saw your paintings at the Ars exhibit. I thought the same thing then. Why not paint people? Why not paint Elsa or your daughter?"

"I don't paint them," he says curtly. "I've never painted them."

"Maybe you should."

"And maybe you should come to my course at the university. I'm going to be lecturing on Jackson Pollock."

"Pollock makes me nauseous."

"Too many colors?"

"Too much dripping paint, a mess, as if the world were a pigsty. What his paintings need is a scrub brush and some pine soap before they put them on display."

He laughs. I look him right in the eye for a second. Another. The moment stretches out.

"Good," I say finally. "So when you're done with this . . ."
I look at his paintings, let my gaze wander over the jars and paintbrushes, the bottles of turpentine and oily rags. ". . . when you're done creating this world, you can come downstairs. Where a cupboard's still a cupboard and an apple's an apple. But don't think that I'll make you anything to eat. I'm sure a man who spends his night creating new realities knows how to butter his own bread."

I close the door behind me, triumphant, hotheaded—this is the first phase of love, but I don't recognize it!—without staying to see the effect of what I've said.

WE MEET ONCE by accident. I'm on my way to my last shift at the hat counter. He's coming toward me. I see him from far off, but he doesn't yet see me. His walk is carefree, hands in his pockets, smoking.

There's a conflict in him between anxiety and generosity. Mostly he's easygoing and carefree. He's anxious and demanding only when he's holding his daughter in his arms or painting, or sometimes when he's reading.

But now he glances across the street and sees me. He smiles, strides across the tram tracks to where I am.

He throws his half-smoked cigarette on the ground. Without acknowledging the thought or reading its message I think how beautiful he is.

"Hello, Eeva," he says.

He must have looked exactly the same when he was thirteen and the neighbor boy tempted him to go around the corner and smoke a cigarette and Loviisa the beauty, a typist from across the street who all the boys were in love with, walked by. He must have looked exactly like this when he greeted her, lifting a hand to his forehead solemnly but with a twinkle in his eye, shamelessly looking her in the eye without lowering his head.

"Hello."

"On your way to work? Aren't you done working at the department store? Or have you secretly changed your mind about taking care of our enfant terrible?"

Without realizing it I'm propping up layered selves he's already left behind. If I knew what I would learn later, I would have known to brace myself. This is the first phase of love, when you see the other person whole, when you can pluck every fear and desire from their gaze like ripe fruit.

I let the warning signs flit past me like house sparrows.

"My shift doesn't start for an hour yet."

"How about I buy you a cup of coffee?"

LOOKING AT HIM across the table I can see that he's been thinking about me. He's been thinking about the shyness of the first week, when he surprised me in the bathroom, accidentally opening the door while I was brushing my teeth, and said something about the brightness of the early summer day to hide his embarrassment.

He thinks about our strange encounter in the attic, in his studio. Was it an argument or just playfulness? He doesn't know. It was a poor exchange, he wouldn't want to repeat it. For the first time he doesn't want to withdraw into his work. The next time I come, he'll suggest a trip over the weekend. He'll drive us to Tammilehto and we'll . . . what?

He doesn't know. He hasn't thought it through. He's allowed himself to think of the beginning and of us, but he doesn't know what to do with the thought.

"What about your classes?" he asks. "Are you done with your exams for this year?"

"Yes."

I'm defying him, unwilling to concede. It's a strange game.

"And are you going back to . . . to where you're from?"

"Kuhmo."

"You're spending July there, aren't you? What will you do there? Burn clearings, that sort of thing?"

"Burn clearings? Where'd you get that idea?"

"From Finnish movies. You'll be frolicking in the fields, cavorting with golden-haired boys? Hiding in the haystacks?"

"I'll be frolicking, frolicking in the fields. Exactly. Skipping into the barn now and then for some kissing."

He stirs sugar into his coffee with a jolly look while I spoon Alexander cake into my mouth.

"Do you think that I wouldn't cut it there?" he demands. "That I'd fall through the ice in the winter and drop the oars in the water in the summer and have to call for help?"

"You'd get lost in the woods. If a bear came along you'd gripe about it. A wolf would eat your leg off."

"But not my hands," he says. "I could use my hands to paint the light. The lake will be a mirror, right? With just a few astonished trees rising from the pine woods?"

I laugh. He starts to laugh, looks out the window. An old gentleman outside the window raises his hat to me.

"You probably don't like my work."

"The lines and circles? I think they're a little affected."

He raises his eyebrows. I'm being cheeky again. He ponders how to respond. He doesn't know whether to find the cheekiness infuriating or admirable. He suddenly wonders what I might look like naked. He's flustered by the thought and looks out the window. I don't know his thoughts. I think this is just his way, to look away when he's thinking how to compose what he wants to say.

"What do you like, then? What kind of art?"

"Edelfelt. And Schjerfbeck. Gallen-Kallela. That kind of art."

"They are good," he agrees. "But perhaps a bit old-fashioned. Dull. I liked them when I was fifteen."

"Dull?" I glance at my watch, spoon the last bite of cake into my mouth. "Do you want to see the light, the landscape, where I come from?"

"I do," he says.

When he says I do, he looks me in the eye, beyond my eyes, and I think that a person's face is actually a kind of opening, like a clearing in the forest. When a person says what they want, every wish and request, fear and even secret joy, the joy of childhood, opens in their face like stepping from the shade into the light.

"I still have half an hour. I think we should make a quick visit to the Ateneum and confront the dullness of the paintings there before I go to the hat counter. If you want to see the landscape of my home."

WE WALK UP the echoing staircase to the third floor. I go first. I glance at him. He follows me smiling as if I were leading him to a carnival ride that he's decided he'll not set foot on.

I go into the hall and stand in front of the painting. For a moment I don't want to say anything, I want to stand here silently. In my first Helsinki autumn I came here whenever homesickness started to flow from the corners of my eyes. I came to this echoing hall and stood for as much as an hour in front of this painting.

There's a second forest painted on the surface of the lake, the precise outline of the trees, the brow of the ridge. The sky is pale; summer's bright, pale light. The sky spills milk over the trees, it coats the crowns of the spruce trees in sunset. In the central painting Aino is fleeing from the man's grasp, the pale skin of her thighs reflected in the surface of the lake, melting into the water as if she had always been kin to the fish.

"Like that," I say, not looking at him, looking at the landscape.

For some reason the man reaches out his hand and touches my back lightly.

"I'd fall out of that thing," he says, pointing at the tipping boat.

"You'd sink to the bottom."

"I'd make my home with the bass and the bream," he says.

"And old man Kemppainen would catch you in his fish trap, but he'd throw you back. He has no use for a helpless thing like you."

"Maybe I'll go there some day. You can teach me how to use a fish trap."

"Gladly."

I turn my head. He's said too much, he knows that. He doesn't regret it.

"I do know how to fish," he says. "But I've never had a close acquaintance with cows. You've beat me on that one."

"Oh, is this a competition? Prove it, then. Prove that you know how to lower your nets."

"I can take you to Tammilehto," he says. "In August. I can show you then."

"Agreed."

The solid walls of the museum recede from me. For a moment I see only the painting, the landscape.

I don't know how much time goes by. Finally the man touches me lightly on the shoulder.

"Still think it's dull?" I ask.

"No. No, I don't."

I look at my watch and realize that I'm late. We run to the door and out into the open air. The world cleaves the silence of the museum.

At the corner he hands me a piece of paper. He does it carelessly, as if he were handing me a cracker or a butter knife. It's a sketch on thick, rough paper.

"Here," he says.

There it is again—his smile for lovely Loviisa when he was thirteen.

"What's this?"

I'm about to turn it over, but he stops me.

"Look at it later," he says.

"Why?"

"Just because."

He takes a cigarette out of his breast pocket and lights it. He blows the smoke at a slant, takes a few steps backward and raises his arm to say good-bye.

When he has disappeared around the corner, I turn the paper over. He's drawn me from behind and in quarter profile. My turned-up nose, the arch of my cheekbone, the plump edge of my upper lip.

I stand at the intersection and let the cars drive past. The warning signs flit by like sparrows, but I don't take hold of them.

THE BEGINNING OF love needs dreams. It needs to wake up from a dream, thoughts that you can't quite pinpoint right away. It needs distance, remoteness that you can bring up close by giving your thoughts the other person's details: this kind of mouth, this chin, this kind of hollow at the wrist. And those eyes! And that smile! And that remark about the trees!

You have to row to an island, warm the sauna, and think: I want to come here with him, I want to row with him across the lake and see a fox flashing through the pines. I want to show him the spruce trees in the yard and say, Don't they look like friendly storybook characters guarding the past?

IN JULY I go to Kuhmo. I travel by train across the landscape. He and Elsa are in Paris with their daughter. I don't know anything about them during those weeks, I don't know that they have happy days together, the kinds of moments when he kisses her neck and they meet old friends. I don't know that there are also mornings when he walks alone along the Seine, goes into a museum or a cafe and lets the thought come: Eeva. All right. Eeva in her entirety, point by point. He orders coffee and smokes, watches the waiter, the people, the cars, the dog doing its business at the corner, the woman in gloves bending over the dog doo as if it were a rare jewel. He laughs at that. He'd like to take a picture of it but he doesn't have his camera with him. He looks at all of this, smoking calmly and building me in his mind.

Her mouth, what's it like?

Nose? Hair?

And her smile. Above all her smile.

The longing is an empty place under his breastbone. It feels a little like heartburn, he thinks, amusing himself. He plans August. He'll bring me to Tammilehto. He plans the winter, too, the winter days: frosty, shouts, sledding hills, me in a white knit hat with a pom-pom and ski pants—he wants to see me in a hat with a pom-pom on top. He mostly doesn't notice that he's planning his winter with me. Not Elsa.

Everything's already begun. Everything's already in motion.

EVERY MORNING IN Kuhmo I take up the nets with my father. A mist hovers over the lake so you can't see the island, a loon calls somewhere. The oars clunk in the locks.

My father's rubber boots are big—sometimes as a child I would try them on and shuffle around the yard, unable to lift my feet.

"Back up," my father says. "Now row," and then, "No, back up," and again, "Row."

"Which is it?" I ask. "Should I row or back up?"

"Row," he says, and I row, but I'm not thinking about the lake.

I'm thinking about the pines growing on the opposite shore—astonished trees.

"What are you grinning at?"

"Nothing, nothing."

I think about Elsa. Her caterpillar eyebrows, her smile. It upsets me a little that I can get her into my mind so easily.

"Back up, now, back up."

I turn the oars forward and back up.

"Now row."

The oarlocks knock. The oars' blades are wet, the boat plows lightly across the lake. The wake closes up behind us and the lake is again a mirror that has never seen a father and daughter.

"Those pine trees," I say. "Do they look astonished to you?"

"What?"

"The pine trees over on the other shore, do you think they're astonished?"

"Talking nonsense," my father says.

In the evening I prepare the sauna. I have to use several stovefuls of wood, and I sit on the dock while they burn. The sky spills over the trees, the lake is silent. There's an echo from somewhere—maybe it's old man Kemppainen gone out to check his fish traps.

I sit and remember the man's chin. That kind of chin. That kind of laugh, the things he said.

Then I take a sauna. I throw steaming water in the washbasin, wash my hair, pour the whole basin over me, it splashes on the floor, the stove hissing under the drops of water.

I go for a swim, wade out deep, the water halfway up my thighs.

It begins here: the astonished pine trees rise, the sky is pale, the moon climbs across the sky, and I think, If it's coming, let it come.

ELSA CALLS ME in August when they've come back to town and tells me about a party that they have every year at the end of summer. She encourages me to come, I hesitate a bit because I'm intimidated by the kind of people who'll be there—artists and scientists and authors.

They'll talk about the world as if it were an object they possessed, their voices reaching up to the attic and down to the cellar. Eventually someone will get up on the table and yell, and I'll shrink to the size of a toy, a doll, paralyzed from sheer shyness.

"What will I tell them?" I ask Elsa. "Should I say I'm your nanny, or that I'm a student at the university?"

"Something more," Elsa says. "You're more like a friend of the family. You're one of us."

"I don't have anything to wear."

"Sure you do," she says. "You have my dress. The one I gave you."

I PUT ON Elsa's dress. Arrive with uncertain steps.

A storm of noise greets me at the door. There are narrow neckties and shoes, high heels, beehive hairdos and ruffled tops, false eyelashes, cigarettes. I look around the room, looking for the little girl, the man, Elsa. I finally see the child: she's playing behind the sofa with a girl her same age.

I see the man in front of the window, he's talking to a friend, a glass in his hand, laughing. He glances at me and looks quickly away.

He's thought the same things about me, I can tell. Elsa comes over to me. She has her hair up, she's relaxed and happy—she seems to have put her professional self away in a drawer for the evening. She hugs me and is about to say something when her attention is taken by a woman unknown to me and her sentence is left unfinished.

And someone else, a man, comes and introduces himself. We talk for a minute about poetry but he can't keep my interest at the moment. I want to see the little girl, find out what she's been doing, thinking. I want to play with her.

"Hey, Ella. Hi," I say, bending down to her level.

She's wearing a dress with a starched collar and patent leather shoes.

"Do you want to play?" she asks. Without waiting for an answer she gets up, takes my hand, and leads me through the throng of guests, reaches for a latch and opens a door.

The room is dark.

"Turn on the light," she orders excitedly.

I fumble for the switch, finally find it and click on the lights.

The little girl kneels in a well-practiced manner next to a cradle. Molla is sleeping in it. She covers the doll with a little blanket and rocks the cradle.

"Sing her a song," she says.

"What song?"

"A poop song!"

"Not poop," I say. I already know how to instruct. "A lullaby?"

"Yeah," she says.

I start to sing a song my mother sang to me. The little girl droops where she's kneeling, her head to one side, listening. I'm startled to hear a noise from the door. It's him. He smiles. I don't know how long he's been standing there watching us.

The little girl runs away and we're left alone. Him at the door, two wineglasses and a bottle in his hand. He hands me a glass, pours. He's suddenly at a loss for something to say, and I enjoy that. I'm opening him again, layer by layer. I see him eight years old, running home after a long day of play with the boys in the neighborhood, gathered to play ten sticks, the evening a broad continent stretching out from their boundaries. I notice his arms, he looks as careless as ever with the sleeves of his shirt rolled up, and it charms me. There's something horselike in his legs, I notice it and like it more and more.

He sees that I'm thinking about him, becomes more embarrassed, starts to look for something in his pockets. In my awkwardness I don't say anything either, I lean against the wall and turn my head. He takes a cigarette out of his pocket. Those oval fingernails, I'll bet he moves his finger from line to line when he reads sometimes, and rubs his temples now and then.

He lights his cigarette. Sucks in the smoke, holds the cigarette between his thumb and forefinger as if he were in a hurry. Rebellious. I see him as he was in high school, he must have had big dreams, longed to be elsewhere, cherished all kinds of dreams, practiced smoking roll-your-owns in the park, not going home until night came. He would tiptoe past his mother's bedroom thinking about the girl he'd kissed, too excited to notice the moment of happiness, the irretrievable perfection of the spring evening, everything within reach and nothing certain. The next day he realized it, and the next week still better.

Now he understands it so clearly that it's painful to think about. And still more painful to understand that he's almost forgotten those kisses now, those restless smokes under the budding trees and all the habits he could have built for himself that were randomly rejected, because he chose others.

"How was Kuhmo?"

"I frolicked in the meadows."

"And the pine trees?"

"Astonished."

He laughs.

"You're good with Ella," he says. "She's talked about you a lot since you came here."

He looks out the window, then at me. I see that he's examining me.

"What did you think of that drawing?" he asks, a little breathless, as if time were running out.

Suddenly there is all the density and concentration and weight that both of us will later call pure happiness when we come back to this moment.

I don't hide my thoughts, I let them shine through my smile.

"No one's ever seen me that way."

THE EVENING CONTINUES. I look across the room, watching him chat with someone I don't know. He's talking about politics. The words are light compared to what he would like to say to me. He kisses Elsa beside him. The stranger comes to talk to me again, a friend of his who introduces himself as Lauri. I chat distractedly about this and that, my head turning to search for him.

I smile. Everything is light.

He peeks at me over shoulders, between hemlines and wineglasses. His look is quick, a mere glimpse. I see his gaze search me out, find me, turn away.

This is where it all begins. Later I realize that it was right here, when he was getting glimpses of me. There's a hint of dread in his gaze. Me on the sofa, sitting next to Lauri, who would later carry our secrets for years in an unspoken agreement that men sometimes make with their friends. Elbows, hands holding plates and glasses, beehives, button earrings.

Lauri's question: "So, you're the new nanny?"

"That's me."

I answer absentmindedly because I've already begun my journey to something else.

I pluck his gaze from among the wineglasses and Lauri's indifferent talk. It's careless, hardly even stopping at me before passing on.

But I know about that.

IN THE SECOND week of September the summer is more itself, the days warm and transparent. The evenings are windy, but the day's warmth lingers. I come back, carrying my things in a suitcase.

On Saturday we drive to Tammilehto. We've packed a lunch—sandwiches wrapped in waxed paper, soda and wafers. I open the window a little in the car and let the wind come in. The little girl screams like we're at an amusement park. She soon falls asleep on the back seat.

The place isn't a cabin, it's a summer house. Where I come from, the summer cabins are gray shacks, red if you happen to have some paint. Here there's a main building, a shed, a sauna looming on the shore. I walk to the edge of the yard and back. I can see the water.

"So! Let's start by making some coffee," he says.

We spread a blanket on the beach, the little girl sits down in my lap without a moment's hesitation. I put a sweater on her, plus a hat and some mittens, which she pulls off immediately. The sun is still shining. I take off my shoes and socks for a minute and sink my toes in the sand, braving the autumn.

The three of us make six sand cakes at the edge of the water and whoop with joy and disappointment when the waves wash over them.

She wants to make them over again.

"Where did they go?" she asks. "Did the lake eat them? Why are they there and then they're gone?"

"The lake eats them."

"But where do they go?" she says again. "Do they disappear?"

"They just go away where we can't see them," I say.

"Where do they go when they go away?" she says.

"They go home."

"Where's that?"

"On Liisankatu."

"Are you going to Liisankatu today?"

"Not today. I'm here today. I'm staying here."

The little girl falls asleep on the blanket with Molla, the man lifts her in his arms and carries her inside. He's gentle and patient in this way. He's tender with his daughter.

"Shouldn't we be going in soon, too?" I ask.

"Not yet. We can wait a little longer. The girl's sleeping."

We share the same thought. We must use the moment wisely, receive it graciously. I look at the lake. I say I might feel like a swim. He shakes his head. Don't, he says. It's cold, you'll go numb.

"Are you going to stop me?"

"No," he says with a smile. "I won't stop you."

I take off my skirt. My blouse. I don't look at him as I take off my bra.

He's thinking that he can't take his eyes off me. Everything's already decided—it's as if someone else had made the decision for us, and this is just a little drama that reflects the inevitability of it, the way we lay claim to our intimacy. I step into the water. The water's cold. I keep going, not letting out a sound. I wade until the water's up to my navel, then I lower myself completely and swim.

The water's amazingly still, the clouds in the sky the color of bruises. I swim five strokes out, five strokes back. I stand up.

"Was it cold? Your lips are blue."

"Then they ought to be warmed up."

He picks up the towel from the blanket and opens it for me like an embrace. I come close to him without any hesitance. He lets go of the towel and I dry myself. He looks at the birthmark on my neck, forcing his thoughts there, away from everything he's just seen.

His breath is trembling a little. I'm trembling with cold, and perhaps also anticipation.

"Shall we go in?" he asks.

As we walk inside, Elsa is still between us. He's thinking of Elsa as we walk across the yard, about what she would say. She would say something about the little girl. She might be a little tired, might rub her neck and say she's going to go check on the little girl. Once they were inside, she might go into the kitchen absentmindedly, wonder aloud if she should make something to eat. Quite a nice day, she would say.

I see the doubt in the slope of his shoulders.

But Elsa is already changing into a picture. If the telephone has rung while we've been away, if it rings in the apartment in Töölö dozens of kilometers away, we won't hear it. Water drips from my hair. The walls protect us, and the night. Everything's already begun, it all began when I rang the doorbell, it began when I stepped over the threshold. Maybe everything began a long time before that, even. It's all as old as time.

The kiss, too, is both ancient and new. I know it's strange, but just before the kiss, I say something about Elsa.

Elsa is at a dinner with her colleagues, laughing. Before going to bed she stretches her neck, pulls the bedspread up and puts her glasses on her nose to read her notes for tomorrow's presentation one more time.

We don't know this. Elsa is far away, but she lingers between us for a moment longer. We stand facing each other, looking into each other's eyes.

I think about Elsa as he comes closer to me. I think about Elsa, and I say, "Does she usually kiss you in the evening, before you go to bed?"

That same doubt flashes in his eyes, I can see it, but then he says *shhh* and comes closer, and we don't talk anymore.

10

INDUCTION, INTUBATION, EXTUBATION.

They were still at the intubation phase. The patient was in a deep narcosis, Eleonoora was finishing up the suture. The surgery had been an easy, routine operation.

Riitta, Eleonoora's favorite anesthesiologist to have in the operating room—quick to smile, a little odd but intently focused on her work—checked the patient's status, decreased the anesthesia and nodded approvingly. There was time to make a careful suture.

Even after twenty years in the operating room the mystery of artificial sleep never ceased to amaze Eleonoora. She saw it every day and knew the history of its attempts and failures in detail.

No one knew how the mechanism of sinking into sleep actually worked. All that was known was that certain substances caused sufficient unconsciousness and numbness for an operation to be performed. There was no way to measure the dose beforehand. The same amount could cause deep narcosis in one patient and leave another merely drowsy, at the edge of wakefulness. Most people didn't remember what happened while they were under anesthesia. But there were those who remained alert during the surgery and described stepping outside themselves and watching the operation, feeling the incision.

A patient once told her of an experience of grace that exceeded her comprehension. "It wasn't an angel or God that I saw, but it took me in its arms and I felt like I never had to be alone. It was absolute safety, like a child in its mother's arms."

Watching a patient sleep, Eleonoora often thought about where they were while they were under. Riitta had once said that patients went toward birth and death at the same time when they were anesthetized. It has its own time stratum, that's what I think, Riitta said. All of your memories are there, all the people. Think about how it would feel to hold your whole life up, see it in its entirety, from a little distance. If all the patients remembered their mental state while they were under anesthesia, that's what they would tell you they saw. I think it's like the state a person is in just before they die. To know everything, see everything clearly. It's too bad people so rarely come back to the rest of us with the information.

Maybe it's a blessing, Eleonoora thought. Maybe we'd be crushed by the knowledge. Maybe only God is meant to see life in its entirety, if there is a God. And the dead, if there is life after death. And writers, who put themselves outside of life and diligently follow each character's every thought and feeling and shine a spotlight on everything that happens.

Eleonoora finished the suture and Riitta started the extubation.

"How's your mother?" she asked when the operation was over and the patient had been taken to recovery.

Eleonoora had told Riitta about her mother in early spring, when her brief cancer treatments had ended.

"She wants to be at home. We've been trying to manage it for a few days."

Riitta touched her shoulder gently. A familiar feeling flooded over her from somewhere in the most secret, guarded part of herself: gratitude for her concern. There was a touch of surprise in it. People were endlessly good, wise, and gentle in the midst of all the hurry, the conferences, the dinner invitations, the smell of disinfectant, the meeting reminders.

She would have liked to tell Riitta what she had tried to say to Eero every day in different ways—nagging him about going to the grocery or cleaning the wrong way, complaining that no one else in the house ever seemed to wash the dishes: *I don't know if I know how to be motherless, and I don't know if I can learn how in the weeks we have left. It feels like it will take the end of my life away.*

"Time is growing shorter," was all she managed to say.

"That's the way it always is," Riitta said. "Talk to your mother, reminisce with her about what's been. And when the time comes, let go."

There it was: let go. She hadn't let go of anyone, not for a second. She had always clung to everything, tried to keep everything together. Where did this worry come from? Why did she think she was the one who should hold up the whole world?

One tear, then another, rolled down her cheek.

Riitta hugged her.

———

HER FATHER ANSWERED the phone after three rings.

"Did the home care people come over?"

"They took some blood and brought a pain pump. The nurse showed me the dose but your mother still won't agree to use it. Apparently there's no need yet."

"Has she eaten?"

"Not yet. She's feeling a little poorly."

Eleonoora felt the floor pitch. She fixed her gaze on the bar of soap at the edge of the sink.

"What is it?" she heard herself ask.

"Just something," he said. "She spent the morning resting and hasn't really wanted to get up."

Eleonoora sensed other meanings behind his words.

"I'm going to drive to Tammilehto this evening with Anna. Don't touch the pain pump. I'll come look at it on the way there and see how it works."

She knew her bossiness annoyed her father, but she couldn't help herself. She changed clothes, opened the door, walked down the corridor. The hospital carried on with diligent industry around her. The vendor in the cafeteria was putting berliners on a tray, a nurse walked quickly by and nodded at her.

She dialed Anna's number. The phone rang six times. She remembered that Anna was at work, and left a message.

She chose Eero's number. She let the heaviness come. She let it come two seconds before Eero answered, but for some reason, she didn't really understand why, her tone of voice changed at the last minute to something slightly bored, demanding.

"Where are you?"

"At work," Eero said. "I'm on my way home."

Eleonoora couldn't say it. She always wore a mask that Eero had to come and remove, patiently, over and over.

"We'll be at Tammilehto. Buy something for you and Maria for dinner."

"OK," he said.

"But don't use the grill yet. Maria said she'd wash it today, but I want to be there when we use it for the first time."

"OK."

The line was quiet, an invisible cord stretched between them.

"Are you all right?" Eero asked.

She didn't answer right away. Tomorrow evening when she came home she would close the bedroom door and press herself against him and let the tears come. She would tell him what she was keeping to herself now. They would keep the door closed, let the walls shelter them, go to bed and build a fort, pretend there was no death for a brief moment.

"I'm fine," she said.

ELEONOORA'S MOTHER ASKED her to bring her some water. Eleonoora asked her father to leave. She wanted to examine her mother, but she didn't want him to see it. He preferred not to see her take the doctor's role. But what else could she do? It was easier to palpate her abdomen than bear the blunt pain of worry.

The home care worker had come again because Mom hadn't been feeling well. Mom was cool and polite through

the whole visit. She only gave in to her petulance and annoyance after the nurse had left.

Eleonoora poured some water into a glass. Her mother
tried to drink, but the water made her feel sick and she
wanted it taken away. She told her to open the drapes. That
wasn't enough—she wanted the drapes taken down so she
could see the whole sky. When Eleonoora had done this,
standing on the windowsill, twisting her neck wrong, reaching up till her arms ached, her mother lay for a moment enduring the rays of sunshine, then asked her to put them back
up again.

"What's the matter with you?" Eleonoora huffed. "You're
like a child."

"Out. Get out of here," her mother yelled. "Leave me in
peace."

Eleonoora was closing the drapes, her hand halfway
raised, paralyzed by the command. She looked at her mother,
baffled.

"Why don't you get crabby with Dad? Why are you never
like this with anyone else? Don't you know how hard this is?"

The question came out as an accusation. Suddenly her
mother looked angry.

"So this is about your pain now? I'm the one who's dying."

"And you won't let anybody help you. You just make it
harder to help."

"How are you supposed to help me?" Elsa said. She
waited a moment, then said the heaviest thing: "Everyone
dies alone."

For the first time Eleonoora saw helplessness in her mother's face. For some reason she answered it harshly, maybe

because she wanted to quickly bury her mother's words with her own: "And you can die all by yourself if you keep this up. Let me know when you've decided whether to accept any help or not."

She closed the door louder than she meant to. Tears came as soon as she left the room.

She had cried in these rooms when she was five years old, shouted accusations at her mother as a teenager, slammed doors, maybe this very door. She had run out into the hallway and raged. It seemed like it had all happened just a moment ago. Sometimes she had been so vehemently angry with her mother and father that even she wondered where it came from.

She went into the kitchen, opened the dishwasher, ran water in the sink. This was an old habit, washing dishes and crying and feeling she had been mistreated. When she washed dishes she could court martyrdom, the running water and choreographed movements helped the feeling come. There were two wineglasses on the counter with a little wine in the bottom.

She opened the trash cupboard door. There was an empty Syrah bottle.

Before she had time to think she had grabbed the bottle and was on her way to the bedroom.

"What's this? Have you been drinking wine?"

Her mother looked as if she didn't understand the question.

"You drink some wine and then you complain that you don't feel well, is that it? Who with, Anna?"

"With your father. I'm a grown woman. I can have one glass of wine."

"Not when you're in this condition you can't."

"You don't know anything about this," her mother said in a strangled voice. "You think you know about this kind of pain, but you know nothing. You know nothing."

Eleonoora was quiet, the bottle dangling from her hand, dripping red drops on the floor.

There was anger in her mother's eyes. The thought came to Eleonoora that she would be relieved when her mother died, secretly relieved, if not downright happy. She shoved the thought aside in the nick of time, before it had a chance to show itself.

"You wouldn't believe how happy I would be to take some of your pain for you. If it were possible I'd even take all of it."

Suddenly she remembered the helplessness that had surrounded her when Anna was small and experienced her first pain.

Sometimes it had felt like every one of Anna's cries carried her farther away.

When Anna was two years old she had burned her fingers on the oven. They were making gingerbread cookies and she had been careless, letting Anna watch the light-brown stars puff up in the heat of the oven. As Eleonoora took the pan out of the oven, Anna pointed with her little finger at one of the star's points. She'd turned her back for just a moment, a second, leaving the oven door open behind her. And while her back was turned, the little girl grabbed the oven door for support.

A stupefied look, bewildered. As if she felt betrayed. Eleonoora felt like *she* was the one who had betrayed her. *She* had made her daughter believe that baking would be fun,

that life would be fun. There she stood with her gingerbread, smiling, while her daughter was experiencing horrible agony. Being betrayed, the incomprehension at being
left alone, the reality of her own pain, all of it showed in the
little girl's face for a hundredth of a second.

It was the first time that Eleonoora had simply seen Anna
for her own self. My daughter, who came from me, but completely her own self.

At the same time Eleonoora realized she would never be
able to completely protect her from harm. Then Anna had
started to cry.

They had to take her to the hospital—the burn had
formed large white blisters. They had to lance the blisters
every night for a week and coat her hands with thick medi-
cated cream. And every evening Anna cried bitterly.

Anna always stopped crying once Eleonoora comforted
her long enough, always. But Eleonoora could always see
that stranger inside Anna, that other person developing little
by little, differentiating herself with every sob.

Eleonoora looked at her mother and reached out a hand
helplessly. "Tell me what I can do. Tell me."

Her mother was quiet for a moment, then patted the edge
of the bed. "Come here."

She took Eleonoora in her arms. She gave in. They would
lie side by side like this when Eleonoora was a child.

"Your father can't bear this," her mother said. "He pre-
tends to be strong, but he can't bear it, I can see that."

"He'll be all right."

"You don't know."

"What? Hasn't he always been here? Decade after decade. Hasn't he always stayed close to you? That's not a small thing."

Her mother looked out the window, her face closed up.

"No," she said. "It's not a small thing."

They lay side by side. Eleonoora lifted her legs onto the bed and stretched out.

She tried to put a different tone in her voice. "Did you get quite drunk?"

"No," her mother answered. "Hardly drank any at all. Three glasses."

"Three! You're not dying, you're hungover."

"Well, you know what they say," her mother said. "A hangover is a small death."

"That's what they say about orgasms."

"Oh, is that what it was?"

Eleonoora finally got it out. She dropped the sentence carelessly, as if it were one of many: "I don't want you to go."

"I'm not going yet," her mother said. "Not quite yet."

They heard the front door open. Maria yoo-hooed to them, came to the bedroom doorway. Anna followed her.

"How are you feeling?" Maria immediately asked.

"Just gathering some strength here," Elsa answered.

"More pain meds?" Maria asked Eleonoora, as if she were her assistant at the hospital.

"Something else. Medicine's not what we need," Elsa answered lightheartedly. "We need a song. My sedimentation rate's over twenty and my CRP has risen to a hundred. I ought to get a song for that, 'The Ballad of CRP.'"

Anna was finally brave enough to come into the room. She went to the foot of the bed and pinched her mother's toes affectionately.

"We brought a song with us, just in case. How does that rhyme go?"

"The rhyme for when you're hurt," Maria said, pleased. Eleonoora said the first verse.

"Uh-huh," Elsa said, suddenly glum.

"What?" Eleonoora said. "Don't you want us to say it?"

"Haven't we heard it enough?" her mother said.

"What do you mean?" Maria asked, uncomprehending. "What do you mean enough?"

Eleonoora looked at Maria, then at Anna. Anna's hand was still on her foot. Anna looked at her, then at her grandmother.

"What is it?" Eleonoora said, looking at each of the girls in turn. "What's going on here?"

Elsa shrugged. "Nothing. Nothing at all. How about a funny song?"

Anna smiled and Eleonoora made a note of the nervousness on her face.

ELEONOORA DIDN'T START to cry until they were walking to the car.

For some reason the car alarm went off. She quickly tried to punch in the code, but the siren shrieked, piercing, reached whining into their ears and stayed there, ringing.

Maria asked something over the noise, and then the tears finally came. Maria came around the car to where she was and took her in her arms. This was the kind of daughter she'd raised. This girl who came without question, as if it were the most natural thing in the world that mothers break down sometimes, mothers who have to worry about the groceries and the dishes and the cleaning and the medicines and the car alarm, all the while enduring their own mother's temper and peevishness that only just manages to hide the reality underneath—the slow but inevitable journey toward oblivion.

The lights flashed, the siren howled.

"Shhh, it's all right, it's OK," Maria said, as if things had always been this way, as if she'd always had her arms around her.

Eleonoora looked at Anna, recognized that same helplessness in her gaze that she'd often seen when Anna was in pain. On the day of the oven door when she was a child, on the day when she said she'd been lying on the floor for more than a week.

She saw Anna's hesitation, then she closed her eyes and left the world alone for a moment.

11

ANNA IS SITTING on the sauna bench next to her mother.

Her mother throws some steam on the stove. Nothing bad can happen as long as the steam surrounds them. The walls of the old sauna sigh.

"It heated up all right, even though the floor's rotten," her mother says.

They've driven west in the car, stopped at the village store, exchanged the news with the shopkeeper, bought a fish twice as big as they need out of politeness. The cabin door squeaked as it always does. The mice, if there were any, ran away. Her grandfather's paintings greeted them, carrying all the winter moments they'd spent here in empty rooms with no one looking at them.

This is where her grandfather brought his most daring experiments, the ones where the moment of creative vision stood out, left raw and half-finished like the rough knots in the floorboards.

Impasto experiments, combinations of different mediums that had proved unworkable. A strange, obsessive series of canvases where he'd practiced splatter-and-drip techniques is stacked under the old bed in the basement. Splashes like wine thrown against a wall, color after color, then scraped with a spatula or palette knife to bring out shapes, notches, scratches, outlines of figures.

There are more works from over the years in the shed, not all of them his. Sometimes an artist friend of his from Lapland would stay here for weeks and paint, drunk and feverish, covering the walls of the shed with images—a reindeer swimming across a lake, the sun shining like a ball of fire.

"I think I'll shake off my winter coat," Anna says.

It's a challenge.

"You're crazy," her mother says laughingly.

She recognizes the tone in her mother's voice. More goading than dissuading.

"Will you wash my back first?" her mother asks.

There's goodwill everywhere. On the walls, in the washbasin, in the bar of soap, still doggedly mint green in spite of changing fashions.

Her mother stands in front of her. Her back is humble. You can see in it that she doesn't make a fuss about her own worries, but she gathers up the sorrows from other people's pathways and crossroads.

"Your back's quite narrow," Anna says impulsively.

She pours a ladle of hot water into the washbasin and squeezes in a mixture of marsh tea and jasmine scent. The bath mitt is stiff. She dips it in the basin and feels the water come in and wet the spaces between her fingers. She rubs clockwise in long, gentle strokes. A memory comes to her. She was sick one morning, threw up before it was time to leave for day care. Her mother told her to lie down and rubbed her back. Broad, gentle circles until the bad feeling gradually subsided.

If someone had asked her, Anna would have been able to draw all the marks on her mother's back on white paper. Two moles down low, a scar farther up that she got as a child in the fire at Tammilehto. A flaked cross shape, like a brand.

Anna strokes the surface of the scar. As a child she wanted to hear the story over and over. It was as fascinating as the story of her birth. Her mother as a child—that alone was incomprehensible. How could her mother have been a helpless child, a child in danger?

Who rescued you? Anna would always ask.

Dad. He ran inside and found me in the smoke.

Just in time, right? Just before you were going to . . .

She couldn't say the word, but she had to go toward it. She couldn't conceive of it: a mother who wasn't yet a mother, her mother as a child, in danger of dying.

Where was Grandma?

In the sauna.

But she didn't see that the cabin was burning?

No.

What happened then?

Then they took me to the hospital. Mom and Dad sat up next to my bed, and when I woke up I saw Mom looking at me, and I've never seen such relief on anyone's face.

And the house burned to the ground, didn't it? Poof, it just burned to the ground and you had to build a new one.

It didn't quite burn to the ground.

But a little bit, a little bit to the ground, right? And it left a mark on you, on your back, a magic mark that protects you forever and ever and ever from anything bad so nothing terrible can ever happen to you again?

Yes, it might be that kind of mark.

Anna draws a tender circle around the scar with the bath mitt.

"Does this ever hurt?"

"Sometimes," her mother says in a faint voice, lost in herself and in the moment. "If I'm in the sun too long."

"You should put lotion on it," Anna says. "I'll put some on after the sauna, once you've dried yourself."

How small her mother is, like a baby chick, hunched a little, with her arms wrapped around herself.

"Did I tell you about when your father and I were in Istanbul last year, and we went to the Hagia Sofia? Did I tell you about the woman who came up and talked to us?"

"No. You told me about the murals you saw there, and the church with the mosque layered over it. Dad talked about it for weeks afterward."

Anna imitates her father's lecturer's voice, the way he pours out facts and paints broad strokes of thought whenever he gets excited. "There's no other place where Europe is such a caricature of itself as in Istanbul. The soccer match, the church, the mosque, the cafe, go anywhere and you see an inadvertent microcosm of Europe. You have to go to the fringes to see what's in the center."

Her mother laughs. "Not bad. He was already preaching about that while we were on the trip."

Anna sees her mother in profile. She looks just like a child when she laughs. Whenever Dad starts speechifying a tenderness comes into her eyes.

"Your father wanted to go upstairs but I had to go to the restroom so I left before him. And while I was standing in line I took off my sweater, and this woman came up and spoke to me. I think she was American, from her accent. She said, 'You bear a cross on your shoulder. Did something horrible happen to you?'"

"Strange woman."

Her mother is quiet, leaning her back into the sponge like a cat leaning against the person petting it.

WET FEET ON the gray wood of the dock. Anna runs to the end of the dock, the familiar sound of the boards banging. Her mother comes after her, protective and encouraging at the same time.

"Don't go too far!"

The water's cold. It locks up her breathing for a moment. The shock bursts out in a laugh that spreads across the surface of the water. There's a bashful, early summer moon in the sky. The laugh reaches all the way to its skewed crescent. She breathes, gasps a little and feels a cool mass of water take a gentle stab at her belly.

"Is it cold?" her mother shouts excitedly.

Cold, old, the forest echoes.

This might be the most valiant thing that Anna has ever done. Her mother on the dock and Anna here, in the arms of the water, as safe as if she were floating in a womb and yet precarious, at the mercy of the world, out of her mother's reach.

"Yes!" she shouts.

"Turn around now," her mother coaxes.

"In a minute," she breathes, not looking at her mother.

She turns around and notices that she's surprisingly far out. She swims in long strokes through cold and warm walls of water as if she were wandering from one underwater room to another. This is what it's like to be a fish! The thought comes to her unexpectedly, with absurd certainty. She rises up out of the water, her mother reaches out her hand and she takes it. For one small moment there's nothing else.

They stand on the dock.

The summer breathes. The torn surface of the lake heals over and goes still. The silence settles on its invisible hinges and the landscape sinks back into self-sufficient sleep.

"Good," her mother says. "Now back to the sauna."

The loon is already here, marking its territory with its soft call. The sauna crackles, the evening darkens outside the window. Anna squeezes thick cream onto her fingertips from a metal tube and smoothes it over her mother's back.

Her mother holds her hair up with her left hand, her head slightly bowed, her breasts humble.

"Is it red?" she asks.

"A little."

Anna smoothes the cream, it escapes the edges of the scar, spreads pearl-like across her mother's shoulder blade. These feelings for another are born at the very beginning, maybe they're already in the bud when a mouth gropes for the breast for the first time, when one flesh first separates itself from the other. But now Anna feels it powerfully: it's from her, from Eleonoora Ahlqvist—Ella—that she knows what it is to bear the worry and fear and pride.

"Is that good?" she asks.

Ella nods. "You take care of me like you're somebody's mother."

Anna is silent. The movements of her fingers accelerate a little. Little circles; the cream layered in transparent ramparts on the skin. She hopes her mother won't ask the question that she knows is coming. But she does ask it: "Have you seen that little girl Linda lately?"

How easily she says it. *That little girl.* Linda.

"No, I haven't."

"Doesn't she have a birthday about now?"

"Next week."

"How old will she be?"

Will she be, she says, not *would* she be. Linda will be blowing out candles on a cake somewhere this year, too. Her mother will smile and say, Good job, you're such a big girl. All this is true someplace else.

"Five," Anna says. "She'll be five years old this year."

She has to turn away. The ink flows into her as if it's filling a bottle. When Linda turned three she bought her cotton candy at the amusement park. It was as if that had happened to someone else.

She puts on her underwear, her jeans. Her mother lifts her head, looks at her for a moment.

"Would you like me to braid your hair? It'll give you curls like when you were little."

"Sure," she says carelessly, smiling.

She sits on the sauna stool. Her mother divides her hair into three parts.

And now she is herself again. And her mother is her mother, strong-handed, determined.

THEY ROAST THE fish over the coals, flavoring it with olive oil and salt and pepper and letting it sizzle in its foil wrap. Her mother makes a sauce from butter and onions for the new potatoes. They take the linen tablecloth with its regular folds out of the cupboard and spread it on the table and lay the plates on it.

Her mother pours white wine into glasses and checks on the fish now and then and Anna opens the door and steps out into the early summer dark. She's going to clip a few apple blossoms for the table.

She walks down the narrow path to the shed. The stones of the path feel smooth under the bare soles of her feet. A loon somewhere on the opposite shore has tuned its call to a yet more penetrating note. A blackbird on a branch sings its yearning song with a familiar melancholy that has always sounded to Anna's ears like it was in a major key.

The shed shimmers in the murky darkness. The door creaks. The familiar smell of turpentine and sawdust and gasoline fills her nose. She sinks into the smell for a moment like stepping into water.

The garden scissors are hanging from a nail. Anna turns on the light. Old powdered pigments, empty linseed oil bottles, dried-out glue and paintbrushes. Wooden stretcher bars on the shelves.

Anna lets her gaze wander over the room, the shelves of stacked charcoal drawings, the color experiments. It's mostly sketches. Still, they shouldn't be left lying here at the mercy of the damp. Any art museum would be glad to buy them for their collection.

Rejects, canvases that look like they've been painted over many times, straggle along the rack at the back of the shed. She goes to them and flips through the pictures absentmindedly.

Anna has a half-formed, careless thought about all of this. The forest, the sky, May, the shed stubbornly standing there day after day, year after year, a squirrel perhaps creeping onto its roof sometimes, the moss pushing out its sprouts. And there were the half-finished paintings, pieces of their own reality, here amid all the activity of the world.

She closes the door a little reluctantly.

She cuts a few branches from the nearest apple tree. They snap like bones as they break.

Her mother is out on the porch when she returns.

"How'd it look in there?"

"The same. Just as chaotic as ever."

Her mother sighs with good-natured weariness.

"Someone should organize the shed, sort through the art," she says. "Dad doesn't value his old pieces enough to take the trouble."

Anna shrugs.

"Maybe I can come with Matias, do a real spring cleaning."

"That would be nice. If Grandma makes it here again, you could clean it up before she comes."

"Agreed," Anna says.

She puts on a smile without effort and hands the apple blossoms to her mother, who reflects the smile on her own face and says, "Well, let's eat."

1964

KERTTU IS WAITING at the corner. September, the sky a high dome, the air thin. The city doesn't yet know about winter.

Kerttu has a new style—she found it this summer when she went to visit relatives in San Francisco. A black turtleneck, jeans, eyes hazy, as if she's decided to let the unpredictability of life show through her gaze. She has combed her hair till it shines, hanging on either side of her face. It takes me a moment to get used to this Kerttu. Just this morning she had on seamed stockings and a short skirt.

"All right then," Kerttu says. "Let's go create a world."

She cajoles me into this—I wouldn't have the time or the desire for it, exams are pressing on me and I've only just discovered the girl and the man, my own days with them. But Kerttu doesn't give in. I quicken my steps beside her.

"Where exactly are we going?"

"To a meeting," she says, and doesn't explain any further.

THERE ARE A handful of young people when we get there. Thick-rimmed glasses float by, everyone smells like cigarettes, unspoken hopes condense near the ceiling, dreams that no one knows how to shout out loud yet. A girl in red beads says something about the Vietnam War, but a boy in a green shirt isn't listening because he's painting a sketch of his plans for the evening in his mind.

Isn't it exciting? Kerttu whispers in a low voice just before we step inside. She doesn't let her smile split its seams.

A girl in the corner recognizes her, takes note of her pants. Happiness goes through me and settles in my fingertips. I'm with Kerttu—me—I'm her friend, so I'm new, too.

We sit in the front row next to a boy who smells of hair oil and yesterday's red wine. I remember him from the university—his name is Tapio. He lent me a pen in the introductory lecture for social science theory, whispering, You heard it from me, Rousseau's making a comeback.

The speeches start. It's like in parliament, only the fervor and the size of the waistlines are different. A man in a corduroy jacket with hair receding from his temples talks about Mao.

"These people admire China?" I whisper in Kerttu's ear. "Don't people go hungry there?"

"That's in Africa. There's a famine there," she whispers back. "Just listen."

Everyone is in agreement about Vietnam. One of the boys gets up and recites a statement that sums up the whole state of affairs in the form of a poem.

He receives nods of approval. Hands are raised in support. I raise my hand, too, although I'm only half there. I don't tell anyone that part of me is still on Sammonkatu. What would Kerttu think if she knew? Suddenly I remember his hand. I think about his belly, the place where the hair begins. It's a real triumph to know those places on another person, those unexplored regions.

For one absurd moment I have the whole world within reach as I think about his belly. These people think they know. They're planning a friendship trip to Berlin, arguing about whether a singing party is an appropriate way to express their opinions. But they don't have the whole world—it's mine.

The girl reached her hand toward me yesterday, climbed into my lap, and I held her. I fed her and put her to bed. Her hair smelled like apples, her skin was slightly musty. It's her own smell. Her breath is a little sour in the morning. Her backside is sharp against my thigh and I have to adjust her a little so the two childish chisels of bone in her butt don't cut into me. Then I wrap an arm around her. She leans her head against me. Eeva, I wish you were always at our house!

Yesterday, once she had gone to sleep, I went and stood in the doorway without speaking.

He came to me. He didn't need to ask anymore. We didn't turn out the lights. Before I tasted him, I looked at him up close. This world is just a thin veil, sparsely knit, compared to that.

To end the meeting a woman sings in a clear voice, an inexplicably strange song like nothing I've ever heard. She looks into my eyes for a moment and I see her longing. She looks like she really is longing for the Black Sea, though she's never set foot on its salty shores.

When the meeting's over, Kerttu is impatient.

"Let's go to a bar. I need a drink."

I don't see him until we've taken off our coats. He's sitting with his back to me. Lauri is explaining something, making broad curves in the air with his hands. Later I learn that Lauri already knows. He's one of those people who eases over the steepest parts of the truth by accelerating his speech.

"There's your artist," Kerttu says.

"He's not my artist."

Months will go by before I dare to say it: mine.

Kerttu walks to their table as if she owns the world. This is a situation that will become familiar to me later. I have to ask permission to sit next to him with my eyes. He smiles. If something has begun, he doesn't show it.

Two realities penetrate each other. One reality, the reality of dreams, hovers above our heads. It's true right now if we just take hold of it. We let it be.

Kerttu isn't shy. She nods toward a wineglass.

"If you gentlemen will treat a couple of women to a glass in lieu of a meal, we can tell you the state of the world."

He smiles. Later I learn that this is a defensive smile, reserved for situations where a woman he appreciates is challenging him. I'm never there when he gives Elsa this smile. I'm not there on the days when he and Elsa quarrel and make up by means of this gaze. When Elsa asks, What if I do go for a swim? Are you going to try to stop me? and he looks at her like this and they know, without saying anything, that they haven't needed to dream about each other for a long time.

But this smile is for Kerttu.

"Who're you?" he says.

"Hasn't Eeva told you about me?" Kerttu turns to look at me and says with genuine hurt in her voice: "You don't talk about me!"

"Eeva talks about what she wants to. She says everything she wants to say." Now he's looking at me.

"And now we wouldn't mind having some of that wine," Kerttu says.

He nods to the waitress.

KERTTU THINKS UP a reason to go to the women's room and asks me to come with her.

"I see what's going on here. Don't try to deny it. But don't imagine that this is anything new. Don't imagine it's never happened before."

"Are you angry?"

"Why would I be?"

"Because he's married."

"Marriage is for cowards."

Kerttu suddenly turns around and looks at me. "You ought to introduce me to his friends. He knows everyone. I'd be very happy to exchange a few words with that poet."

"You shouldn't start up anything with him. You haven't heard him talk. Say one wrong word and you could end up in court."

"But he's a thinker," Kerttu says. "He knows more than other people."

"What does that have to do with anything?"

"It has to do with *solidarity with the peoples of the world.*"

"Is that so?"

Kerttu is silent for a moment. Then she asks, "Do you love him? Are you already in love with him?"

"What if I am? Are you against that, too?"

Kerttu hugs me. "No, I'm not. I'm not against love."

When we get back to the table, she interrogates him.

"What do you intend to do to make the world better?" she asks. "Besides those paintings of yours?"

He's used to people coming up to him in restaurants and demanding an explanation for everything in the world, demanding a position, an opinion. Kerttu knows that he moves in circles where new ideas are simmering. She wants to catch some of his spark. More than that: she wants to create the spark.

"What do you think I ought to do?" he says, looking at her across the table.

"Don't ask me. You ought to know, since you know people."

"You mean them?" he says, pointing to a corner table across the room where the stage of drunkenness is rising to the level of falsetto. "I'm not part of the inner circle. They don't tell me their most important insights."

I already recognize when he's being sarcastic. It settles around his mouth, and if you're not used to it you can mistake it for an ordinary smile.

"Although they do occasionally let me drink a glass or two at their table," he adds.

"What do you think about Vietnam?" Kerttu asks eagerly.

She still has the idea that he's at the forefront of change because he knows poets and things. Vietnam is a key question.

He smiles. "You ask big questions."

"The world's a big place."

"All I know about Vietnam is that I oppose the war," he says. "I oppose the Americans' activities in Vietnam."

Kerttu nods. "And?"

"And that doesn't mean that I support everyone who opposes them."

Kerttu sniffs, disappointed, and drinks down the rest of her wine.

She thinks for a moment. Sniffs out the quickest dig, the sharpest barb she can toss across the table. "Keeping your Schjerfbecks upside down in the corner doesn't make you any less bourgeois. It's because of middle-class people like you that this whole country's going down the toilet."

He laughs, charmed. He glances at me. He knows I'm the one who told her about it. Then he's annoyed. "What do you suggest, then?"

"We should think up a plan. Make our voices heard. We should sing and dance, do anything, be seen. Why should you hide in your studio? Why not do something?"

"Listen," he says. "I've seen this before. I saw it in Paris when you were still carrying your books to school. I saw that it doesn't get you anywhere. Politics and art are best kept separate— otherwise one will diminish the other. Art turns empty when it's only about one truth. That's what I think. It's best to keep art open to the struggle between different points of view."

Kerttu has no answer to this. He looks at me, asking with his eyes, Who is this girl, this sassy friend of yours?

I'd like to try to explain. But Kerttu doesn't really need any explanation.

"Good," he says. "Now let's have another round. Let's drink to differences of opinion."

AUTUMN AWAITS WINTER'S pardon. I'm happy. My happiness is new. It comes from the strange pact I've made with the man over the weeks and months. When Elsa's away, I have a family. I'm still learning about them, but I already love them.

There are two realities.

There's the reality where I'm a student of literature and French who eats one-mark sandwiches and drinks cheap wine. In that reality I'm the same Eeva who ran across the meadows and recited spells to nourish the world, the same girl whose mother scolded her in her harsh moments, the one who fell in love with a boy in the second grade who didn't get a single Christmas card at the Christmas tree festival. His name was Heikki, and the girl named Eeva fell in love with him because she didn't yet know the difference between love and pity.

And then there's the other reality, the other woman who has the same name as the first, and who is very much like the Eeva who lives on Liisankatu. But the woman of this other reality is a little more capable than the one who ran through the meadow with a spell on her lips. In this other reality Eeva has a daughter and a husband, a house with stone walls and nights when she creeps in to lie beside him.

This other reality has strict boundaries. It closes up and stays shut away waiting for the next time she will return. This reality is a dream world, and its Eeva is a woman of the world of dreams, although I don't yet know to call myself that.

And this Eeva doesn't yet have doubts. I don't yet feel myself caught in the squeeze between these two worlds, and he hasn't yet become sick with guilt, and the little girl hasn't yet begun to ask her timid questions about what's going on.

THE DOORWAY BETWEEN these two worlds is always the same. On the last night before Elsa comes home, he and I look at each other as if we've both just awakened. We know what's coming. We prepare for Elsa's return by not touching each other, by turning polite and guarded.

Elsa usually comes home on Mondays. I make my long good-byes all Sunday evening.

"Where do you go, when you go away?" the little girl asks as I pack my things. Blouses, skirts, and stockings.

"I go home."

"Can't you stay here?"

"I'll come back."

She nods and lets go of the hem of my skirt.

WHEN ELSA RETURNS, I smile as we drink coffee at the table and tell her about the little girl's new words, how she cried a little the first night but then calmed down, how she hit a boy in the park with a shovel and I had to tell her about right and wrong.

I turn my gaze to the window, as he does, and we both take note of the flamelike leaves on the trees. He kisses Elsa. I watch, unable to turn away.

I pour Elsa some coffee, because these days I've learned to act like the lady of the house. My hand trembles.

Then I take my few things and go by tram to Kruununhaka, to the apartment on Liisankatu. I hold tight to my suitcase, sit on the edge of my bed, and don't know where to begin. The evening opens up outside the window. Kerttu's great-aunt's bed, the wardrobe heavy in the corner, filled with superfluous clothing, the clock on the living room wall about to strike, night about to fall, the last tram screeching as it turns the corner, and I sleep with the weight of his hand a ghostly ache at the curve of my waist.

I'll continue this other life, meet some boys now and then, have parties, pass my exams as I should, and not yet know how to wish for anything more.

"MOMMY," THE LITTLE girl cries after I've left.

She's pleased that her mother has returned. For her the world is uncomplicated: Elsa comes back, Eeva leaves.

"You like Eeva, do you?"

"Yes," the little girl says.

She climbs into Elsa's lap.

"I missed you, Mommy," she suddenly sputters, hiding her tears in Elsa's neck.

"Did you?" Elsa says, touched. "Mama's darling," she says, and cuddles the little girl.

In the evening before going to sleep Elsa tucks her in, reads her a story. The man kisses Elsa's neck. He feels regret. The guilt is a black spot inside him—he uses this tenderness to hide all the things he's done while Elsa was away. He's thinking of me, of the way my thighs pressed against his sides.

Suddenly he's baffled by his own strange desire for me, thinks of it as a temporary disturbance. My moans ring in his ears and cause him to tremble with both passion and horror. He looks closer.

He goes over my features, my breasts, which are small, my belly, which is perhaps a bit too white, my smile, which, now that he thinks about it, is perhaps a bit too impudent and flirtatious.

The little girl frets and whimpers because she's missed her mother and won't go right to sleep. And when she finally does fall asleep, he undresses his wife in the bedroom and they do what they have the strength and tenderness to do.

As they lie side by side, Elsa asks, "How did things go this time?"

"Good," he answers, and his voice is faint.

"What about Eeva? Was she a help? Did you enjoy yourselves?"

"Yes, Eeva's a great help. She's a fine young woman."

Elsa soon falls asleep. He lies beside her awake. He decides to put a stop to the whole thing.

HE CALLS ME. He's lain awake all night next to Elsa, re-proaching himself. He's made a decision.

"This has to end," he says as soon as I answer.

I don't say anything.

"So," he says, "let's end it, all right?"

"All right," I say.

"You'll come . . . you'll come the next time and it'll be like nothing has happened. Agreed?"

"Agreed."

He hangs up the phone. He thinks that when the next time comes, if I'm still even their nanny the next time Elsa's away—he could always make up some excuse to get a new one—he'll treat me like he did Hilma. Businesslike. Cordial, but without affection.

THE FOLLOWING WEEK he rings my buzzer. I feel like I'm catching a cold. I've spent the morning at home drinking tea, bored, wearing my mother's old wool socks. It's afternoon now and the sun is shining brightly, one of the last times it will that year.

I open the door into the hallway. I'm not surprised to see a glimpse of him coming up the stairs.

There's no return, it's impossible to turn back.

He has the requisite gift with him, a paper bag full of cinnamon rolls, which he knows I like. He smells familiar, pungent and soft at the same time.

"Have you come to set the rules?"

"I came looking for a woman," he says. "She was raised at the edge of a burned clearing."

"There are only women of the world living here."

"What kind of world?"

"A dream world."

"It can't be entirely a dream world," he says. "The woman I'm looking for is so filled with affection that it flows out of her fingertips."

"Oh, her. She left. Went to another city. She told me about it before she packed up."

"What did she say?" he asks.

"She said she thought she might be in love."

"Really?" he says. "Then what's the problem?"

"It's complicated. That's what she said. The man wanted to end the whole thing before it had even begun."

"Idiot," he says. "A guy like that deserves to get lost in the woods."

"A wolf'll eat his leg off."

"But not his hands."

"No, not his hands."

"What do you think this woman plans to do?" he asks. "When she gets back from this other city."

"She'll ask him in, offer him some coffee. They'll talk to each other like strangers for a moment."

"And then?"

"Then," I say carelessly, as if I were talking about the movements of clouds. "Then it all depends on him. On what he wants to do."

"What about her? Doesn't she have any say?"

"Of course. But she's one of those people who thinks that no one can afford to let love pass them by. She's the kind of person who thinks that no one's rich enough that they can afford to walk right by love. That's why she keeps the door open."

He steps over the threshold, comes inside easily, as if there were no threshold.

I measure some coffee into the pot, watch as it brews, the foam rising to the top, and then take it off the burner. We eat half a cinnamon roll and drink the coffee, though the grounds haven't yet sunk to the bottom.

He lights a fire in the tiled stove and finds one of Kerttu's great-aunt's books half-burned in the grate, titled *My Love*. We speculate about who loved Kerttu's cantankerous great-aunt. The wood in the stove catches fire. I change the record on Kerttu's player. The light lingers in the corners, the old clock on the wall strikes—one hour has passed. I go to him. It seems self-evident somehow that I should lean against him a little.

Soon I ask him into my room.

THE CLOCK STRIKES four. The sun is setting. People are coming home from work. The trams are packed full of afternoon hope, and I'm not cold anymore. The burning wood, sticks of spruce, sputter in the stove.

My father always says that spruce isn't good for heating—too much pitch. I like the popping sound, it's like the starting gun for something, dividing time between what's past and what's new, not yet formed.

As he's leaving, I sit for a moment on the windowsill. I ask him for a cigarette. Smoking makes me cough, but I smoke anyway. The pungent fall air comes into the room from the slightly opened window and gives me goosebumps. The dark hasn't come yet. I sit at the window until it does.

I'll take love. It's what I want, and I'm going to take it.

There's another feeling that takes shape as I sit here on the windowsill. It's bound up with the melancholy that hovers behind the feeling of love. It concerns Elsa, and its name is guilt.

AFTER THAT FIRST time, we occasionally see each other even when Elsa's in town. He comes to my house in the afternoons. He stays for two hours, sometimes three. The walls are the boundaries of our world. We rarely go out. He brings me rolls, sometimes bread. Our existence is like a long outing, we broaden the space of the day from the inside out, first by buttering the hard-crusted bread he got at the bakery and brewing strong coffee, then by closing the door to my room.

Time slides away from us, out under the bedroom door, and we slide into each other.

THE LOVE FOR him belongs to the new Eeva. Something else that develops more secretly is the love for the little girl.

When autumn ends, I've already learned her. She scratches off her scabs when they start to heal. She fusses when she's tired, hits me and kicks me. Sometimes she's unmanageable and I have to tell her no. The first time I do she flies into a rage. I get even more angry, and afterward I cry in the bathroom.

But she accepts me in spite of my prohibitions, or maybe because of them, because when I tell her no she can test its strength and position and see that it's a wall that's always in the same place.

Right away, in the first few weeks, she wants me to put her to bed, wants me near her before she goes to sleep.

She always falls asleep suddenly, just the way she did the first time I was left alone with her. She wants to hear one more story, even though she's already sleepy, insists, begs drowsily until I agree. I make up a story and watch as she slips into sleep little by little, sometimes waking for a moment, as if to make sure I'm still there, and I continue the story to assure her that I haven't gone anywhere, I'm still right here beside her.

A T THE END of October, on an ordinary day, the little girl hurts herself. We're playing tag while her father is busy with his work. It's her favorite game: again and again she evades my grasp, squeals when I'm just about to catch her, giggles.

After dozens of dashes to freedom, her sock gets caught on the threshold. She falls on the floor with a smack, her hands in front of her, and bangs her head on the edge of the door.

"Uh-oh," I say.

She's quiet at first, for two seconds, three, then she gets up and looks embarrassed. I think for a moment that she's not going to cry.

"Did you hurt yourself?" I ask.

She shakes her head, then opens her mouth and begins.

Her crying is quiet and hoarse at first, then it grows into a loud bellow interrupted by gasping breaths. I remember all the times I cried as a child, when I couldn't catch my breath and snot ran into my mouth, those moments when I believed that nothing good would ever happen to me again.

She gets up, runs to the space between the cabinet and the radiator, rolls up in a little ball and bellows. I go to her, try to touch her, but she bats my hand away.

"Did you hurt yourself, sweetheart? Where does it hurt?"

I see a throbbing, shining bump on her forehead.

"Mommy," she says. "I want my mommy."

"Your mommy's not here right now."

"Where is she?"

"Mommy's on a trip, but I'm here."

Her crying grows stronger, the sound rising a note or two. Something is sprained inside me—I don't know what to do. I'm insufficient. Her crying sets off every ghost and goblin of my childhood, all the times I woke up alone in the dark and couldn't feel my own boundaries.

I shove my own terrors aside and act. I find the words.

"Will you let me blow on it?"

I reach out my hand. She gets up, stumbles out of the corner toward me and stands beside me at first, not letting me pick her up yet.

"Come here."

I sit on the floor. I take her in my arms. Her little body is hot, the pain has brought a sweat to her skin. The lump on her head is turning red, thin red threads under the skin like a spider's web.

I remember the rhyme my mother said to me. The words rise from my healed wounds and hover in the air. She listens.

I blow, recite the rhyme in the little girl's ear just like my mother did, and her mother before her.

She's not crying anymore. The paths of her tears are shining red on her cheeks.

She's very quiet, looking straight ahead at the corner and resting her head slightly against my chest. She's heavy here in my lap, letting her weight press against me little by little.

If this feeling had a color, it would be yellow, and a touch of blue.

I remember my mother's smile, those languid moments when I sat on her lap and she comforted me this way. I saw her from the outside then, I didn't guess that the feeling was like this, so complete.

Something stirs inside me. I'm much bigger and brighter on the inside than I've ever been before.

12

THEY'RE DRIVING THROUGH the countryside. Now and then Matias puts his hand on Anna's thigh.

They had a strange argument at home before they left. The words they said still linger in the air. The beginnings of the fight had been simmering in Anna's mind for days, springing up at odd times—irritation at something Matias said, some gesture, the way he takes off his socks, tugging on the ribbing with his toes against his Achilles tendon and tossing one sock, then the other, across the living room, or how he mutters *mmm*, and reaches his hand to the fluff at the base of her abdomen, as if discovering the boundaries of her body hair never ceases to amaze him.

"What's this?" he had asked as Anna was packing.

Anna looked up. He was waving a piece of paper in the air.

"I don't know," she said.

"It was over there on the desk," he said. "Did you write this?"

"No," Anna said, before she had time to think. Then she said, "Yes. Who else would have written it?"

"I read it," Matias said.

"Why? Give it to me."

Matias held the paper over his head and looked at her. She thought she saw sarcasm or something like sarcasm in his eyes. But it wasn't sarcasm. He was serious. How could she never have seen him like this before—angry? She looked at the text. She recognized the writing, read the first few lines.

When I saw Linda for the first time, I wasn't prepared. There had been a mix-up of dates and he had to go to work unexpectedly. I told him I would watch her for a few hours. They were standing in the doorway, Linda wearing a backpack. I hadn't looked at a child up close like that in a long time. Pure was the first word that came to mind, but not in the sense of being free of dirt. It was something else, something fresh. Her eyelashes were surprisingly long, her eyelids were plump, her nose looked soft, rising from her face like a ripe berry. She already had distinctive expressions, but sorrow hadn't yet found its way onto her face. I could see that it hadn't. Seeing this was not like other seeing—it was seeing something that doesn't yet exist, but that you know is coming. Give her some bread and juice, he said. Don't let her eat candy from the table. You can play, maybe go to the park.

So we did. As we were crossing the street I wanted to run to the shelter of the arched building entrance, not put the child in any danger, not shatter that face into unrecognizability.

Linda interrupted my growing terror by taking hold of my hand. So simple: her trust made me believe.

When it was all over I realized that she would survive this. I was the one in danger, the one who wouldn't survive as well. Maybe it had been that way from the very beginning. She was the one who drew the sorrow on my face. It was her disappearance from my life that left me limp, lying on the floor for days without moving, unable to get up.

"Something I made up," Anna said. "A story."

Matias looked at her, not turning his head, trying to get hold of something.

"What does it say about me that you wanted to leave this out?"

"What are you, the truth police? Can't I write what I want?"

"You left this out because you wanted me to read it, that's what I think. Leaving something like this on the desk where I can see it can't be an accident."

"What kind of nonsense is that? What right do you have to go snooping in my things?"

"It was right there on the desk. The desk that we share. Don't pretend that you didn't think I would see it."

"But you still shouldn't read a person's diary."

Matias gave her a significant look. "A diary. You just said that it was a story."

"Same thing."

"This is about things that happened to you. Your last relationship. The one you don't talk about."

"Everything has to do with my former lovers in your mind. Try to get over it."

He laughed. "You're the one who can't get over it."

"You're the one who brought it up."

"Because you won't talk about it. I think that's strange."

"What should I say about it? What should a person tell their new lover about their old lover? Do you want to read the notes on last year's calendar, or the year before that, so you know who I went to coffee with two years ago January? What do you want to know?"

He shrugged. "You're the one who knows what I should know, if there is anything."

He laid the paper back on the desk. It was between them. Anna looked away.

NOW MATIAS IS putting his hand on her thigh and not taking it away. This is their making-up ritual.

"Should we stop at the Prisma?" he asks.

He looks at her affectionately.

"Let's."

In the parking lot she thinks that she could easily stay here, by his side.

She sees their lives. Children skipping along ahead of them, yelling, begging for ice cream.

Ordinary moments, not sad, but not the kind of moments that you mistakenly thought represented happiness when you were a teenager dreaming about the future. Moments when you feel boredom, when a word like happiness doesn't apply. She knows that at some point in the future, happiness will seem like an overblown, childish word, once she's learned these other moments of . . . not happiness, but some other word—more ordinary, flat, skin-deep. Contentment.

They both secretly like the Prisma supermarket. They like the big shopping carts that you push down the aisles like steering a ship. They like the mountains of fruit and the foolish impulse buys—a hula hoop, a barbecue mitt shaped like a crayfish. They like the touching families, meekly buying ten liters of fat-free milk and two cases of yogurt, all of them wearing Crocs.

Anna picks out a whitefish from the seafood counter. They wander absentmindedly among the shelves, choose some vegetables for the grill, charcoal, lighter fluid, marshmallows, ice cream.

THE ICE CREAM is melting in their bowls. They're sitting on the porch with their arms around each other.

They talk lazily about Godard's *Pierrot le Fou*, which they saw last week at the film archives. Matias thought it was fragmentary and overly arty. Saara thought it was chauvinistic. That's Godard's idea of what a woman is, she said, with exaggerated incredulity. Nothing but temperamental princesses! A line from the movie has tattooed itself into Anna and she doesn't want to shake it off: *We are made of dreams, and dreams are made of us.*

She doesn't know if the line refers to the woman, whom the man can't understand, or to the time that the characters in the film are living in, or to dreams, which people can't live without, or to all of reality, everything that happens between people.

Anna's overcome with a surprising feeling of well-being, as if she were entirely herself and at the same time someone slightly different. The blackbird's call has a friendly, familiar sound, louder than before, but she can't find its dark shape among the foliage anymore.

"I'll tear up, that floor tomorrow while you clean the shed," Matias says, looking satisfied with himself, the way a man who performs mental labor every day sometimes looks when he has a chance to putter with his hands, build something, discover hidden abilities.

"Don't start dismantling anything by yourself. Wait till Dad gets here."

Anna's mother, father, and her sister Maria are coming tomorrow. Her grandparents are coming, too, if Grandma's condition will allow it.

Anna hears her mother in the commanding tone of her voice, the same tone her mother uses with her father sometimes, which always makes him angry. Now these emphatic words give her a secret joy. She's exasperatingly like her mother, and it doesn't alarm her at all.

"I know how to do it," Matias says. "I'll pull up the floor, then we can get started nailing down a new one right away."

"Well, all right," Anna allows, pretending to be the one giving in, but pleased.

Her father suggested reflooring the sauna porch when they saw him last week—he had a manly discussion with Matias about it at the front door when they arrived. Anna thought for a moment that maybe her father had always wanted a boy. With Matias he could talk about boards and nails and percussion drills and look out across the lake and say magnanimously, There's beer in the fridge if you want some.

THEY TAKE A sauna in a mood of goodwill, the words of their argument dissolving in the steam. Matias rubs lotion on Anna's arms and back afterward, spreads apricot scent on her legs, and it all leads to where they guessed it might.

A mist floats over the lawn, Anna can see it from the window before she lies down on the linen blanket, a little damp from the sauna. Matias comes into her amazingly carefully and passionately. It suddenly feels like they are different people, who are doing this together for the first time. Anna herself is a little more passionate than at home, Matias strong and gentle.

What does the loon think, or the blackbird, when they hear this, Anna thinks just before she reaches her peak, rising and dropping at the same time.

Afterward they sit on the porch and Matias strums the guitar. Anna drinks Sol from the bottle, pulls her knees up against her chest. It's a little cold, but not too. She reads a copy of *Seura* that she found in the bottom drawer of the chest in the dressing room. A middle-aged writer and a pop singer telling about their new happiness.

Anna reads the writer's words aloud: "*I finally know what love is.*"

"What year is that from?"

"Ninety-seven."

"Does he tell?"

"Tell what?"

"What love is?"

"No."

THE MORNING IS rainy. Clouds hang dreary above the treetops. The blackbird has disappeared. Matias puts on his old jeans and takes his tools to the sauna. Anna follows and watches him cheerfully begin his work.

She goes back up the path. Opens the door of the shed. The same smell, the same charcoal drawings on the shelves and half-finished paintings on their easels.

She doesn't know where to begin. She moves the boxes, paint cans, and gardening tools out of the way.

The orange painting strikes her eye almost immediately. It's unfinished. It looks so ordinary that she nearly passes it by before she realizes. It's a picture of her, with all her budding seriousness, bushy-haired, dark-eyed.

An irresistible feeling comes over her: she suddenly knows that she can't go on living if she doesn't have the painting for her own. She has to bring it home. She has to hang it on the wall. The photo that was on her wall in the apartment on Pengerkatu for two years—the tasteless Aino pastiche—can collect dust in the closet. She's going to hang this picture on the wall.

The painting is a condensed version of her, somehow. It holds all that she was as a child and all that was still just germinating inside her. If she leaves the painting here in the garden shed at Tammilehto, at the mercy of visiting squirrels, she'll be leaving herself here. Or worse yet, she'll be leaving her childhood, those shapeless fears and hopes that she can't name but which she nevertheless recognizes as her own.

She takes hold of the painting carefully, puts it in front of the others. When she looks at it from up close she notices that her grandfather has mixed the paint carefully in the eyes to create the right darkness. Maybe there's also something other than ordinary oil paint in the eyes. He's good at that sort of thing, mixing in who knows what—aluminum powder, ashes, sawdust, sometimes even silver. Anna is taken with the idea that in her eyes, at the place where the change in hue expresses hope, at the place that reflects all that hasn't yet been realized, all that a child carries inside her, there's a pinch of silver.

If Anna tries hard enough, she can clearly remember what she was thinking on the day her grandfather painted her eyes. She was making a precocious decision not to tell lies, because she had been grounded the week before for tricking Maria. She had made up a story of kidnappers who drove a red car and snatched children away from the street where they lived and Maria had been afraid to come out from under the bed all afternoon.

Maria cried about it to their parents in the kitchen that evening, and they had to use some harsh words. She had been to Fazer for ice cream with her grandpa—she'd reluctantly eaten a meatball at dinner for the privilege, a dinner she still remembers: ketchup and meatballs and the clock in the kitchen ticking. She'd read *Tintin* on the living room carpet. An ordinary day, a prototype of childhood, of hopes and secret worries veiled in songs and games.

Anna decides she'll take the painting, perhaps in secret. She'll have it framed and hang it on the wall because she knows that it is more her than she could ever be.

"Ready to eat?" Matias asks behind her. He's been working a good while.

Steam is coming off him. In these few hours he's acquired a workingman's cheery bravado. Anna goes to him and kisses him.

"So, have you had enough?"

"No," he says lightheartedly. "I'm taking out the wall. It's taking awhile, because it's lined with old newspapers. I spend half the time reading. You wouldn't believe the journalism in the old *Uusi Suomi* or *Helsingin Sanomat*."

Anna gently pinches him.

"I should make a note never to hire a historian to do demolition."

"Did they remodel the sauna, when the main building burned down? The newspapers in the wall are from the late 1960s. What year was the fire?"

"August 1967. I don't know if they rebuilt the sauna, too. You should ask my grandparents. Maybe they decided to renovate the whole shebang."

Matias looks at the orange painting.

"What's this? Is that you? This is like the one at your parents' house. Is this the mate to it?"

"Yes. I've been pestering my grandpa to tell me where it was for aeons. It's been right here all these years. It's a little unfinished, but I was thinking about taking it to have it framed anyway."

"And hang it on our wall?"

"Why not?"

Anna notices herself searching Matias's gaze for his opinion of the painting. Is it tasteless? Is it pointless, garish, as garish as the Aino photo? Or maybe Matias just doesn't want to see her on their wall, sad-eyed, looking out with a child's gaze at everything that happens. Her storytelling, truth-mangling, six-year-old self watching over their lives.

"Why not," he says finally. "Let's take it with us on Sunday. We can drop it off at the framers on the way home—if your grandfather will give it to us, that is."

"Of course he will."

13

HE WAS TENSE. The last time they'd been here was in the fall, when Elsa was still strong.

"Should we buy some water?" he said, to have something to say.

It was strange to be tense around his own wife. He felt as if they were living some very old time, from fifty years before, all over again. He had listened to Elvis the day he met Elsa. Suddenly he remembered Elvis, how nervous he was. His hands gripped the steering wheel, fifty years melting away.

"Why?" Elsa said. "I'm sure the water there is working."

He looked at her surreptitiously, and she turned her head. A little smile.

"Just let me know if you get tired."

"I will, I will."

He was pleased when he didn't see any cars as they pulled into the yard; Anna and Matias were out shopping for groceries and Eleonoora, Eero, and Maria hadn't yet arrived. He could have a moment alone with Elsa.

It had rained. The trees in the yard held the drops proudly, as if aware, devoted to the task. Elsa stepped carefully out

of the car, felt the ground for a moment, then walked pur-
posefully toward the sauna. Where did the illness show? Nowhere, really. Her legs were sticks under her pants, but you
didn't notice it if you didn't look closely.

"The whole floor will probably have to go," she shouted
from the sauna porch. "And part of the wall," this time from
inside.

He opened the door of the cabin. He was pierced by his
fondness for Tammilehto and their shared days here. He remembered the smell of all the breakfasts, bread and butter
and ham, the smell of coffee and cucumbers and sun shining
in the window.

Anna learned to walk here one summer, and so did Maria,
a few years later. Eleonoora and Eero had been married in
the yard. How long ago was it? Twenty-five years. He had
walked down the aisle with Eleonoora. He remembered her
damp hand, her slightly terrified smile. She had stopped for
a moment, as if she were having second thoughts. She wants
to call it off, Martti had thought. He had already seen it all in
his mind—they would drive away together, go to the service
station, the veil still on her head, like a meringue. He wouldn't
ask why, since it wasn't a father's business. They would buy
cheese sandwiches and coffee, not caring if people stared.

But Eleonoora had said, Well, let's go.

Eero had looked at her across the yard and she had smiled
at him, a little dazed, as if she wanted to say, This is stupid,
it's insane! I want to embark on this crazy thing with you!

He picked up a cookie from a plate on the table—a Dom-
ino. The damp had made it leathery. He liked the way it
tasted. It was right for this place.

Elsa came inside.

"Let's make some coffee," Martti said.

"The boy's torn up half the sauna," Elsa said cheerfully.

"If it's rotten, it should be taken out."

"What if it was rotten from the start?" she said.

He searched her face for a sign in her words, for the familiar, hurt expression, the crease between her eyebrows.

He pulled her closer.

"We were in a hurry to have a new sauna. In a hurry to rebuild."

"You were the one who was in a hurry. We didn't have to repair the sauna at all. It wasn't necessary."

"Maybe. Maybe it was me."

He was quiet for a moment, letting his gaze wander.

"I ordered some new paints," he heard himself saying. "I bought canvases. Paper, other materials. I got a little carried away. I could start up a little shop of my own with everything I bought. So I'll have a lot of materials to choose from if I want to try again."

Elsa raised her eyebrows. "That's wonderful."

He had gone the week before to Rautalampi's art supply store. He didn't actually know what he intended to do with the supplies. Did he even want to start again? The whole thing felt somewhat frivolous. Still, he'd put in an order. Rautalampi had chuckled when he saw him.

"Going to try it one more time?"

"We'll see. I might buy something. Pigments. Maybe you could order me some of the powdered ones from France, the ones I used to use. Can you still get those?"

Rautalampi had run the same art supply store and frame shop on Uudenmaankatu for decades. A lot of people ordered things from the Internet these days, but Martti had doggedly stuck with Rautalampi—there are some things that shouldn't change. I knew you'd come back, Rautalampi said good-naturedly. I kept telling myself, Ahlqvist will come back. I'm sure he'll want to work again some day.

A strange, pleasant sense of shame had rushed over him, the same feeling he remembered from his younger years, the ·first few times he got caught drawing in his sketchbook.

They'd had a cup of coffee in the back room and smoked a pipe of good tobacco. As he was walking out of the shop he'd felt the same enthusiasm for painting that he'd had when he was young.

Elsa went into the kitchen and looked in the cabinets.

"Good. Anna and Matias bought some fresh coffee."

She poured water in the pot, smelled the ground coffee with her eyes closed as she usually did before measuring it out. Martti picked up the gesture and drew it precisely in his mind. Elsa saw his look, flipped the switch of the coffeemaker with a smile. It made a crunching sound and then started to gurgle.

"Maybe I'll just sit here," Elsa said, sitting down at the table. "I'll just sit here and you can take down all my essentials. If you're thinking about painting, you could try painting me."

He laughed. "I wouldn't know how."

"Try," Elsa said.

She crossed her legs, leaned on her arms, closed her eyes.

Here was Elsa's whole face. It was so rare to be able to see her whole, all of the versions of her at the same time.

He remembered one time like that. Elsa had been packing her clothes for some trip. He saw her back, which he had always looked at tenderly, always stroked as he passed if he could. He was thinking about how he'd never cared particularly what Elsa looked like from behind. No, that wasn't it. What he had thought was: that woman could be anyone, a stranger.

The thought had suddenly taken on the strength of a horror. Elsa had evolved a series of gestures and expressions that he wasn't a part of, that he could never make his home in, and now she was suddenly a stranger.

The realization had a weirdly triumphant flavor. As if he'd been given a reason for his vague feelings of hostility. If I feel this much hate, he thought, love must be a lie.

He remembered how he had believed that he hated the way Elsa popped a bite of sandwich in her mouth, her way of combing her hair or dishing vegetables onto a plate to cover exactly one quarter of its surface.

He also hated the way she took care of Ella when she came home. She monopolized her, invented her own rituals with her daughter so that he was left out of them. And the little girl turned to Elsa like the sun, always staying close to her, wanting to be held, cuddled.

Their bitterest fights had been in those days after Elsa returned home. When they were fighting he would make a note of her every gesture, every rise and fall of her body, like a clinician gathering observations for a report.

Often days would go by in this strange, rarified atmosphere. Elsa would gaze out the window, caress the girl but speak to her only a little, and look like she longed to be back at work, traveling, away from here.

And then, out of nowhere, a fight would start. Elsa would lash out at him with the words they always used, familiar words, finding just the right ones.

It had been one of those evenings when he stood in the doorway watching her perform some ordinary task.

He let the thought come into his mind: I don't love you. At the moment that he let himself think that, he was able to see Elsa whole.

This woman: brown hair, glasses, her skirt a little tight around her thighs, heavy breasts that had fed one child placid under her blouse. A woman who had a whole store of the right words, many of them gentle ones, a woman who could hide her tiredness better than anyone he knew. Elsa was always careful not to show herself to strangers. This woman absorbed in some activity, ironing a shirt, folding sheets or leafing through papers. Sunk in her thoughts, starting to slump.

What is it? she had asked. Have you been standing there long?

She had looked up at him as if she were embarrassed that he was watching her without her knowing it.

You're beautiful.

Ah, she said, flustered. She smiled, bent down to pick up another piece of clothing—she must have been ironing, not leafing through papers.

I don't know if I love you anymore.

She looked at him, surprised, received the words like a sudden slap, not yet realizing their power.

He had thought, this is the crossroads. If he continued life the way they were used to, if he thought of her as the girl she'd been when they met, he couldn't be close to her.

You have to learn the other person again all the time.

IT WAS AS if Elsa knew his thoughts. She opened her eyes and looked at him slightly reprovingly.

She let out a little sigh, light. For a moment he waited for words, blame, a reminder of something a long time ago. When it didn't come, he asked, "Are you angry?"

"What do you mean?"

"You look irritated."

She got up from the table, walked over to him, and took him in her arms. They stood that way for a long time without saying anything. Finally she said, "I miss the days when I had time to be angry. Now it feels like death will come before I even have a chance to cuss."

"I'm sure you have time for one damn it. Give it a try."

Her breath felt hot and damp through his shirt.

"Damn it," she said gropingly, questioningly, like a child.

"Look at that. See?"

"Are you ever going to paint me?" she asked.

"I don't know. Would you like me to?"

Lightly, as if she were talking about the end of any period of time—picking strawberries before the damp days of late summer, digging potatoes in June, while they're still small and flavorful—she said, "I don't know. But if you're going to do it, you'd better hurry."

———

A HAPPY DAY, like they used to have. There was life in the cabin, Anna and Maria were bustling around upstairs, cleaning the shed and cutting the grass, coming now and then to help with the sauna. Elsa sat on the porch and seemed to be enjoying herself.

"I'm looking at things really closely now," she said. "It seems to me that I ought to get a good look at every tree and hollow."

Matias played the guitar after dinner, teased Eleonoora by playing "Eleanor Rigby," which she didn't like.

"It's such a sad song," she said. "I don't want a song like that for my namesake."

"It's pretty," Matias insisted.

"Everybody in it ends up alone," Eleonoora said. "Play something else. Play 'Blackbird.'"

Matias played "Blackbird" and everyone liked it. Elsa turned to look at the tops of the spruce trees and the lakeshore. Eleonoora reached out her hand and stroked her mother's back. For a moment they had the feeling that it didn't matter that they could never return to this moment. For this once, it was that complete.

THEY TORE UP the entire floor of the sauna. Anna wanted to keep the newspapers. She spread the whole last part of the sixties out across the dock, weighing the pages down with rocks, and sat half the day bent over them, as if she were examining a rare plant through a microscope.

Later she came to the door. The others had gone to eat and Martti was tossing the last of the planks into a pile.

"That fire—did it start quickly?" she asked.

"I guess so," he said. "It burst into flames."

She swung her wrists, shifted from one foot to the other. She had on tennis shoes and jeans, a hooded sweatshirt, clothes she would have worn when she was twelve. Maybe she was smarter, more perceptive than he had realized. Children change without our noticing. First they're one or two years old, then they're five. They're frolicking around the yard with an inner tube in their skinny arms, and everything's already begun. They've already begun to understand about the world. The years go by, they wear different clothes, find new expressions, gather information in secret, and carry it quietly within them.

"What about those paintings in the shed?" she asked.

Martti bent over to pull up the last board from the corner. It cracked as it came away. The crack made him feel satisfied in a way he couldn't name.

"What about them?" he asked.

"I was thinking that I might take one home and put it on the wall."

"Why not, if it suits you? Take whatever you like. You can take those old etchings, too. It was something I tried for a while. A lot of work, but I enjoyed it."

"Thanks. I looked through them yesterday," she said. "There were a few really good ones."

He realized he missed her company. When was the last time they went for coffee, sat and talked?

"Do you still play the tram game?" he asked. "The one where you make up lives for people?"

She took hold of the shared memory, smiling. "Still do."

"Shall we try it?" he asked. "Like we used to?"

"As soon as we get back to town."

He bent to pick up a newspaper page. It was the same year as the others. The headlines were about demonstrations.

"Look," he said. "A rebellion."

She reached out, took the page, glanced at it. "The rebellion is alive under the floorboards," she said with a smile.

14

WAIT. I HAVE to get my wallet," her grandfather says. "In case we decide to buy up the whole town."

Soon they're boarding the number three tram. He gives Anna a questioning look as soon as they sit down. Who?

Anna looks around.

"What about that one?" he says, gesturing to the left side of the aisle.

"Who, that girl?"

Anna tests the girl for a moment. She has reddish brown hair and a shy half smile. Anna shakes her head. The girl has an ordinary story. Writing university papers, a fear that pounds to the beat of her heart, fear that something important is happening someplace else. The endless dreams of sunny spring days as she rides her bicycle through the woods, the shadows of spruce trees cutting across the path like tall figures bending over her in a childhood dream.

"Not her," Anna says.

Grandpa nods in agreement.

A tattered man gets on at the next stop. Not a reeking human wreck, younger than many drunks, perhaps a little over forty. Grandpa glances at her. What about him? She nods.

They both lean forward a little. The man sits down next to the entrance and takes a cell phone out of his pocket. It's a recent-model phone, but very used, covered in duct tape.

Anna leans toward her grandfather and whispers, "His name is Vesa."

Grandpa looks at the man with interest. "A mechanic? Or maybe a construction worker?"

Anna looks at the man for a moment. "No," she says suddenly, with absolute certainty. "A lawyer. A former lawyer."

Grandpa nods, approving of her decision, and starts to sketch Vesa's character.

"Studied at Helsinki University and Cornell. Was married to a doctor. It took a long time for his wife to realize. She used to boast that he knew how to drink like a European."

Anna takes up the story: "She didn't realize that meant not just wine with lunch and dinner but also a bottle every Friday."

Grandpa: "When it occurred to her that there is no country where the drinking traditions include falsifying a prescription for spirits, she left him."

"After the last binge, before he lost his job, his ex-wife checked him into rehab, but he escaped, claiming he was too busy at work."

"And he was. There was a business trip to Hamburg, and it would be his last. He woke up on Reeperbahn—he'd been robbed by a Croatian stripper and all he could remember about the evening were the tassels on her breasts."

"And then his boss had a talk with him."

They have Vesa, Vesa's whole life. Vesa has given up fear. Being free did that. But he's also given up hope. He no longer has dreams or fantasies, and it worries him a little because he remembers what his mother told him when he was a child: When you stop dreaming, you start dying.

Vesa gets off at the railway station. They both turn to watch him go. Anna looks at her grandfather out of the corner of her eye. She can see the same exhilaration that she feels.

"The best thing about the tram," he says, "is that nothing ever ends."

"Yeah," Anna says. "Everything is happening—nothing is beginning and nothing is ending."

"Want to go to Torni?" he asks. "All the way to the top, to the place with the view, like we used to. You have a Jaffa and I'll have a coffee."

"I drink coffee, too, nowadays."

"You? Do you take snuff, too? Blithely baste your stomach with a drink in the morning to kill your hangover?"

"Is that what pleasurable things lead to?"

"In the end."

They share a smile. Anna thinks, some things never change—they're not allowed to change.

"Let's," she says.

THE CITY STRETCHES out to their right and left, changes to woods after the Olympic Stadium, offering its southern edge to the sea. The ships look like hopeful animals on a journey abroad, ready to forget momentarily where they came from. If you look closely you might be able to see all the way to Tallinn. Coca-Cola costs four euros, even a coffee is three.

"Did you use to come here when you were young?"

"Sometimes. But I mostly went to Kosmos or Hansa."

Anna thinks about Eeva again. What if she just asked him directly? The question lurks at the back of her throat but something in her grandfather's expression prevents her.

"Look," he says, drawing the landscape with a gesture from edge to edge. "Pretty as a picture."

"But you'll leave it at that? You don't intend to paint it?"

This makes him laugh. "A landscape? No. Landscapes aren't my thing. My work has always been more abstract."

"Why don't you paint anymore?" Anna asks abruptly.

He doesn't seem bothered by the question.

"I don't know. Maybe I thought I was concentrating on life. Making art can become antithetical to life without you noticing."

Anna remembers one of her grandfather's many art openings. She was sixteen and didn't want to participate in the family celebration, staked out a protest with her eyes like one of the Fates. Grandpa was in excellent spirits, enjoying the attention, explaining to a journalist that some of his paintings were made by leaving a canvas on the floor of his studio so that when his paint dripped or spilled it would create unanticipated art. That part was apparently true. But then he continued: sometimes I might add some lunch to the mix, some pea soup, ketchup, that sort of thing. Sometimes a bit of cardamom bun at coffee time becomes part of my materials—it makes interesting raised areas in the painting. I look at my works in process like mysterious maps, throw myself into their incompleteness like getting lost in the woods. The reporter nodded uncertainly, still smiling.

Grandpa glanced over his shoulder at Anna and smiled and then she knew he was joking.

Anna realized that humor was her grandfather's shield against nervousness. Afterward he had some cognac in the back room, looking happy and melancholy at the same time.

The exhibition was a success. As Anna was reading a review of the show in the paper over breakfast she had one of those moments when she realized that her grandparents were out of the ordinary.

Anna remembers the dreamy hours when Grandpa was painting her. He was familiar to her, but he was slightly different when he was painting. She sensed the difference without being able to name it. It was in his gaze. He sat her down under the window and she played with a doll or drove a toy car over the floorboards. She could tell when he had begun painting just from his gaze.

He would whistle as he mixed thinner into the paint. Anna would watch him as he went to the window. Then he would walk back to his easel. His chin would lift a little, his sleeves rolled up to the elbow. He would make a stroke, look, and begin.

"How's your dissertation coming?" Grandpa asks. "Has your project to explain the world moved into its theological phase yet? Or are you just wallowing in the sixties?"

"Wallowing deep in the past. My adviser says I should tie the theme more to other political movements. Just the change in the status of women isn't enough."

He laughs. "Well, you've got a storehouse of information right here. Ask me anything and I can tell you the answer. I'll give you eyewitness testimony."

"I can cite you in my source list as 'a certain grandpa.'"

"Information inherited from certain grandpas ought to have its own category in the citations list."

He digs a cigarette out of his pocket but doesn't light it. "It was all a lot of noise when you look back on those years. A crazy time. Every time I went to Paris something had happened, my old classmates had thought up something new. Finland felt like the boondocks, although we had our own circles here. But they were a little homespun and tame compared to Paris or Amsterdam. In Finland we were reinventing everything that my friends in Paris had already been through in the fifties and early sixties. There were all kinds of movements in Paris over the years. I was at some of the meetings. I kept my distance from that crowd when I was in Finland."

"What did they do at the meetings?"

"They created guidelines for reality."

He says this with overemphasis, as if he were talking about a party that's got out of control. The kind of party that you reminisce about, embroidering events, shaking your head but nevertheless yearning for that time—a time when we were so sweet and wild!

"You always had to be thinking up something new. It often felt like just when I'd mastered some technique or style, they'd start doing it some other way. Painting was out of style, supposedly. You were supposed to analyze the world some other way, through provocation. Or at least use mixed media. Sometimes I felt like politics was more important than art in that crowd. Not even politics, really—just spectacle for spectacle's sake. That sort of thing annoyed me generally."

"Too modern for you?"

"Maybe. Or maybe I thought that too much attention was paid to shock value, that careful, uncompromising work was disappearing. When the ideas that had been going around in Paris came to Finland I felt like I'd already heard it all. Maybe they sounded a little childish to me. But a lot of my friends were in that group."

They're quiet for a moment. Grandpa lets his gaze drift over the people in the cafe as if to say, why talk about the past when this is going on all the time—the world, life! Compared to this, every work of art is trivial, a sand castle.

"What about that woman?" he says, nodding toward a table in the corner. "What can we tell about her?"

"Who?"

"The one eating chocolate cake."

Anna turns to look behind her.

"The sad one?"

The woman has the mouth of someone who's given up—creased at the corners, as if there isn't a thing in this world that can touch her. She's drinking coffee and spooning a piece of cake into her mouth with her eyes closed.

"What do you think she's sad about?"

Anna can see the woman's eyes. She takes hold of the edge of the sadness. The woman looks like she's invariably a little amused at how the world keeps going, how people come here and order a coke, take the trouble for such a trivial thing. How other people take the trouble to print the newspaper that they sell at the counter, and others do their jobs, wipe the tables and say thank you and have a nice day.

"Maybe she's lost someone," Grandpa says. "Her father? Her mother?"

"No," Anna says. "Someone else. A child."

"You think so? What makes you think that?"

Anna doesn't hear his question. "It happened suddenly, last summer."

"Was it an accident?" Grandpa asks. "A car accident?"

It happened suddenly, in the time it takes to say the carefree words "See you tomorrow." That's how suddenly the woman's world was put in parentheses. Suddenly everything changed into this grotesque drama in which other children continue to be led across the street, carnival rides spin all summer long, and garish photographs advertise digital cameras on the sides of the bus stops. Grandpa looks at her, examines her expression. The sun beams down. Anna bends over and picks up her sunglasses and puts them on.

"It's bright," she says.

"Well," he says. "What now? What else shall we make up?"

The chocolate cake woman gets up, glances at them before walking to the door. As if she knows. No smile. Just a glance before she's gone.

Anna turns her head. Her grandfather tries to see what she's thinking. She sees those other faces in his face, young faces, the ones she's never seen before, the ones he's nevertheless carried with him across the decades. He raises one eyebrow, smiles, lights his cigarette, blows smoke. Gestures that belong at the edge of a soccer field or under a courtyard arch. Gestures that have charmed people, caressed them, got them to agree to things. Gestures that could make broad lines on canvas, try new techniques. They belong to youth.

On an impulse, Grandpa takes up their old game: "I met a girl," he says, not looking at Anna.

Anna plucks the sentence from the air like a shared memory: "What kind of girl?"

"She carried sorrows around that she never told anyone about."

Grandpa looks into Anna's eyes now. She can see that he knows.

"She had eyes like pools because they'd collected so many tears," he says.

One tear, then another, roll down Anna's cheek, under her collar into her shirt.

"Maybe she should tell someone about her sorrows, then," Anna hears herself say.

"That's what I told her—the girl that I met."

"And she will, too," Anna says. "Just as soon as she's ready."

1965

AS SOON AS we're in the taxi an abyss opens up between us. The flight to Paris is leaving in two hours, we're still on the cobblestone streets of Helsinki and the driver is calling me Mrs. as if I'd always held that position. I'm shaped like an apology, quite motionless, like a statue.

He's already regretting this. What insanity! Traveling with an assistant, and this punk calling her Mrs.!

"She's not my wife. This is a business trip."

I turn and look out the window at the stones of the street, not wanting to read the thoughts on his face. He's thinking: isn't this what he wanted? To show me the city? After all, he loves me, doesn't he? The love started at the party. It started in August, when he looked at me from across a room. It's a sickness. He still hasn't recovered. He never will.

How could he not have known that love is a fever, a drug, needing to have the other person near you. Why hadn't he felt that with Elsa? Was it because they'd always had their own separate selves? It feels to him like he'll perish if he can't be mine. He'll cease to exist if he can't be in me, inside me. If he can't see me smile in the morning, still a little sleepy, he might as well put parentheses around the world.

He tries to reach a hand out to me, but can't. An objection forms in his mind and takes Elsa's shape. He sees Elsa right after she gave birth—and he's surprised because Elsa is usually quick and compact, not giving up any of her self. She was walking down the hospital corridor a little unsteadily, porous, the belly that was just carrying their daughter still ample, like life. Elsa in the hallway, reaching out her hand: come on, let's go look at the baby, I want you to see how much her nose is like yours.

He remembers how I lied to Elsa about the trip. I told her I had a lot of studying to do, made up a story about a trip home, without looking her in the eye. That's a shame, she said.

"You shouldn't have lied," he says when the driver has picked up our luggage and we're alone at the front door. "You didn't have to lie to her that much, anyway."

"Just a little would've been better, you mean? Lying just a little?"

He turns away toward the rushing crowd.

We've been talking about the trip all winter. Was it possible? How much of a deception would it be? Would it be more deceit than either of us was ready for? His friend was having an exhibition in Paris, that was our cover story.

At the airport he measures the weight of the clouds with his gaze, as if sketching the possibility of escape. We sit side by side without speaking, like two strangers. I no longer dare to touch him.

"This is my first time flying," I tell the stewardess.

Something about her comforts me, perhaps her smile, perhaps the thought that here, above the clouds, safety and comfort are concentrated in the coffeepot she's holding.

"Are you afraid?" she asks.

"I'm nervous. But the takeoff was lovely, like a carnival ride."

She pours me some cognac. I gulp it and excitement flashes through me suddenly, unexpectedly. I don't care about him with his face turned away anymore. What luck! What joy! To be traveling toward possibilities and know nothing about them except that they exist.

WHEN WE ARRIVE, there are plastic tubes leading up and down, like in a science fiction movie. People constantly being paged. We step into a tube. He still doesn't look at me.

An Arab woman is standing next to me, her eyes drawn in charcoal. She's swathed in meters of fabric, eyes shining like two emeralds. A curtain of incense surrounds her. I catch a glimpse of her fingernails. They're as red as her lips. There are such things! The kinds of things I've only read about in books! All those dreamy evenings in Kuhmo, up in the attic, a bee buzzing in the window and me reading about faraway countries. Now those countries are becoming real. I love the woman for that moment, her abundance and her hard, hoarse voice that doesn't ask permission.

She says to me in French that my skin is so pale it's as if a lamp were burning inside me, and she smiles. I've studied the language for six years, I can read Balzac and order coffee and orange juice and a medium-rare steak, I can talk about the weather with subtle turns of phrase and exchange opinions about welfare and economic development, but I'm still amazed that this has been going on somewhere all this time, this language. I talk with her and he looks at me, smiling for the first time.

"You speak as if you've always lived here," he says.

I put my hand in his. He takes hold of it, but he can't shake off the feeling of strangeness. Who is this woman? He might mistake me for any Parisian. Like that girl there, with the ample bosom.

Actually all he wants to do is leave, pick out a few souvenirs for Elsa and his daughter from a department store and go, as if I don't exist. He wants to go back to Helsinki and forget that he was ever so stupid, so thoughtless and heartless as to sneak away on a trip with me.

He has no intention of introducing me to his friends, either. He'll send me out alone to see the sights, go to dinner with a few friends out of a sense of duty, get this whole absurd thing over with and buy me a return ticket on another plane.

That's what he decides to do as we hold hands and he hails a taxi.

In the taxi I force the guilt out of my mind for a moment, because Paris is coming to meet me. House after house, and houses being built and suburbs already constructed, their courtyards nursing hopes of fame, of extraordinariness. Fates formed from dreams, indifferent to conventionality, hidden within their walls. And everywhere laundry drying in the air shafts, an endless, festive flag to a trifling Tuesday.

Then come the wrought iron balconies and the *boulangeries*, the Paris I've seen in pictures. I yelp involuntarily.

———

HE'S THINKING ABOUT Elsa, the times he's spent in Paris with her. When they were in their twenties Elsa studied in Helsinki and he studied in Paris. She would come to see him whenever she could get enough money together for an airline ticket. Sometimes she came on the train. They would walk along the Seine and go to museums on Sundays. They would sit in cafes, he would read the paper or explain something in an eager voice, Elsa would read her textbooks, because she was determined to succeed and she didn't want to let up for a minute. They would walk in Luxembourg Gardens and buy crepes from a stand, stop for a while to watch a tennis match. They were young, their love was still new. They had fights, misunderstandings, doors slammed in protest. Often he was the one who got angry, got fed up with her about something. She would contradict him and he couldn't stand it. He would leave, wander the streets, stop to buy cigarettes in the Latin Quarter and take pleasure in being misunderstood.

He would walk around the Left Bank, go down to the level below the street and make the acquaintance of a passerby walking along the river shore. If there's any place where arguing can be beautiful, it's in Paris. They unconsciously struck up a ritual for making up. After the first, hours-long period of estrangement, he would get hungry and go to a small bistro on a square at the Sorbonne and order an omelet or a warm, toasted, stuffed baguette. The first time was an accident. Elsa wasn't looking for him, she just happened to be wandering along St.-Michel, saw the windows of the restaurants beckoning, and opened the door to the same bistro.

They wouldn't make a scene, wouldn't behave like people in a movie—that didn't fit their straightforward style. Elsa would just sit down across from him, smile, and order something for herself, maybe the same omelet or sandwich. Both of them would gradually give in and the fight would dissolve into the background, ridiculous.

The evening would already be turning dark when they walked to the metro station and neither of them would need to say out loud what they both were thinking: life, even a happy life, once you get used to it, is plainer than it is in dreams. And also heavier.

THE HOTEL IS more Parisian than any postcard sent from Paris. Narrow hallways, little elevators, steep stairs, cast iron railings outside the windows. The walls tempt us to tenderness, we should be sweating against each other's skin, but we go to sleep like brother and sister. I can't sleep. The room is an abyss.

I get up during the night, go to the toilet, can't find the light switch. I do my business in the dark. When I open the door, I run into him. He's a shadow—I don't recognize him at first.

I yell. My voice shakes the window on its hinges. He takes hold of my shout as if it were a request and takes me in his arms.

"Shhh. It's all right. Everything's all right," he says.

I'm trembling, can't stop shaking. "You hate me."

"No."

"You do, I can see it."

"I don't hate you. I love you."

"That's just a word."

"But it's still true."

In the morning he's quiet again, as if he's made of wood. He wants to meet some friends alone, to explain to them who I am before they meet me. I'm left with my anger in the hotel room and muster some curiosity to replace it: I'll go out alone.

I spend the day wandering in a museum. I find a painting that I linger over for an hour. It's a Rembrandt. The woman seems to be floating toward me. Her skin glows. No one knows anything about her hopes, her joys, her affections, but they still light up her face as if a lamp were burning inside her.

I go to the movies. I see a film about some people on the run from professional killers who escape from Paris to the south and end up in all sorts of difficulties. The man in the movie doesn't understand the woman, he says that all he sees is an image. Maybe the woman doesn't even want to be understood. Sometimes she goes dancing, sometimes she commits crimes. Sometimes she just saunters around on the shore with nothing to do. She wants to dance and doesn't care about anything else. She just wants to live, but the man doesn't understand that. She's amazed that people in photographs are always thinking unknown thoughts, about the past, the future, basketball, anything, and the people who look at the pictures will never know anything about those thoughts.

I think about Rembrandt's woman at the Louvre, about all that's inside her that I'll never know. I think about the people in all the pictures, in all the paintings in the world. A whole world behind their smiling faces! The crust of bread they ate that morning! A sneeze! A confession of love waiting to be spoken!

After the movie I take the metro north. A smell of toasted sugar and a swirl of stuffy air in the underground tosses me onto terra firma beside a white church. Suddenly the world is filled with song, steam, and rays of sunlight, the shouts and smiles of street musicians.

Men yell after me, a child runs toward me and offers me a piece of her bagel. The church is ridiculous, pompous, shameless. But I don't want a sanctuary, I want the world—splashes on the street corner and smoke curling on the horizon.

I go up some stairs and walk along a little side street and get lost. I arrive at a square filled with a fragile little park. It covers its melancholy in bright colors that are repainted every spring. There's a Ferris wheel, a carousel, and a row of little elephants going around and around in a circle forever. I pay a long-faced man with a billed cap and gray stubble a franc to rent binoculars and climb into a bright green basket. It rises up into the air. Suddenly I have the whole city, the meandering streets and the tower rising up in the middle of it all. People are bustling far below, crying, laughing, loving and betraying each other, making up, eating a meal.

I could live behind one of those windows. I have the language. No one here would smell the barn on my fingers. I could finally learn to pronounce *aujourd'hui* so that not one syllable would sound like I spent my summers and winters next to a pine forest. I would become a woman of today.

Yesterday would become a word I pronounced without nostalgia.

THERE'S A MESSAGE for me at the hotel reception, the clerk hands the note to me ceremoniously, like a jewel. It's an address and an apology. Under the name it says, Will you come?

I go as if I'm a stranger. Paris has wrapped itself around my gestures, the pine woods are just a memory. His friend's art opening is over, and the celebration reaches all the way to the ceiling. Someone has climbed up on the table, someone else is playing the piano, although they don't know how.

He comes over to me. Hands in his pockets, not hesitating but testing the climate.

"So," he says.

"So."

"Do you know anyone here?"

"One person. He's an artist. You know the type."

He sizes me up. This is the moment when he realizes that he doesn't really know what I'm thinking. The thought rises up inside him, stays in his mind, off to one side, like a persistent insect. I might hate him. How would he know if I hated him more than I love him?

He asks, not seriously, just challenging me to a game: "And what's your opinion of him?"

I speak carelessly, as if I'm discussing the endive: "Somebody said that I love him, but that was an exaggeration, because he keeps my heart in a metal box among the dust and the pocket change."

"A metal box? What an idiot. Someone ought to teach him a lesson."

"I already hired a few roughnecks I met on the Left Bank, under a bridge. They'll be here at any moment. I sold our whole love story to a street musician in Montmartre for a franc. He's singing it to the tourists for small change now. He gets some of the details wrong—you wouldn't believe the tasteless things he throws in. As lightweight as the bread around here—airy and meaningless."

He opens his hand in a gesture of surrender. "Then he must have lost the game, this artist."

I hesitate over my answer. "Not completely," I say finally. "There's one thing that separates him from the others. He can see me. He can see me better than anyone else can."

I'm introduced to the others. I meet René and his wife Yvette. Julien and Oscar, who think artists should be involved in politics, preferably by going wild and throwing their clothes in the corner and coating themselves with blood, or why not semen?

Evá, they call me, and I like the sound of it. Suddenly our evening is complete. We move our tables and chairs aside and the restaurateur carries a record player out to a side table. We dance.

Finally, when they can't dance any longer, I dance alone. I carry all of Paris in my arms, lift it into the air like a globe and don't let it fall. I stretch out one hand and let my skirt rise halfway up my thighs.

He's thinking that this is how he'll see me if this thing ever ends. The gentle curve of the soles of my feet at this moment, as the balls of my feet lightly brush the floor and then lift into the air until I look like I'm floating. My neck that sparkles, my smile intended for the whole town.

When night comes creeping into the evening and I've danced until my feet hurt, I sit at the table and listen to René say to him: "Your new woman is exquisite."

He nods, smiles. He doesn't deny it. And he doesn't deny that I'm his. Maybe because René said it in French: *ta femme.*

They start to talk about art. I hear someone toss out a pronouncement of what should be done, how the world should create itself again. Maybe it's René or the eager Oscar who seems to have a firm idea about reality: "Not just one image, but many overlapping ones. You have to account for all the layers of reality. Shadows, sadness, seriousness, along with happiness. And don't forget cruelty, comedy, and banalities. No one can afford to fall into the trap of clearly delineated images anymore. Reproduction is the key word. Copy, copy, copy, that's what it's all about. Icons into the Dumpster, and stacks of copies in their place."

Someone asks, "Do you intend to paint Evá? Do you have any plans to do it?"

I don't see his expression when he answers but I can hear the tone of his voice. There's pride in it, even tenderness.

"Eeva can tell us her hues herself."

THE MORNING AFTER the party we walk along the paths that the street sweeper opens up. We come into each other's space. There's no time, no distance between our skins. I come into his arms, he puts his hands on my buttocks. He slides a finger inside me. He opens me completely, that little notch inside me. He works the edge of his hand into the angle of my vulva and for a moment I'm nothing but a rising sound, a bright whirl that rushes from between my legs to the edge of my scalp.

Is it him or me? Do I make him see worlds that he's only seen from outside before, standing at the threshold? Or is he making me real?

I lower onto him, he's deep inside me, the city shelters us. Sometimes we feel like all this is just a dream. But in this city, just now starting to talk about change—a city that in three years' time will shake up the whole world—right now, we are made of dreams and dreams are made of us.

By wrapping ourselves in dreams, we make each other real.

AFTER THE TRIP he invents a jealousy. He starts to ask me about my past. When Elsa's in town and I'm staying on Liisankatu he calls me in the evening to make sure I'm at home. He asks me about my days as if he wants me to give him a report.

"What did you do?"

"What do you mean?"

"Tell me about your day."

"I went to class, sat in the library, then went for a walk with a friend."

"Who?"

I drag out my answer, wanting to bring him to the brink. There he is, on his knees, pleading, and I enjoy it without knowing why. I drop a picture in front of his eyes for him to latch onto: "I would have liked to go for a walk with you. I was thinking about you."

"Who did you go with?"

"Kerttu."

He's quiet, weighing my answer, wondering whether he can trust me.

"Can I see you?" he asks. "Can we meet tomorrow?"

"Maybe."

I know this game.

"OK," I say finally. "Let's meet tomorrow."

He comes to my house the next day, we close the door, and for a brief time it's like the world doesn't exist.

IN MAY HE holds a book he's found on the table in his hand like it's a dangerous animal that he's rendered unconscious. He's standing in the living room door with a remarkable look on his face, testy and frightened like a little boy who's done something wrong but doesn't know who he's done it to.

I'm on the floor playing with the little girl, telling her what to do, when he asks his question.

"Who gave you this book? Your boyfriend?"

I look at him and smile as if I don't understand. My smile betrays me. The book is from a boy I met at the university. He walked me home. He gave me the book and wrote a dedication on the inside cover. Why did I leave it lying on the table, right under his nose? Was it so he would pick it up and see a strange name that would taunt him? That's exactly why. Exactly.

"I want you out of here," he says calmly. "Out."

"What? I can't go anywhere."

The little girl looks at her father, frightened. Then at me. The man yells "Out!" and I get up. The little girl runs into her room. I see her looking at us from the doorway, like a bird that's fluttered up to a branch for safety. He pushes me into the apartment foyer.

"No. I'm not going," I say.

"Get out of here."

"I've never even met him."

"Out."

He pushes me out into the hallway. I laugh, flabbergasted. I realize that there's nothing I can do or say to make this strange performance end. When he's got me out the door and into the hallway his anger subsides and he looks surprised at what he's done, because now I'm crying. He can't back down now. He decides to stay angry, because the fight has to be gone through all the way to the end, each sentence hanging in the air must be plucked, every cruel word must be thrown like a little dagger.

"Go to his house, if that's what you want."

"There is no one."

"You're lying. I saw the name."

I sit in the stairwell for half an hour. The woman who lives next door walks by and says hello. She's heard the fight, knows exactly what's going on. But she tells me to have a good day and walks on.

I see the end. I sit on the steps, unable to get up and leave, not daring to ring the doorbell, and I see the end. I can't let myself see it yet, but I know that's it's in exactly this kind of hollowness.

He opens the door when the half hour is over, apologizes, and I don't know what to do but go in and shape myself to fit his apology. He takes me in his arms. We stand in the foyer, silent. He strokes my back, I fit myself in against his neck.

We already have the complicated rituals of fighting and making up of a man and wife. As he holds me and we construct our mutual consolation he thinks that our rituals are surprisingly similar to the ones he and Elsa have. The same role is reserved for him with both of us, first to be cruel and then, at the end of the argument, tender.

Elsa is quicker to argue than I am. She has more complicated sarcasms and hurtful clear-sightedness. She knows every part of him and uses the knowledge ruthlessly when they fight.

But he and I are starting to get good at it, too.

I can see all of his weakness at these moments. The anger that will later twine itself into me in an aching knot and make me imagine the various ways I can humiliate him begins in these rituals after an argument, which in those first years still ended with no boundary between my skin and his.

But I've already learned his pettiness. I make a note of his every physical and personal failing and take pleasure in their variety.

LATER ON THE little girl comes to sit in my lap. I'm at the kitchen table, hours after the argument, but she still remembers it.

"Are you going to go away? Out in the hallway?"

"No, honey."

"Can I sit in your lap?"

She looks at me pleadingly, and it's at that moment that a feeling takes root in her that will later define her. Gradually, over the decades, scenes from this shadow theater of her childhood will shape her into a worrier, someone who covers her uncertainty with meticulousness and strong opinions and doesn't know how to show her husband her need for affection

except by getting sick. She'll get a fever when her boss repri-
mands her at work. When her daughters confront her with
unreasonable accusations, as daughters always do, she'll get a
migraine. She'll lie in her room in the dark and the light coming in from between the drapes will make her retch.

When she gets sick, her husband's patient, uncomplicated
tenderness will astonish her. He'll peek in the door and ask
her what she would like, what he should be, how he should
help her. It will make her cry. Actually, she'll be crying because she's so incomprehensibly lucky to have found this
man who overcame gravity by eating an orange.

Bring some water. And stroke my hair. These are her requests; she'll come no closer to a request in all of her adult
life. And her husband will come and stroke her hair, bring
her some water, sit beside her and rub her back with steady
strokes. Did something happen with the girls? he'll ask gently. A fight or something?

Mm-hmm, she'll say. He knows her. Her migraines, no
matter how genuine and unfeigned, are clever disguises her
body devises to allow her to make a request. How lucky she
is that she has this husband who loves her, day after day,
through the night, through dreamy Sunday afternoons and
tense Tuesday evenings. Year after year he peels her patiently
to find the child who stood with her doll in the kitchen doorway when she was three years old and asked to be held.

But it's a journey to all of this, a decades-long trek. Right
now she's still three years old. Her request is naked and I
answer it, taking her in my arms without hesitation.

———

THAT EVENING HE wraps his arms around me. Again it's easy for me to believe that it's always been like this. The day's argument is a melancholy gap between us. He tries to close it up with words and caresses. Finally he gets up, sighs, and goes to the window. He takes a cigarette out of his pocket, sits on the windowsill, opens the window. I give in a little, sit up on the bed, and lean my head against the wall.

"You shouldn't put up with this," he says suddenly. "You should go with him, whoever he is, this other man."

"Why do you say that? I don't want to."

For the first time I see pain in his face, the pain I'll learn later.

"This won't end well," he says. "That's why."

"Don't say that."

"You should love someone else."

"Don't ever say that. Don't ever tell me to love someone else."

15

THEY WERE WAITING in the glow of the apple blossoms for the guests to arrive. Eleonoora's mother wanted to throw one last party for her friends. The apartment on Sammonkatu smelled too much of illness, so they decided to move the party to Eleonoora's garden. Besides, Mom said, what better place for the perfect terminal party than under the apple blossoms?

Mom and Dad had come well before the guests arrived; Mom wanted to poke her fingers in the dirt one more time, insisted they let her plant the morning glory seedlings, a variety called Thread of Life. Now the threads of life poked drooping out of the earth under the window, in shock from the light, sucking up moisture from the mulch. Tomorrow they would perk up, and in a few weeks, when the apple blossoms had fallen from the trees, they would reach as far as the windowsill.

The two of them were in the kitchen making salad. Mom had changed into bright red high-heeled shoes and was contentedly tearing lettuce leaves into a bowl.

"A woman needs two things in life: a sense of humor and a pair of red high heels," she said. "A Ph.D. is good, too, but not essential."

Dad and Eero were priming the grill outside the window, the girls were mowing the lawn. The door was open, swinging in the breeze. Eleonoora was in good spirits. There was nothing she needed to worry about at that moment.

"That's your final statement?" Eleonoora asked, laughing.

"Yes. Write it down and see to it that it's put into my obituary."

"Well, let's not start writing eulogies quite yet."

"Why not? I have a fantasy of a snappy obituary. It reads: Elsa Ahlqvist, pear-shaped until very recently, adequate breasts all the way to the grave. Mother, grandmother, and professor emerita. Infallible taste in shoes. In short, never fear, she died happy, and never turned down an offer of ice cream."

She rippled with laughter.

"A little less terminal irony, please."

"Irony suits me. I've noticed that. People often want me to talk about the redemptive power of love, but I've come to the conclusion that talk of redemption is only appropriate for men with full beards."

She rinsed some cherry tomatoes and started cutting them in half. Maria came inside, grabbed a piece of mozzarella from the plate, and hugged her grandmother, who kissed her on the cheek and waited for her to go back outside before saying what she'd been planning to say: "I probably won't see those threads of life full grown."

Eleonoora pushed her sadness away with a sigh. Some day they would talk about her mother and sigh like this. Next year when the apple trees bloomed they would sit under the trees and eat a salad made with the same ingredients and say: Mom would have liked this.

"Maybe not. But you're coming over next week. By then they'll have taken root. They'll grow well there."

"I could be buried under them."

"Mom. You're not going to be buried in a flower bed."

"I think I'd be happy in a flower bed," she said lightly.

She got out a box of foil and started putting together packets of vegetables for the grill. Each one got its own tomato, chunk of mozzarella, oil, and basil.

"This is nice," Eleonoora said. "Just like when I was a kid and we used to play together. Remember? We could spend hours playing with nothing but a pair of mittens, or your leather gloves. Those red gloves you had. I was a clam with my mitten and you were an evil, unpredictable fish that would swim inside it."

"Really?" Mom asked.

"What happened to all those games?"

"That's how it is," Mom said. "Things are forgotten, new things come along."

"Maybe they disappear when childhood ends," Eleonoora said, suddenly feeling an overwhelming longing for those days.

She didn't want to be five years old. She didn't want to be a child. But she wanted her mother to be the kind of person who would surprise you with a game, the kind of person who would invent crazy stories about cabins of the four winds and princesses and witches and magicians. She wanted her mother to be the kind of person who, on a dark path in the woods, would suddenly whisper in her ear: the bogeyman, and then run with her, slipping on fallen branches, bursting with fear and joy. She wanted her mother to be a young, giddy girl, with the years still ahead of her. Her father would walk behind them with his hands in his pockets, shush them good-naturedly, although he liked to see his two girls running and hear their squeals of joy as much as they did.

Mom opened one of the bundles up again.

"I've been thinking," she said.

"What?"

She looked out the window at Dad. He had gone back to where the grill was. Judging by their expressions, he and Eero were in a heated discussion about the optimal temperature for grilling.

"I made a mistake," Mom said.

"What do you mean? What mistake?"

She sighed, searching for a shape for her words.

"I don't know. I feel like I haven't told you everything that I should have. That's what I feel."

"What? What should you tell me?"

Mom shrugged her shoulders. She didn't stop moving— new foil packets were still forming under her hands. Suddenly she poured the contents of one out onto the plate.

"I don't know if I've been a good enough mother to you. I didn't know how to change. I didn't know how to be more motherly, to stay at home."

"How should you have changed?" Eleonoora said, bewildered. "I've never said that you ought to have stayed home."

"You survived, didn't you? You did well."

"Survived? What do you mean?"

Mom got quiet and looked at her as if she wanted to say something more.

"What is it?" Eleonoora asked.

The lawn mower chugged, the noise covering up Dad's and Eero's voices. Mom turned to look.

"My womb was torn in two when I had you. Not completely, but almost. It was torn, so that I couldn't have any more children."

She said it suddenly, breathlessly.

"I didn't know that," Eleonoora stammered.

"I grieved that loss for a long time, busied myself, got involved in all kinds of distractions."

She looked at Eleonoora.

"You've been a good mother," Eleonoora said. "I couldn't have wished for anything different." At that moment, it felt important to say this directly.

"Thank you," her mother said.

She turned back toward the bright evening sunlight shining through the window and closed her eyes, looking fragile and happy. Like she's made of silk paper, Eleonoora thought.

"You know, I love the moment when an airplane takes off," her mother said. "When you pass through the clouds and the sun shines on your face. I always missed that terribly when I was home. I never could admit that I would have felt smothered without it. Waiting for the rush into the air and the smile of the stewardess, conversations with strangers in the next seat. Maybe that was my weakness."

"Why in the world would that be a weakness? You loved to fly."

Mom looked a little impatient.

"I wanted to be on the move all the time. What if I didn't want so much to change the world, to make it better, to help those children and do my part to advance science? What if I just wanted the thrill of taking off, of travel? Over and over. What if that was my reason for going?"

The question sounded agitated, pleading.

"What if it was?" Eleonoora felt a worry at the corners of her mouth. The sound of the lawn mower had stopped, the girls had come to join Dad and Eero. "What does it matter? What's the matter with enjoying taking off?"

"But what if I liked it the most? What if I wasn't so noble, so altruistic? Maybe I just wanted to enjoy myself. I was restless and bored, I couldn't stop. What if my own family appalled me, the motionlessness, the same thing all the time? Slushy November evenings! Always the same expressions. And I went and helped other families, so I wouldn't have to face my own."

"What are you saying? You had a notable career. You weren't afraid of your own family. You were always present whenever you could be."

"Well," her mother said. "I guess I was."

Eleonoora felt she should say something more. Her mother needed reassurance. She needed a final view of herself, the most fundamental assessment.

"That's what happy people do," Eleonoora said. "A happy person enjoys herself, has fun, and changes the world at the same time, almost as an aside. You had it all. You had a family, and the thrill of taking off, and the whole world—that's the kind of person you were."

Maybe the roots of the threads of life had already started to attach themselves to the earth. The apple blossoms in the trees, their innocent glow, slightly surprised at itself, like a child barely past the age of confirmation putting on a miniskirt and realizing her power of attraction. Everything in its place for a moment, just where it belonged. Everything important had been said now. Her mother's smile reflected thanks.

"That's the kind of person I was, then," she said.

They hugged for a long time. The foil packets lay fat on the table. Soon they would be sizzling on the grill.

"My daughter," Mom said. "All grown up."

A stunning thought went right through Eleonoora: this is the moment I've been living for.

"Is everything ready," she said, "for the guests to arrive?"

"Everything's ready. I'm going to celebrate with my friends like it was my last day on earth, and if I get tired out, you can worry over me."

"Good. If you get tired out, I'll worry over you."

16

THE TELEPHONE RINGS three times before a woman's voice answers. Anna has been putting this off for over a week.

"Population Registry," the woman says, somewhat demandingly.

For some reason Anna needs to preserve her anonymity. She doesn't introduce herself.

"You can use an old name and address to find a new address, right?"

"Yes. If you have the person's name and year of birth."

Anna's hand is shaking.

"Her name is Eeva Ellen Ronkainen. She was born in 1942, from what I can tell. I don't know where she's been living. One of her addresses was on Sammonkatu, in Helsinki. She was born in Kuhmo. Her last name may have changed if she married. Ronkainen is her maiden name."

"All right," the woman says. "Let's see what we can find."

Anna can hear her typing something into a computer.

"She's not a relative of yours, then?"

"Not exactly . . . In a way. In a way she is."

Hesitation reaches out over the phone line.

"Why do you want information about her?"

An awful idea occurs to Anna.

"Am I required to give a reason?"

"There are cases where we ask," the woman says. "Not all information is public."

"It's for genealogical research. Sort of."

"Fine."

Anna hears a mouse click. She imagines the arrow on the woman's screen pointing at a group of Eeva Ronkainens, then Eeva Ellen Ronkainens. There may be two of them, or more. Anna can almost hear the system's process of elimination, leaving just one in the end.

"Yes," the woman says. "We seem to have a record of the person in question. Would you like me to read you the information?"

Anna hears herself say yes.

"Eeva Ellen Ronkainen," the woman says, then pauses for a moment. "Born in Kuhmo in 1942. There are some addresses here, although none of them are on Sammonkatu. Maybe it wasn't her official residence. All of her addresses are in Helsinki, including the last one . . ."

"The last one?"

The woman pauses a moment, sighs, then reads, in a declaratory, emphatic tone: "Died in Kuhmo in 1968."

Anna hears Frida, the three-year-old who lives downstairs, crying defiantly. On rare days Frida smiles at Anna in the elevator, shows her her toys, and makes pronouncements of truth. *I live downstairs and you live upstairs but that's not the same thing as heaven.*

"How did she die?" Anna asks, bewildered.

The woman laughs. Maybe she's the kind of person who likes shocking people, or maybe she's just one of those people who has no empathy. People who are embarrassed and laugh when they ought to sympathize.

"We don't have any of that information, of course. We have records of births, marriages, addresses, children's births, and deaths. We don't have the resources to record the cause of death. Or the permission, actually."

"What do I do, then? What should I do?"

The woman laughs again, types on her keyboard some more. She really is someone who's embarrassed by the role of messenger. She stops typing. Anna can't say anything. The line doesn't hum. Just silence.

"Well," the woman says, "if you don't know her relatives, I can't help you." Then she says, a little surprised, "She died when she was twenty-six years old."

"Yeah."

"Sometimes people die young. Accidents, illnesses that can whisk you off in a week, unexpectedly."

"Yeah," Anna says. "All sorts of things."

The woman is quiet for a moment. Anna realizes that those people who work at the Population Registry must have a specified way of expressing condolences. Then the woman surprises her and says with a sigh: "I've always thought that if I die young, in a car accident or something, maybe in the summer, on a summer road, driving through farmland, I'd die happy. Maybe she died like that."

"Yeah, maybe."

The woman reads her the last three addresses again. Anna writes them down. She says thank you, good-bye, ready to end the call. Now the woman says it, a little strained, as if she's speaking a foreign language: "I'm sorry."

She's young. Anna didn't realize it until now. Maybe just a little older than Anna herself. To those still living out their youth, words of condolence are a foreign language and it hurts a little to speak it. Young people think, That's not for me, it never will be for me.

She hangs up the phone and listens to the silence. There's an ad for a dentist on a flyer that came in the mail. A yellow slip of paper with Matias's grocery list from yesterday. "Coffee milk" is underlined twice. Matias can't stand a morning without milk for his coffee.

Anna stands in the entryway. Her strength seems to be draining out of her. The black stain that had been shrinking starts to spread again. She's pouring ink on the floor, pouring herself into the cracks between the floorboards.

Without knowing what she hopes to accomplish, she dials the Population Registry again. A man's voice answers. She's a little disappointed that she can't present her question to the woman she just spoke to: "Eeva Ellen Ronkainen. Born in Kuhmo in 1942, died in Kuhmo in 1968. Can you tell me whether she had any siblings?"

1966

BRIGHT DAYS, OPEN spaces. Elsa is away for three weeks from June to July and we make a home in the country. We check the fish traps every morning. I put on his rubber boots and row. He sits at the back of the boat with the little girl and they make up stories and laugh.

One day I get a pike from the trap, it struggles but I keep my hold on it. The pike brings greetings from the bottom of the lake, the little girl laughing as I make up words for the fish.

"Is it cold at the bottom of the lake?" she asks, giggling.

"Yes," I answer in a fish voice. "It's cool and quiet there. Nothing ever changes at the bottom of the lake."

He sometimes draws me while I'm rowing. More often he lets the days and the fish be, without trying to capture them. The sun rises and sets. The world is frozen in place. The oak trees in the yard grow dense with leaves from one day to the next. The blackbird has already quieted, the warblers are still singing. Now and then one of his friends drives into the yard in a car uninvited, but that doesn't bother us. Some of them bring a bottle of wine with them, some want to make a party of it. Sometimes families come. We stay up late into the night with the wine and chocolate they've brought and all sorts of talk—the child often falls asleep in my lap.

We begin to take turns speaking in big words.

But the world . . . , someone says. This country . . . , someone else answers. This era . . . , someone adds, and once again we're talking about humanity and where it's going.

No one will admit it but all of us are actually more interested in the lake and the sauna and the half of a blueberry pie on the table than we are in the fact that reality is being created at this very moment in offices and meeting rooms and on speakers' platforms and who knows maybe underground in the kinds of groups whose names have only just been thought up.

Kerttu spends time at these meetings. She doesn't care at all about blueberry pie. She eats it if she finds it in front of her, but she doesn't waste her time thinking about it. A loon is just a word to her, from a bygone time.

But there are those of us who are content with the beginnings of sentences and the call of a loon as it rakes across the surface of the lake.

"But the world . . . ," someone says.

He looks at me. The little girl is asleep on my lap with Molla under her arm and we don't need to say it out loud: the world is right here. Somewhere else, at this very moment, the jungle is bathed in napalm and a lot of people are upset about it. So are we, as long as we can keep our blueberry pie. In Paris, an all-consuming indignation at the general state of things has already begun, now they're trying to dress indignation in a suitable shape for the masses.

Alongside all that—the indignation, the seas of flame and horror, solidarity and unmetered verse—somewhere a long-legged, short-haired girl is wearing a yellow dress. Her eyes are pools, but she shows them off more than before. She puts on false eyelashes and pictures are taken. I see the pictures in *Hopeapeili* magazine, the "Silver Mirror," and wonder when it was that this dumbstruck expression came into fashion. That's happening right now—new fashions are being created. But we don't care about that because we have the spruces and the oaks, the blueberry pie, the beginnings of sentences. They're all that we need.

One of our summer guests pours himself some more wine and says, "Everything is going to have to be looked at from an angle of hope first. Kind of like what Martin Luther King said."

"Not King, Kant," someone corrects him. "We should look at Kant again and ask ourselves what we can really hope for. Only then will we be able to ask ourselves what we can do about it."

The others nod. Kant is approved, but most of the gazes are aimed at the blueberry pie and the clumsy bee that's decided it wants a piece, too.

SUMMER HAS COME to a halt, the sky stands still, the grass grows without making a sound, the wild strawberries grow heavy with dew and light, swelling from day to day toward the earth. The little girl picks them every morning, they patter into an enamel cup like blind, happy grubs.

"Shall we put them on a stem of grass to make a necklace?" I ask.

"How?" she says.

I string her a strawberry necklace, and another for Molla. She wears it around her neck until the berries are soggy. She stains the curtains with the juice and a red drop runs down her neck and between her shoulder blades and one of the summer guests says, Child, you look like something's pricked you.

"It's Eeva's prick," she says, pleased with her jewelry.

"Don't talk silly," I scold her.

"Eeva's prick is silly," she says, and I threaten to wash her mouth out with soap like my mother sometimes did to me.

I wrap the threat in a grin and she laughs and runs away.

THE MAN DAWDLES over his work. He prepares everything he needs to begin, but he never gets started. One of his friends brings him some canvases, which he stretches on wooden frames he's built. He studies new techniques in the shed on rainy days, the ones they talked about in Paris last year. How about combining photographs and oils, what about that idea? Should he try it? He sets up his camera, ready for anything, but he doesn't take any pictures.

"What are you doing?" I ask sometimes, standing at the door after the guests have gone and before any more have arrived.

"Practicing," he says without turning around.

"Practice with me. I'm bored. Ella's taking a nap and the rain's going to melt me soon if something doesn't happen around here."

"Sit down there, then," he says.

He draws the outlines of my features in rough, careless strokes, starting with a soft lead pencil on paper, and it's not bad. He doesn't think of it as art, as a work of art, he's just experimenting. I keep him company, sit there looking at him. He lights a cigarette and takes a drag, turns on the radio. I turn back to the book I'm reading.

"So that's the way it is," he says after a moment.

"What's the way it is?"

"This scribble."

"Are you drawing me?"

"I'm trying."

An hour goes by, sometimes two. He mixes paints, makes a few strokes. Thinks maybe he should try ink after all, maybe he could bring out my features better that way. It's a half-formed thought—mellow and careless. On porous paper, maybe. He decides he'll try it later if he feels like it.

The rain patters on the roof and neither of us would change anything about this moment, not even the fly making its way down the window pane on suction cups when we're not looking.

The rain, the sprays of blueberries in the woods, the red bucket in the sauna, the little girl in the house napping and dreaming. The two of us, completely without plans. We talk about something, but not about anything important. We talk about what we'll do tomorrow on our way into town to pick up the mail from the apartment. Or maybe not, one or the other of us says. Maybe the day after tomorrow, the other one says.

Dreamy, lighthearted, a cigarette in his mouth, he looks like he's entitled to achieve immortal visions through half-careless glances.

He doesn't think he'll paint me, but then he just begins.

ON ONE OF these days, when the sun is shining warm and time doesn't exist, when you can hear the strawberries ripening, Kerttu comes to Tammilehto. We've been in the country for two weeks by then. We have a week left before Elsa comes back. I haven't thought about Elsa or Kerttu—just the sky and the blades of grass and the strawberries and evening walks to the vendor's truck with him and the little girl. Kerttu comes unexpectedly. She's with a man named Pennanen, an assistant sociology professor who's taken to drink.

I haven't seen Kerttu since June. She's been in Stockholm, re-creating herself. Bangs, thickly lined eyes, a skirt the size of a pot holder. Boots, even though it's summer.

Pennanen and the man are old friends. Kerttu was in Pennanen's seminar in the spring and started an argument or two. Kerttu and Pennanen think they're mortal enemies, but conflicts can sometimes give birth to strange friendships.

They bring a gigantic pork roast, wine, and a bottle of Koskenkorva with them. Pennanen strokes the pork, brags about getting the best cut. He looks at Kerttu. She glares at him and I don't know what's going on between them, whether it's anger or mere teasing or something else altogether.

Just butchered today, Pennanen says. Let's cook it up.

He drinks and smokes the whole time and has a dirty mouth. Kerttu likes being able to put a man like him in his place. They fight constantly, argue about anything at all. Kerttu annoys him on purpose and he annoys her.

We roast the pork on the shore. The little girl demands that Kerttu make herself a strawberry necklace, and Kerttu takes her up on it. They sit on the sauna porch sharing secrets not meant for me.

The man stokes the coals under the roast and I chop potatoes into the salad while Pennanen starts to show signs of increasing drunkenness. He ticks off his points: the direction of the country, the threat of war, nuclear weapons, Vietnam, the status of women, artistic trends.

He's one of those people who start talking about revolution whenever they get some Koskenkorva in them. He's also one of those who talk about good women and bad women.

He's trying to straighten Kerttu out.

"Why aren't you more like her?" he says. "Like Eeva? Accommodating."

"Eeva isn't accommodating," Kerttu says stiffly.

Pennanen raises an eyebrow and snorts. "She's here taking care of other people's children." He empties the bottle before finishing the sentence. "And other people's husbands."

The man is on him in two steps, throws the bottle in the lake, pushes Pennanen up against the wall of the sauna, next to a fishnet hanging from a nail.

"Drop it," he says. "That's the last mention of it."

He lets go and Pennanen straightens his collar, a bit bewildered, as if he doesn't know what hit him.

The little girl watches all of this, sitting on the sauna porch. The strawberries glow on her neck like red, forsaken eyes.

"It was a compliment," Pennanen mutters. "I mean a compliment to you, Kerttu. In a way."

"Start cultivating some other kind of compliments," Kerttu says.

LATE THAT NIGHT I take a sauna with Kerttu. The men are sitting on the porch and the little girl's already asleep. I don't ask until we've cooled off after the steam.

"Am I accommodating? Is that how this seems?"

Kerttu hugs me. "Don't get hung up on that. He was just talking. Drunk."

"But do you think I should be more demanding?"

Kerttu studies me. There's a crease between her eyebrows. "When is Elsa coming?"

"Next week, on Wednesday."

This is the first time Elsa has been mentioned at all. The little girl talks about her sometimes, but the man never does. Kerttu looks out at the lake and seems to be thinking of what to say.

"Well," she says finally. "When fall comes maybe you can do something."

"Like what?"

"Like maybe focus on your studies. You'll be starting your thesis, right? Come to the university with me. I've met some new people. I can't wait for you to meet them."

"He loves me."

"That's not a small thing," Kerttu says.

"And the little girl. She loves me, too."

"I can see that."

We swim across the bay and slowly back again, our voices echoing over the surface of the water. When my feet strike the bottom, just before I come up out of the water, I think that in the fall something has to change.

AS THE EVENINGS start to darken, I do it. He doesn't even notice the change at first. He thinks I'm busy. Even in their apartment on Sammonkatu I go from room to room with a book in my hand.

Maybe Eeva's looking elsewhere, he thinks. She turns away more than she used to, but that doesn't mean anything. He comes and kisses me. I can't turn completely away. I answer his kiss.

But in the weeks when I'm at home on Liisankatu, I don't seem to hear the telephone when it rings, and if I happen to answer, I rattle off simple sentences. Yes, I say, the days are short, it's getting darker than you'd expect. No, I say, I haven't been to the movies. I've been sitting in the library. Yes. Busy.

I hang up the phone. I walk out the door, go down the street, take routes I've never taken before. I go to bars I've never been to. I meet people, but mostly I just walk to the library or into the quiet of the lecture hall to open my books and toil away.

I think that maybe I could be a teacher. I could easily apply for a position in the fall. Why not?

November brings snow, December, candles in the windows. I have evenings when I don't think about the man once, perhaps only once about the little girl. But I still carry them with me everywhere, hauling them around like a moving van looking for a home.

I remember him even if I do walk down different streets. His smell is on me even if I am wearing new clothes. When you learn another person, you learn everything, the line of their jaw, the way they brush their teeth. Once you've learned the way someone mutters in their sleep as if they're speaking some difficult ancient language, it's hard to forget it.

I know his sore spots and cruelties, the complicated pattern of his occasional joys and his sometimes surprising melancholy. I carry it with me all through the autumn as I try to live my own life. I carry it like a useless, awkward, heavy treasure. What can I do with it? Bury it in the park?

I'd like to travel far away with the knowledge of how he curls his toes when he reads. I'd like to throw it off a mountain and see it bounce off the rocks below. And what about the way he sneezes? Or the little girl. The way she giggles! I could sell my memory of his sneezes or her giggles to a stranger on the street for a mark. I could trade it for a bottle of soda some Saturday in town, because I've started to feel like the memories are making me heavy and unwieldy. No, not heavy. They're making me light, transparent.

17

W**HAT ABOUT THAT** one?" Grandpa says, pointing at a woman sitting in the lobby with a baby carriage.

He called, talked about the weather, then asked Anna on a tram ride, a little shy so that she interrupted him, answering quickly, with a smile in her voice, Let's go.

Now they're sitting in the last seat at the back of the tram. Anna sounds out the woman with the baby carriage in her mind for a moment, then shakes her head.

"No. She has a child. She looks happy. She should have a crack in her, but I don't want to think of her that way. Let's leave her happy."

Grandpa nods. "I'd rather think about love," he says matter-of-factly, as if he were talking about picking out some cheese.

He puts his hand on the back of the seat in front of him, taps on it like he's practicing an étude, then looks fixedly at the door. The tram is coming to a stop. A teenage boy and two middle-aged women, one of them talking on a phone, get on. A man in a suit glances at the other passengers with something restless in his eyes, ruthless proposals for business deals on his tongue. Grandpa leans toward Anna and says jokingly, whispering, dramatizing his disappointment:

"No, not love. No love of any kind, not the beginning of love or the end of it."

"Do you want to get off?"

"I think we have to."

They step off the tram at the next stop.

"I've got it," Grandpa says. "Love begins with ice cream."

"That's original."

"Prove me wrong."

"All right. I can't. Let it start with ice cream."

They find an ice cream stand. Anna chooses nut chocolate. She's trying to get him to try a new flavor, salmiakki-pear. He tells the vendor, "She could get me to eat garlic ice cream if she told me it was this summer's flavor."

He pays for the scoops of ice cream, taking out the bills with a flourish. They go to sit on a park bench.

"Now, then," he says. "I'll just bet you that something's going to happen." He tastes his ice cream. "Quite good."

"See?" Anna says. "Stick with me and you'll be as fashionable as a fifteen-year-old."

"Then I'll be a pretty modern old dog."

Five minutes. Ten. People walking dogs, joggers. A father with a child on a tricycle. Finally, a couple. The boy isn't holding the girl's hand, the girl is smiling, the boy is explaining the laws of political economy.

Grandpa looks at Anna with raised eyebrows and says, as if giving a report, "Love begins with ice cream and inflation. What do you say to that?"

"I'll make a note of it. I'll also note that their names are Rebekka and Aleksi. Age: twenty-two. Third date. They've got as far as ideology, but not as far as kisses."

Grandpa nods.

"There's still time for that. The day will come when they'll feel like they can't go on living if they can't see each other."

"Then the uncertainty and jealousy begins."

"And the fights. One of them will yell, You're smothering me, and the other one will say, Your love is impossible to bear."

"Who left their socks lying around? Who didn't wash their dishes?"

"And still that feeling that you'd die, just die, if the other one ceased to be, that you'd be sick, only half an existence, if . . ."

He stops. The pair—Rebekka and Aleksi, or whoever they are—walk away. Grandpa looks at the cobblestones. The moment stretches out. A bird that Anna doesn't recognize marks the pause in the scene with three sharp syllables. Is he thinking about Grandma or Eeva?

Grandpa looks at the sea. "You know about Eeva."

"Yes," Anna says quickly.

"Elsa told you."

Anna is silent. It feels like she shouldn't say anything. Then she says, "I tried to find out where she lives. I called the Population Registry."

"Did you?" he says, not sounding surprised.

Anna can't decide if she wants to say it, but she does. "Did you know that she's dead?"

He nods. "This is a small city. Of course I heard about it. I would have liked a different ending to that story. Eeva deserved it. I would have granted her that."

He sighs. Anna sees sadness in his face, the same sadness that lodges behind his eyes whenever Anna's mother talks about Grandma's medical arrangements.

"Preserve your separateness or narrow it to nothingness and melt together. That's something that's never stopped troubling me. Which one is it, when you're in love? Sometimes I wanted Eeva to melt, to become a part of me. She had others, too, at least at the end. She lived a free life. She was ahead of her time in that way. Just the thought of other men made me wish we'd never be apart."

Anna says what she believes is true: "Something new. Always wanting something new. Endlessly new, to the point of anonymity, rather than having things stay the same."

Grandpa smiles. "That's what Elsa says."

"That's who I learned it from."

"I feel like I never knew Eeva completely. I certainly knew her as much as you can know someone close to you, I'm sure of that. I knew her well. But still, she remained a stranger to me, somehow. I don't know where that feeling came from."

Anna turns to look at the pale green of the park. The trees bow down. People are creating the summer by taking off their coats, throwing Frisbees and running after them. Just a few days ago Anna would have been looking for Eeva among the people in the park. She would have been thinking, that woman? Or that one?

"I think you knew her," Anna says. "I'm sure of it."

Grandpa stares straight ahead, his gaze downward, as if he's looking at a very old scene, a memory from years back. Anna thinks, I've never seen him this serious.

"You know, sometimes Eeva was downright childish, un-compromising. I thought at the time that she was naive. I thought she was young. But later on I thought that she had a kind of conviction. She wouldn't give an inch. She lived the way she believed."

He smiles tenderly, as if treasuring Eeva's stubbornness. "Love is the only way to make the world true. That's what she used to say. She said, 'No revolution can do it.' Was that childish? I don't know."

They'd finished their ice cream. They couldn't see Rebekka and Aleksi anymore, with their kisses yet to be kissed, their fights, their melding and separating. Grandpa leaned back, put his hand on his hip and suddenly looked as if he might whistle.

"Well, then. We've considered love, and may it do them good. I declare this meeting of the investigative arm of the committee on love adjourned."

"May they find happiness."

"And when the world comes between them, as it always does, may they traverse it patiently to be with each other—but not within each other. Let that be appended to the meeting minutes. Because it's good enough to be within another person's love."

"Like how it is with you and Grandma."

He smiled. "Yes. Like how it is with me and Elsa."

18

"WELL," ELSA SAID, a little embarrassed. "Is this where I should sit?"

"That'd be good."

They had prepared well, as if they were going on a trip. They had cookies, sandwiches, tea in the thermos, music.

Martti liked her embarrassment, which showed in a certain kind of smile she had. Eyes cast downward, neck bent slightly forward. My old woman, suddenly a bashful girl, he thought, and tenderness came over him so irresistibly that he had to turn and look at the colors.

"More than fifty years, and now you want to paint me."

"Yes, now," he said, feigning carelessness, not looking at her.

"Well, it's about time," Elsa said, with a smile.

It was as if he was drawing a person for the first time, although she was so familiar—the most familiar. He picked up a pencil and started sketching an outline. He got the line of the neck easily, the shape of the head, the nose. The years that were layered over her, he gathered them all.

"A little to the left."

"Like this?"

"That's good."

He remembered how he had sometimes drawn the house-keeper, Hilja, as she washed dishes or peeled potatoes. He would sit on the kitchen stool and munch on a sandwich, drink some milk, chat with Hilja the way they usually did.

Hilja was eighteen and he was fourteen. She was a woman who perhaps had suitors, her own affairs apart from being their housekeeper. He was just a schoolboy.

He had drawn her breasts and arms, which were not delicate but vigorous, and beautiful for that reason, something almost thick around the chin, that's what made her boyish. He had transferred her broad hips to the paper, her posture slightly bent over the sink.

Of course he was groping for a turn-of-the-century artistic expression: A Woman at Work. He had already learned that the distinctive quality of artfulness was achieved by being honest to the point of heartlessness. He couldn't idealize, he should depict reality, with all its details, even its flaws.

You're really good, Hilja had said. And then, more tenderly: Just look at that. I knew you had a fondness for something, that you were dreaming of something behind those beautiful eyes of yours, my boy.

He saw that Elsa was looking at him.

"Have you started yet?" she asked almost immediately.

"Have a little patience," he said affectionately. "Or I'll lower your modeling pay to two cookies."

Elsa was quiet, the smile still lingering on her lips. She turned her head toward the window.

"You could have done this before," she said. Not hurt, not complaining. Just stating it gently. "When I die, they'll come and want to do an exhibition. They'll buy this from you. The sketches, too. 'Why did you want to paint a potato sack, Mr. Ahlqvist?' someone will ask. 'What exactly were you trying to express?' Someone else will say that it's a close allegory of society, the growth of the income gap. And you'll answer, 'No, that's not a sack. It's my wife, whom I managed to love for more than fifty years.' Then they'll go have coffee. They'll eat cheesecake and between bites they'll marvel aloud: 'Imagine, for more than fifty years he loved a woman who looked like a sack.' And someone else, some genius who's stuck on his own ideas, will insist: 'I don't believe that it's his wife, when you come down to it. I think he's trying to depict the change in society from the agrarian to the urban. He's depicting urbanization, no matter what he says. It's that crisis, with all its painful aspects, that he's trying to portray through this woman who looks like a potato sack.' So it would have been better if you'd painted me when I still looked a little like a woman, to avoid these smart-aleck interpretations."

"Quiet now," he said softly.

She laughed merrily at her own train of thought. Martti plucked the familiar expression she had when she laughed. He saw it now; it had always been the same. Without commanding his hand he succeeded in transferring it to the canvas.

Now Elsa was looking at him.

"I like the way you're looking at me," she said. "I like the look on your face. It makes me feel like I have secrets to protect."

He smiled. "I'm sure you do."

1966–1967

AT THE BEGINNING of December I find Molla in the pantry. One of her eyes is torn off.

Molla is sitting on the bottom shelf next to a tin of barley flour. Her one eye stares at me in alarm. A scarf has been wrapped around her mouth. It's tight, like a gag.

Strawberry jam has been smeared into her braids, oat flakes from the pantry shelf are stuck to the jam. There's jam in the flour sack and the coffee canister, too, and a sticky splotch on the shelf paper. The little girl has opened a package of pearl grits and dipped Molla's feet in the jam and then into the grits, making a pair of clever booties for her from the mess.

I pick Molla up. She's collapsed in a slouch of pure horror, huddled in the cupboard as if it were a jail cell. The eye she has left is still smiling, her gooey braids sticking out happily in spite of her humiliation, trying to tell me that there are all kinds of wonderful things in the world, like bubble baths and lollipops, like the bright December sun just now coming across the yard, dividing it into darkness and light.

I go to the window.

The horse chestnut tree stretches out its limbs, mute and dreamy in the winter light. The little girl and her friend Teija are squealing in the yard, running to the swing, to the rug rack, then back to the swing again.

They've been playing the same strange game all day. The girl is good at thinking up new rules that change constantly. Now it's become an endless tag where you cast spells and drive off spirits.

I open the window and hear her order her friend to the shady side of the yard.

She's explaining the game. You're not allowed to touch the chestnut tree. But you still have to go near it. You should get so close to it that you almost touch it, but if you do touch it then you have to go to the shady spot for the rest of the game and you can't come out until dinnertime. Or nighttime, she says. You can't leave until nighttime, if you come out at all. She explains the rules feverishly, as if she were reading a sealed dispatch from heavenly authorities.

"Ella!"

She doesn't hear me, or doesn't want to. Molla's jam-covered braid sticks to my shirt.

"Ella, will you come here? I want to talk to you about something."

She turns her back to me. The back of her neck glimmers under a red scarf.

"Eeva's calling you," Teija says.

She keeps talking, raising her voice slightly. She can definitely hear me. She just doesn't want to pay any attention.

"Ella, come inside now."

Teija looks at Ella hesitantly. Finally Ella lowers her head as she always does when she's sulking and walks to the door.

There's a noise on the stairs, they'll be upstairs in a few moments. I take the scarf from around Molla's mouth. A wound is revealed beneath it. The stuffing is poking out of her red half circle of smile as if she were coughing up dry foam. Her face has been cut with scissors.

My hands are trembling. Ella opens the door, stands on the threshold, looks at Molla, then at me. I pull the doll closer, I don't know if I'm shielding it or it's shielding me. Teija eyes me over Ella's shoulder. I see the shocked look on her face.

Ella looks like she's been struck. Then she shouts. "Molla's supposed to be in the cupboard!"

"You've cut Molla. You've taken scissors to something you like."

She doesn't answer.

"Why did you cut Molla and get her all dirty?"

She flies into a rage. She turns red in a second, runs at me. She wrenches Molla out of my hands hard enough to tear her, and runs into the kitchen. I hurry after her. She puts the doll on the shelf, opens up the package of grits before I can stop her, and pours them over the doll.

"Now, Ella. Stop that, now."

I take hold of her arm. I pull her away from the cupboard. She shoves me. She's surprisingly strong, I stumble backward. I hit my hip against the corner of the table. She takes two steps toward the pantry, grabs the coffee canister forcefully off the table, opens it, and pours the grounds over Molla. I can see an almost pure triumph in her eyes.

"Ella!"

I go and grab her by the hair, take hold of the tuft of hair on the top of her head like a bunch of chives growing in the ground and pull. She screeches. I realize then that I've made a mistake. She's already crying; my apologies don't do any good.

She hits me in the stomach with her fist. It's like a sharp little hammer, closing off my breath for a second. I gulp for air like a newborn. She stops yelling and stares at me. She's bewildered by what she's done, looking at me in fascination. Then she starts to cry. She goes to the cupboard and knocks everything she can get her hands on onto the floor. The jam jar shatters, a jar of preserves rolls under the table. Molla smiles on the shelf through it all, covered in jam and flour, the stuffing foam sticking out of her mouth.

I take Ella in my arms. She yells for help, keeps saying no. It doesn't reach just to the walls, it escapes through the window. I close her tight in my arms.

"Shhh," I say. "Calm down, everything's all right. It's all right."

She yells, struggles, finally roars. I can't reach her anymore. When I grabbed her by the hair, it pulled her into the dark.

Snot runs into her mouth, her yells make snot bubbles that pop like muffled emergency flares.

Teija stands in the doorway looking at us in horror. Then she turns, slamming the door as she goes, and runs down the stairs. I can't be concerned about that now. I lift Ella in my arms. She's still yelling. I stumble with her across the hall. She tenses her muscles and I almost drop her.

I put her in bed. She strikes at me. Red blotches come out in her cheeks like they do when she's sick. Her feet flail at my face; one kick lands painfully on my breast. I lie down beside her and hold her tightly.

"I'm here. Don't be afraid. Everything's all right."

"I hate you."

"I'm sure you don't hate me."

"Yes, I do. I want my mom."

"You'll get your mom. But right now, I'm here."

"Go away. I want you to go away."

"No. I'm not going anywhere right now."

Her voice gets louder. She's already hoarse. I hold her, not slackening my grip.

"Shhh."

Her yells gradually diminish; she's exhausted, as if she's run around the world. She takes a breath. Her tears come in waves for nearly another hour. She varies it, like a song, as if in a little while she'll wake up humming.

The clock ticks in the living room. People are returning to their homes. We lie on the bed holding onto each other. She's bathed in sweat. She trembles. I say *shhh*.

She'll remember this later. She'll remember this moment when she's twelve and sixteen, twenty-two and forty-two. Her memory will condense into a sound. She'll wake up at night gasping for breath and not know what's weighing on her. *Shhh*, she'll say to herself and think that it calms her because it reminds her of the sea and her honeymoon in Nice.

Gradually, she starts to breath evenly. Her chest rises feverishly, her heart fluttering wildly. She wraps her arms around me. She doesn't look at me, just lies there quietly.

"Don't go away," she says finally.

I've never wanted to mean anything as much as I want to mean this now. "I won't. I'll stay right here."

HE AND I have fights all through December. I don't speak to him when I come to clean up the rooms, to peel potatoes, to caress the child into sleep in the evening. He's silent, too. The little girl, on the other hand, chatters nonstop and holds onto me. She wants to be near me, as if she's made me her dwelling. I go to take out the garbage and she puts her rubber boots on the wrong feet and runs after me. I give her rides on my back and she asks me to run around the yard like a horse. I gallop, our breath steaming. We go up the stairs, she on my back like a baby monkey. I put her down at the door, open the door, step inside. She asks me to hold her.

"I can't hold you, honey. You're such a big girl now."

"I'm still pretty small," she says, pouting.

Her arms go around my waist, she burrows under my coat.

The small, hot cycles of her breath are little gusts against my stomach, as if she wanted to find a route through my navel to somewhere at my core, to Eeva's center point, from which there is no exit.

He watches me. He's impatient and restless, like these weeks have been. We haven't sat together in the attic in a month. The last time we did, I stared at him unflinchingly, my hands on my hips. He was trying a new technique again, painting over his last experiment, taking photos that he intended to combine with oil paints.

Why not ink? Why give up on ink so cavalierly? He'd have dozens, hundreds of prints, if he'd thought to carve my outline in wood or linoleum. Oil paints are stuffy and old-fashioned. He should have been more open to new methods.

I had no sympathy for his indecisiveness. I didn't let him see any farther than my eyebrows. It infuriated him. Go on, you don't want to stay here, he said, and I went.

Now he sees me and the girl, the girl and me, at the front door, wrapped around each other, and he can't come a step closer. I see that he wants to come to us, to come to the place inside me, into me. I know that when he asks, maybe even tonight, I won't have the strength to say no.

But he doesn't say anything to me; our fight is a stubborn one this time. It spreads into the rooms, over the thresholds, stuffs itself into every corner like a dough that's out of control.

WITH THE CHANGE of the year, I shyly present Kerttu with my plan: I intend to move.

All through the autumn I've been thinking that I need my own walls around me, my own stove and table, a threshold that I can just step over and say: mine.

We sit silent for a moment at the kitchen table. Liisankatu bends over us, the walls wait for the right words.

Finally Kerttu says, "Something's beginning. Something new."

I smile. "And all we know is that it has to be good."

ON THE FIRST day of January, I find a little, lattice-windowed, twenty-square-meter flat on a courtyard on Pengerkatu. It's a converted pantry room, but it's all mine. I pay the first month's rent in cash before I bring the table into the house. I see my reflection in the window—I look like a different woman. Strange, but still the kind of person I can learn to like.

This strange woman, who's not afraid to say her name, is going to get her degree. That's why I have to plug away at my thesis all month while snow surrounds the city from east and west, the freezing weather scraping and sculpting it.

On the sixth of February my thesis is ready, and Elsa wants to take me for coffee and pastries.

"I have a gift for you," she says as soon as we're seated.

A barrette or a powder compact, I'm expecting something like that, but she hands me a check across the table.

"I think you ought to go to Paris. To test your language skills. It's my gift to you."

The slip of paper is lying on the table in front of me. It's a large sum—the flight there and back, lodging in a hotel with white tablecloths in the breakfast room that hold their creases.

"Thank you," I say.

IN MARCH I see the rambling streets of Montmartre again. I take the metro and climb to the surface without knowing what station I'm at. I get to know people in cafes and pose as a Parisian. My gestures become more confident. I test my opinions and smoke Gauloises, although it's not a habit I have. Evá smokes, this woman they know in Paris.

I spend two nights in the hotel that I've paid for with Elsa's check. On both nights I have the same dream about her.

In the dream we're taking a sauna. Elsa is in the sauna, which is full of steam when I open the door. There's a lot of steam and it's difficult to see. I wait for her to come down from the sauna bench. She hangs back, but finally comes down. She doesn't look at me, picks up the wash bucket and pours water into it from the hot water tank. She adds three ladles of terribly cold water from a large basin and sloshes the water over herself.

Then she looks at me—not angry, not disdainful, not embarrassed, not curious. Mostly just confirming: there you are. I see her body—it's beautiful and full. Her breasts are heavy, drops of water from the wet hair on either side of her head flow over her nipples, which are larger than mine. It's almost impossible to look at her. I look away, then at her, then away, then at her again.

You have beautiful breasts, I say.

Elsa's lips part, she takes a slight breath and is about to say something, but then she turns back toward the sauna stove. For a moment I think that she's going to stick her hand into the stove and purposely burn herself. But she pours more water into the bucket. Then she opens the door, turns once more, and steps outside.

Watch out that you don't scatter breadcrumbs on the floor.

I'm sorry, I say. Did I? I can sweep.

Good. That's what we pay you for, Elsa says.

I WAKE FROM the dream shaking, sweaty, and decide that I can't sleep for another night on Elsa's check. I pack my things and sit in plazas all day, walk around the city.

A WAR FAR away in the east has become intolerable in the minds of the Parisians, as it has for many other people. It's expressed in a surprising way, with bright shirts and chants that didn't interrupt the noise of traffic two years ago. The hats and tapered skirts have disappeared, replaced by short, short hems. The men have beards—my mother would say beards a swallow could nest in. In June, a band of English insects appear on an album cover in bright-colored coats surrounded by faded, black-and-white celebrities. No one knows it yet, but copies of their whiskers and round glasses and careless gestures and ideas imported from India will soon flash in the doors of the pubs and out again. The flow of fashion is as easy to catch as a disease or an opinion.

I don't like beards. I don't know what I think of the idea that we should all unite in the battle of love, like the people here are saying. I just want one person. One person who's completely mine. Is that too much to ask? Has that kind of love become old-fashioned?

ON MY SECOND day in Paris I meet Marc at the museum. I'm looking at the Rembrandt painting, the woman I had pined for like an old friend two years before, when Marc comes along and says that we look alike, the woman in the picture and me.

It all happens easily, imperceptibly. This is the way loves begin, I think, as we walk along the river and drink wine in a little restaurant. Marc looks me in the eye—he has brown eyes, without a single shadow!—and smiles. He says, why not trust a stranger, since there's nothing to prove he's not worth the trouble? Life begins when you throw yourself into it.

I throw myself into it in Marc's apartment in the Marais. The whole thing would have been ugly (I'm sure that's what my mother would say—what ugliness!) if it weren't so beautiful. This is called pleasure, Marc says. He has two dark, flat nipples like friendly eyes. As I make my way into him I stare at them like violets. He's tenderer than anyone, a little surprised when he finds the place inside me.

Afterward he makes me coffee and sandwiches in his tiny kitchen corner and brings them to the bed. We have a picnic as if we're sailing the open sea. *Je t'aime*, he says, and I wonder if that can be at all true, because we've only known each other for one day. For him it is.

One day changes to another and then another. Marc offers me a life, like an item on a shelf at the store that you can take or leave.

"You could love me," he says. "Couldn't you?"

"I would be someone else. I don't know what kind of love it would be."

"Beautiful love."

He says it as if it's some Sunday picnic he's preserving in his mind: light and easy. And who knows, maybe it is easy for someone like him. The kind of person who keeps his money in a coffee can on the kitchen shelf, whose door is always open to friends and strangers, who tapes a picture of a beautiful rebel to his wall without asking why or what it means.

The rebel dies in October, far from here. Marc cries that day, lights a candle on the floor in front of the poster. But there will be plenty of time for that.

AFTER FIVE DAYS in Paris, I leave. Will I see you again? Marc asks, and I say *peut-être*. Maybe I'll come again and trust him and throw myself into it, like brave people do.

Because what he says is true: everyone has to find the courage to surrender to the unknown. The world is a stranger to each of us until we have the courage to reach out to it, and then it becomes a friend.

I MARVEL AT how easy it is to forget Marc when I get home. I have his address, promised to keep in touch. I wrote my own address on his hand—maybe he washed it off, or maybe he put it on paper. I wadded his address up at the bottom of my bag where it lay wrinkled like a plum stone—some day a whole tree could grow from it, in other circumstances. I don't think about the address, but I don't throw it away, either. The spring light comes with me from Paris to Pengerkatu. The sun has climbed a step higher in just five days.

On the third day after I get back to Helsinki, the man is standing at my front door when I come home from the store. He's smoking and kicking stones like he'd just as soon not be. He looks at me. My hair is down—he likes it but it makes him uneasy. Who let it down? At that moment he can't bear the thought of Paris breezes reaching to the roots of my hair, it's an offense from the city he once lived in.

"Who are you?" he asks, a little half-grin on his face, like he often has. "There was a girl named Eeva living here. She's from a place where they make potato-berry tarts at the edge of burnt clearings. You, with your hair and your cigarette and that look on your face, seem to be a person from a big city."

I ought to know how to turn away. I shouldn't play this game anymore.

Time after time I distance myself, and so does he. We tear ourselves away from each other just so we can take those steps toward each other again. We're never there—always on the way toward or away from each other.

He leans against the wall of the building like he wouldn't mind much if his weight knocked it down. The hands in the pockets and the cigarette in the corner of his mouth are familiar. I've gone to the center of the world but I don't know how to forget what it feels like to love him.

"Weather's been . . ." he says.

"What?"

". . . picking up."

I shrug. "Hardly. I saw some clouds fall today. Flopped down like fat geldings just down the block. I wouldn't call that picking up."

"Where? On this block?"

"I'm not telling you. You'll just go and try to get them into a picture. You won't leave them be."

This silences him for a moment. He doesn't look offended. He's deliberating about whether to test this game of ours. He decides he will.

"I met a woman," he says, a familiar look on his face.

He raises his left eyebrow. I don't know how he does that, raises just one of them like an eager inchworm. I know I should turn away. Another person, years away from me and people like me, would turn their back on him and refuse to play this game. But I can't be anything but myself, and I'll never get the chance to be different.

"What's she like?" I ask.

"Angry. She picked up some anger in a strange city. She's become unrecognizable."

"That's what really galls a man. When he can't see a woman anymore."

The pain returns to his face. Another person, years away from me and people like me, would harden her heart when she saw that pain. But I'm me, and I haven't learned those habits. I haven't learned how to tell someone no once I've said yes. Once I fall in love, I open myself to that person forever, give myself completely. My hands say no and squeeze into fists, but he opens me again, time after time.

"Can't he?" he asks.

"Maybe once in a while. Once in a while he can see her more clearly than anyone else can."

I smile. He plucks my smile out of the air and makes a home in it.

"Nice. Was it nice?" he asks. "At the center of the world?"

"Absolutely. Like at the circus."

"And it is a circus in that town. I saw your Kerttu, by the way. She was on her way to Stockholm. To cause trouble, I expect."

"What about you? Did you come here to cause trouble?"

He looks around and drops his cigarette butt on the ground, rubs it out with his foot.

"Precisely for that reason."

Marc's address is in my suitcase, the sky is high above us. Thunder has started somewhere, that world has already begun to hatch, the world that will teach people like me, little by little, year after year, to close doors, to keep our walls up.

But now it's the end of March 1967 and I have only con-
cessions for this man that I love. I don't have a single no for
him. I open the door and say, "Come in, then."

WE TRAVEL TOWARD each other all that spring. We have
new boundaries for our affection, because we have the walls
of my apartment on Pengerkatu now. He often comes to my
house. He brings things with him, some object each time—
a disposable razor, a toothbrush, a sketchpad, a bundle of
pencils—so that by March it already looks like he's divided
his life in two.

Mostly we lie in bed and make lazy excursions toward
each other, calm and friendly because we're already so familiar to each other that we're not surprised by what we
find. I should still be plugging away, getting ready for my
final exams, and he should be working, but neither of us can
get started on our own tasks.

Reality can wait while we weave dreams made from each
other.

AT THE END of April, a raw wind comes off the sea as I'm
taking my last test in a cool lecture hall on Senate Square.
Professor Falck evaluates my pronunciation, making me say
whatever occurs to him, and I say it. Heaven seems to be
creaking in its joints, but the church outside the window is
still standing. I pronounce *aujourd'hui* incorrectly.

After the exam I walk across the square, the sky lists, the
earth rises.

Even as reality creaks, Elsa believes in pastries and home-made lemon beer for May Day, served in the back room of the city's most venerable cafe. She insists on taking me to the cafe after the exam, although it's still another month before I'll have my diploma. I agree, without knowing why. My stockings feel tight and my stomach churns. Elsa orders us coffee and lemon *sima* and three kinds of sweets.

"So!" she says. "A toast to the Master."

Behind her smile, she's wondering at herself. The previous Saturday—one of those bustling days when she'd decided to put her house in order—she found my clothes in the bed-room closet as she was cleaning. A blouse, a dress, pants, and a bra. In a moment everything is clear to her: Just as I suspected! I've been pushing it out of my mind for three years! But then she upbraided herself and thought of six or eight different explanations for why my clothes might have ended up in her closet. Clothes get mixed up—socks and things—why not bras, too? Of course I didn't undress in her bedroom. Or dress, for that matter.

As I sit before her, she reassures herself: Eeva isn't a trai-tor. Eeva's good.

We clink our glasses and speak French just because we know how. My lies disappear in the swirl of the *sima*, be-coming unimportant. I forget them just as Elsa forgets her husband turning away from her, her daughter's questions: *If you're my mother and not Eeva, whose mother is she?*

"What do you plan to do?" Elsa asks. "Anything's pos-sible for you now."

I pretend to be full of hope, spread my arms in a sign of openness.

I make my words sound like a request: "I'd like to continue working for you. I'd be happy to continue for the rest of this year."

Elsa nods. I see a thought in her gaze, but I can't see what she's thinking about. She's thinking about last Saturday, when she told her husband she'd found my clothes in her closet. She let the words drop casually. He was just as casual, saying in a critical tone, We'll have to tell Eeva to be tidier.

Elsa had looked at him. She wanted to believe him, and at that moment he actually did believe it himself. She took a breath and spoke of other things, although she hadn't shaken off her uneasiness.

He had looked at her sitting at the kitchen table, suddenly slightly smaller, helpless. Uncertainty made her shrink, and he remembered what she'd been like as a girl. He went to her and took her in his arms.

Love was the denseness of flesh, as self-evident as his hand reaching toward her.

19

SAARA IS DRIVING, Anna is sitting beside her. Saara doesn't believe in private cars, but she loves to drive. They borrowed her father's car. It's not a long trip, a little more than an hour north.

They used to drive like this when they first got their driver's licenses. They would go to the airport and sit in a cafe and watch the planes take off, drinking cup after cup of coffee. Saara was planning to study in Berlin or New York.

Anna still remembers the uneasiness that thudded inside her as Saara talked about her plans. She would leave, would send postcards covered in exclamation points telling about her happiness and about people Anna would never learn to know. Anna would stay home, would never be able to make big changes in her life let alone change the world. She would keep wandering in this two-block radius. From home to the store, from the store to work, from work to home, never daring to create herself someplace else.

"Are you nervous?" Saara asks.

"Yes."

The car eats up the asphalt. Anna feels as if she herself were filled up with the road. Saara hums a little.

"How's your grandma?"

"She's hanging in there. She's planning to start a swing band."

"That's so like her," Saara says with a smile.

Anna has to say it out loud: "The end is coming, though. It may be soon. You can already see it."

Years ago Grandma had said about Saara, Now there's a girl with a strong construction of self. Saara was seventeen, and said she was planning to go into either politics or theater. I haven't decided yet which is the best way to influence people, she said.

"Tell me if you want to talk about it," Saara says. "It must be tough. It's the saddest thing that's ever happened to you."

"How do you know that?" Anna asks brusquely.

"What?"

Saara looks at her once, then once more. Anna continues, although she doesn't want to start a fight: "You can't just tell someone: This is the saddest thing that's ever happened to you."

"Where's this coming from?"

Anna is quiet for a moment, then says, "Every person's sadness is their own. Other people can't understand it."

"There's no point in splitting hairs. Is this about last year?"

"Splitting hairs? Is that what you think I'm doing? You're the one who's overgeneralizing."

She didn't want to start this old argument because Saara would overpower her and she wouldn't have room to breathe. Saara the conqueror, Saara the revolutionary. Saara the bold. Saara the brave. But now the disagreement has been announced, however accidentally, so all Anna can do is take up the challenge: "You think you know more than other people. You're at the center of everything, you push people aside, force people up against a wall."

Saara is struck dumb for a moment but doesn't take her eyes off the road. "This might be more your problem than mine."

"What is? What's my problem this time?"

Saara looks like she's trying to decide whether to speak or not. "You divide all the women you meet into two categories."

"What do you mean?"

"Think about it. They either own the world or they're martyrs. Those who've succeeded or those who've surrendered. Happy or unhappy. Rambunctious or repressed. Uncomplicated or neurotic."

Anna hears herself snort. She feels a woundedness between her eyes. There's a touch of triumph in the feeling— she can throw herself into misunderstanding. "That's really rich. And you're one of the ones who own the world, right? You think I put you in the happy people category and myself with the unhappy ones?"

Saara speeds up to 120 kilometers per hour, as if in answer. "That's what I think you're doing. I don't believe in that. I believe that the whole world is open for people to be whatever they want to be."

Anna feels like opening the car door. She'd like to run away, fly over the tops of the trees in protest. "You don't know anything about me. You don't know anything about what this has been like. You knew me when I was sixteen, but I'm not sixteen anymore."

Fights with Saara can start from nothing. It's the same when she fights with Maria, hurling cruel words in each other's faces. Old friends and sisters need each other to be distorting mirrors, to look at each other and say, well, the mirror tells me time has gone by.

Saara takes no notice of her jab and says lightly, "I can't know if you don't tell me."

They sit in silence for a moment. Saara presses on the gas, passing two cars as if she were trying to shake Anna off.

"There's nothing to tell," Anna hears herself say at last. "It's best if people mind their own business. It's best not to know too much."

"What do you mean 'too much'?"

"So you're not disappointed."

"How? Disappointed how?"

"Disappointed in love."

Saara looks at her in disbelief, completely baffled, as if she needs to make sure that it's still Anna speaking. "When did you get so cynical? When did you start being opposed to love?"

"The world changes a person," Anna says. "Experiences change you. I've started to think that love doesn't belong in this world." She turns her head, unable to look at Saara, and continues, "The world is built according to different rules."

"What kind of rules?"

Anna leans her head against the headrest and says carelessly, striving to sound casual, "Different rules. More realistic, more real."

Saara doesn't hide her bafflement. "Listen to yourself. That's not how you think. You're the one who danced down Mannerheimintie in her bare feet to demand that they give the streets back to foot traffic. You're the one who was kissing strangers at the demonstration against the Iraq war, the one who believed that if there were enough photos of kisses it would nullify the whole justification for the war. You were singing 'All You Need Is Love.' Remember? That was you."

"It was someone else. It wasn't me. That girl was a child. Just a stupid child."

Saara is quiet. Anna looks at her in the mirror. There's a sadness in Saara's eyes and a cold decisiveness in her voice as she lets the words drop like stones: "You don't believe in love anymore."

Anna sits in silence as the words flow into her and freeze her limbs.

Disappointed and furious, Saara continues, "You better straighten yourself out or you're going to become the saddest person on earth. There's nobody who can afford to think that love is childish and believing in change is an illusion."

The road shoots into them and out again, the woods hum.

"You've really changed," Saara says. "It's because of what's happened the past couple of years. And you still won't talk about it."

Saara hesitates. Anna thinks: if she says his name, or the little girl's, I'll collapse, fall on the floor.

Saara says their names.

Anna doesn't collapse. She doesn't turn invisible. She sees herself fall and melt, but she's still sitting there.

THEY PARK AT the corner, away from the house. A yellow house in the shade of a spruce tree. In the yard are an apple tree and a doghouse. Ivy is making its leaves at the end of the house, climbing up the outside of the window.

"What if I went in by myself?" Anna says.

Saara looks uncertain. "Do you think?"

"I think I should."

"Well, if you want to."

"Could you maybe wait for me? You could take a walk."

Why doesn't she want Saara to come inside? Is it because of the fight they just had? Or is it because no matter what Eeva's sister tells her, she wants to hear it alone? Eeva's story is hers.

"All right," Saara says finally, and gently squeezes her shoulder. "I'm just a phone call away. I think I'll walk down that road and see if I can find that famous view."

"All right," Anna says.

She thinks, whatever happens to us, we'll always be friends. Saara the conqueror. Saara the brave. And me.

LIISA ARTEVA, MAIDEN name Ronkainen, a woman Anna wasn't able to imagine as Eeva's sister, opens the door almost immediately, and smiles. Anna is expected.

She quickly gleans Liisa Arteva's features. Eyes blue, with laugh lines around them. These were Eeva's expressions. Maybe the very same smile. Maybe the very same way of holding her wrists.

"Well," the woman says, as if she's been waiting inside the door for half an hour, holding her breath. "Liisa," she says, extending a hand.

Anna takes her small hand. It reminds her of a bird.

"I made tea," Liisa Arteva says, for something to say, and gestures toward the kitchen.

Anna takes off her coat and glances around the living room. She's looking for pictures. There are two on the bookshelf, both of children. Grandchildren? She follows Liisa into the kitchen.

Liisa is one of those sixty-five-year-olds who preserve a girlishness. The impression may come from something around her chin, or from her turned-up nose. Or her lively eyes. When she was a girl, Liisa was the kind who giggled in class, feared laughing fits that she could feel coming, found herself imagining her mother's death, and nuclear war, and couldn't keep a straight face when the teacher played the organ and sang "Give Thanks to the Lord." She and Eeva had a secret language. They ran on their way to school, played horses in the woods, frolicked among the pine trees. They did little things that weren't allowed together—stole the cardamom roll dough as it was rising, fed a pail of blueberries to the cow to see if the milk would turn blue. Once Liisa and Eeva drank cough medicine because they'd heard that it gave you a nice, dizzy feeling. They both threw up behind the barn and vowed never to touch strong drink again.

All through her childhood, Liisa believed that she could cause accidents with her thoughts. In those years Eeva was still a carefree girl, putting her worries up like preserves in silent prayers. When Eeva moved to Helsinki, Liisa wanted to go with her. She studied and got accepted as a nursing student. Only later did she admit to herself that it wasn't her dream profession; she'd done it to help her bear the worry she always carried for other people, to learn how to rescue them.

Liisa Arteva is used to doing what is expected of her. Her pleasures are simple and her hopes reduced. Apple pie in the fall made from the apple trees in the yard—her specialty is to mix the apples with rhubarb and flavor the pie crust with Turkish yogurt, the secret to juiciness!—a grandchild laughing in the washtub on sauna night, her husband making coffee good-naturedly in the morning. One Christmas Eve after another, year after year. It's been enough. Maybe it's been more than she dared to hope for, because she's always been prepared for loss, just in case.

Anna shakes off these imaginings, reminds herself of what Saara just said. She doesn't know anything about Liisa Arteva except what she can see, a small-handed, smiling woman.

"I got out a few photo albums," Liisa says, sounding a little out of breath. "Here they are."

She offers Anna some tea. Anna regards people who don't offer coffee to guests with some reservation.

She has a hard time thinking of a way to begin. She can't say Eeva's name. She takes refuge in the trees out in the yard, the bushes in the garden, as always.

"Gooseberry bushes."

"I make jam from them every year," Liisa says, seizing on the conversation opener with relief. "You wouldn't believe how good it is. Would you like a taste?"

Without waiting for an answer Liisa gets up and opens the cupboard, looking for the jam.

"The secret is cinnamon and vanilla. I've eaten it with cookies that my daughter sends me from France."

She sighs the way people like her do. A little flat, but resigned: the world has always belonged to others.

No, Anna corrects herself. She doesn't know this about Liisa. She's putting her own ideas in, interpreting this woman's gestures according to her own wishes. Liisa Arteva isn't neurotic or docile, those are just Anna's own conclusions from this woman's interest in gardening and her jumpy gaze.

Liisa watches as Anna tastes the jam, waiting for an approving nod. Anna nods.

"It's even better with scones," Liisa says. "First butter, then jam."

IN CHILDHOOD PICTURES, Eeva looks like a brown and long-legged country girl. Braids, a dress, eternal summer. Liisa is younger, it shows in the difference in height.

"We had cows for pets, and cats and dogs, too. We used to pet the calves, and even the chickens."

Liisa laughs. "When she was a kid, Eeva always said that she wanted to stay in the country, live in the same place all her life. Then she started reading and dreaming of going to the university."

"Did you see much of each other in the Helsinki years?"

"Eeva had her own friends and I had mine. Sometimes she invited me to parties or to dinner. We had a habit of going for walks together, often on Sundays."

There's a picture from later years on the next page. Liisa smiles when she sees it. "I remember that one. She'd just fallen in love. I asked her about it, and she admitted it, but she wouldn't tell me who the man was."

"Did you ever see them?"

"Of course. I thought of them as a family. I went to their house often, especially the third year. Sometimes I saw Eeva and the little girl at the park. We would sit on a bench, eat apples, that sort of thing. I think that was toward the end—the little girl was older then, maybe six years old."

Pictures of the last year, a school photo: Eeva sitting in the center smiling and holding a sign.

"The first time I saw this picture I thought she was happy."

"Wasn't she? Happy?"

Liisa's smile doesn't grow stale. "Sometimes I think Eeva loved excessively, unreasonably. I even told her that. I didn't always understand her feelings. She said, 'How do you love reasonably? Why would you even want to? There's no such thing.' Maybe I thought that each person should live so that they won't lose themselves to another person, won't start living entirely other people's lives. It's something a person has to learn in order to get on in life. You can't put someone else before your own survival."

"Did she want to learn to live like that?"

Liisa laughs. "Hardly. She said what was life for if not to lose yourself to other people and find yourself in other people. She said that after they had tried to be together and he had left. I told her that she should have been more careful, should find meaning in her life some other way."

"They tried to be together?"

"Yes. They tried. And when it was all over, when nothing came of it, I said that she should try to learn to live differently, and she said, 'What's the point of being a person then? We might as well live and die alone.'"

Anna lets herself think about Linda. In the beginning Linda ordered her around, and she obeyed because she didn't yet dare to say no. Later she learned to say no, to say no and love at the same time. Was it unreasonable love? Was it excessive?

Liisa picks crumbs up from her plate. Maybe she's thinking that Anna is disappointed in her story of Eeva.

Anna thinks about what Saara said. Maybe she was right, maybe I've stopped believing in love. What kind of person am I, then? A poor one.

Why can't Anna believe in all that with Matias? Why does she turn away again and again?

She can't bring herself to ask Liisa Arteva the most important question: how did it all end?

They say good-bye on the porch the way people who visit each other's lives for a moment do. They hug and say I'll see you, even though they both know that they will never meet again. Anna can almost see the relief in Liisa's eyes.

"Well?" Saara asks when she gets in the car.

"I tasted some gooseberry jam," Anna says. "I got a phone number."

Kerttu Palovaara is just a made-up name. Anna has the real Kerttu Palovaara's phone number in her pocket. The real Kerttu Palovaara's name is Katariina Aavamaa and she lives in Helsinki, in Eira. Anna could call her right now, but she doesn't know if she wants to. Maybe she wants to stick to her imagination.

"So," Saara says. "Let's go home."

1967

SUMMER RIPENS SLOWLY. The radio on the sauna porch is always on, pouring out the newest song by those insects from Britain over and over. It starts with the familiar strains of revolution and then changes to tidings of joy. As July quickens people start to believe in the song little by little, coming together in droves. Girls don't bother to put on undergarments anymore. Men's hair and beards are longer than before. Someone has invented the idea that there'll be no peace without love, and whispered it in someone's ear on a street corner. Everyone's consciousness expands, the heavens ascend to clear a path for new opinions—the earth doesn't quake but hearts beat faster.

We don't know about it.

We need the song's reassurance more than anything, because love has suddenly disappeared from our days, sunk into the cracks in the floor.

He becomes more irritable from one day to the next, complaining about the light and how it changes all the time.

"Sit still."

"I am sitting still. Just tell me how I should be and I'll be it."

"More to the left. Stop turning your head all the time."

"I'm not turning my head. Maybe you are."

"Quiet."

There's no tenderness in him. So different from how he is at night, curled up inside me. The sky refuses to stay put and I'm like a shadow.

"Your face," he says. "It's narrower today."

"Same old face."

"Are you sure you had breakfast? How am I supposed to get hold of you if you're changing all the time? Tell me that."

There's a knife in his gaze.

"This light refuses to settle down. Goddamn light."

"Maybe you just haven't found the right composition. It'll all start to go smoothly once you've found the right composition."

"I'm starting to think I'll never find it," he says gloomily.

I get up and go to look at the piece. It's unfinished, but it's not bad.

"What's wrong with it?"

"I don't know," he says, not looking me in the eye, turning away. "I just can't get hold of it."

"I think it looks quite good."

"You're biased. Besides, you're not a professional. You don't acquire artistic vision by wandering around museums."

Now I'm angry. "Well, what exactly are you trying to do? What are you driving at?"

He runs his hands through his hair the way he often does, sits down, lights a cigarette, takes a drag, looks at the lake, and sighs.

"I'd like there to be something old-fashioned about it. But something else, too. Something else. Some kind of angle."

He spreads his arms helplessly, looks at the painting.

"This is just trivial somehow. Mediocre."

He's already got the eyes—they're recognizably mine. My gaze pierces through, as in those strange portraits from the 1600s that I've seen in museums. I'm floating, like a head blossoming out of nothing.

"The eyes are good," I say. "The expression is good."

"Not good enough."

SOME DAYS ARE different. On some days we forget his work, take the boat out and have a picnic. We have veal in waxed paper, a whole bottle of fresh milk, three kinds of cake, one that I've made and two from the neighbor lady. We have strawberry juice and chocolate melting in its foil wrapper. The little girl begs me for it the whole time; she's allowed to have one piece. It won't come out of its package, she licks it and smiles with smeared lips.

There's a picture of this. In the picture she looks triumphant, with the sun behind her as if it will never set. Later she remembers this boating trip, although she remembers nothing else from the whole summer. She builds memories from the words of others, but she tells her own daughter about this trip, as if it's a precious thing—the nicest part was Mom and Dad and I went out in the boat to the island. Mom usually rowed, but Dad did sometimes. The sun was a friendly fire in the sky, it felt like the world had always been nothing but light and water and melted Fazer chocolate in a blue wrapper and I could lick it off the foil to my heart's content.

"Why don't we stay on the island forever?" I whisper in his ear in the evening, after we've swum all day, made coffee on the campfire, roasted three fat fish that I caught with the rod, found little stones at the water's edge and made a magic circle with them on the beach.

"Yes, let's," he says, and kisses me. "Let's imagine that there's no other world than this."

"We can live here forever and ever," the little girl says.

And I say, "Forever and ever."

No one is thinking about the painting on the sauna porch; it's trivial. No one is thinking about Elsa, not even the girl falling asleep in the tent with her hand in mine.

I carefully ease my hand away once she starts to breathe evenly.

The man is someone slightly different. There are two people inside him. The cruel, ruthless one who gives commands has disappeared without a trace now.

He gently moves the blanket, patiently, as if he's removing layers worn out by the world, getting them out of the way.

He lowers himself, kisses my breasts. This is ours alone, and we can't tell anyone about it.

We become each other and remain the same and I love his sigh when I open to him and invite him in and he comes.

AT THE END of June he decides to try a new medium. He prints ten silkscreens of me, working in town, in the living room of a friend who has the needed materials. Clumsy attempts—even he can see that. The prototype screams out like an exclamation point. His friend says it to him straight, using the worst possible word: cheap. He drives back to Tammilehto in a rage and quells his anger by stopping at the lakeshore on the way. The water is like a mirror, he lets his thoughts drift into communion with it. He eats some ice cream, skips a few smooth stones across the water. He was good at it even as a child—the stone bouncing on the surface of the lake five times, six, leaving a soothing trace of spreading circles.

As he's looking at those circles he gets another idea. He's going to give up the silkscreens, the printing—it was ridiculous of him to even try! Why not continue what he already has? He'll go back to oil painting, but he'll try a new technique. He'll paint over his previous works, layer after layer. That's what he decides to do.

Everything continues as before—I sit in front of him, unmoving, day after day, and I hover on the canvas, ethereal, incomplete.

———

ON THE EVENING when everything ends, the little girl refuses to go to sleep. She runs to the sauna. She has woken up alone in the dark and is sleepy and a little confused.

"What are you doing here?" he asks her. He takes her in his arms.

"You're drawing Eeva," she says.

"That's right," he says. "Except I'm painting."

"It doesn't look like Eeva yet," she says emphatically.

"But it will," he says. "If I work at it enough."

"Then Eeva will be in the picture completely," she says. "Then she won't have to sit anymore. She can play."

"That's right," he says.

"Can I draw a moon?" she asks.

"You can draw on another piece of paper," he says, and hands her a piece. She announces that she's going to draw my nose.

"Then you can put it on your painting, Daddy. Right, Daddy? This nose? I can draw it better than you."

"Yes, you sure can," he says absentmindedly, no longer hearing her because his gaze has become fixed on me.

She continues drawing for just a moment, then comes over to me. She tries to get in my lap, but he tells her not to.

"Ella, come away from there."

She doesn't obey him, and he commands her to move with one gesture. "Go," he says, pointing at the house.

She stamps her foot, grabs his palette in one quick motion, and smears paint on the threshold.

He's severe: "Will you go inside and be good for a little while? Go play quietly. Or do I have to lead you there by the hand?"

"No, I can go by myself."

I'm gentle: "I'll come with you, honey."

He doesn't want me to leave. She makes the decision for me: "No. I'll go by myself."

She goes, her head bowed, a little deflated, dangling Molla from her left hand. Molla's feet plow through the grass and the hem of the little girl's summer dress trails dejectedly through the clover.

The two of us are left alone in the sauna. Nearly an hour goes by before he can get the right angle again. He gets annoyed. His shoulders hunch a little, his lips remain expressionless. He mixes colors, thins them. He adds too much thinner and curses.

"Well," I say. "Here we go again."

"So what?"

He wants me to resist. I don't take up the argument. I leave it to one side, like a cardboard box full of worn-out junk. It sits between us. I look at the lake.

"Look this way," he says.

"What if I don't? What if I look where I want to look? What if I decide I want to go for a swim?"

He exhales wearily. "I've seen it all, I know all your tricks. It's just an act now, just for show."

I sigh. It doesn't please him.

"Now you're pouting."

"No, I'm not."

"Yes, you are. I can see you."

"You're seeing wrong."

"I'm seeing what I'm seeing."

"You think you're seeing what you're seeing. In reality you don't see anything. Reality is something else. You don't have any concept of it."

I use the strongest words I can think of. I want to make him feel crushed. Suddenly tenderness is just a trinket. This is a competition. I want to smash him to pieces.

"You've never known me, not really. You wouldn't recognize me if I passed you on the street."

He throws his tools in the corner. He strides the few steps to where I am and pushes me against the wall. I can feel a bruise forming on my arm where his hand is squeezing tightly around it. It's there for three days, but it's the least of my worries—just a mark from a time when I didn't have worries. But I don't know this yet.

He covers my mouth with his left hand so that I can't utter a word. The wall presses another bruise into my back.

"It's your fault, this stagnation. You're never in the place where you pretend you are. You're always different, never completely here."

He lets go of me. I run. I knock over the easel as I go and notice that he hasn't made any progress—I'm still floating on the canvas like some strange apparition.

I run to the spruce grove and up the ridge. If I stopped now I would smell smoke, but I don't stop.

I go up the path all the way to the top of the ridge, where the boulders are. I don't look behind me. I want to pretend I'm a forest, to hide under the moss. But I stand there, trembling. My arm itches, I can still feel the shadow of his hand against my lips like a gag.

I have to wait a long time before I see him coming up the path. He's full of regret. He stands next to the boulders.

"I'm sorry."

I turn away. I won't give in that easily.

"Love."

"What? What is it? I'm bruised. You gave me bruises. Is that your idea of love? I have a different idea of it, I can tell you."

"I'm sorry," he says again. "I didn't mean it. Forgive me."

"What if I don't?"

"Love is impossible for me to depict. I don't know how to describe it, and everything gets lost when I try, everything essential about you."

I melt a little. I look at him, still not saying anything, delaying my answer. He looks helpless. We stand silent for a minute, two minutes.

The flames are already rising below. We don't see them because the wind is blowing from south to north, carrying the smoke beyond the spruce trees. The forest is crackling. I start to relent.

"Come here," I say finally.

He comes. He takes me in his arms.

We stand pressed against each other. Time passes, centuries twine into us. These fights are as old as the forest. A woman takes a man in her arms and pities him, with everything she has. They press against each other, they don't measure time according to the rules of this world.

I see the flames when I turn my head.

"Look," I say. It's all I have time to say.

For a brief moment I think, almost with exhilaration, that it's surprising how like a drawing the flames are. Then there's a sound, a crackling hum rising with each second, and I realize what's actually happening.

He acts faster than I do. He runs down the hill. Then I run. Through the curtain of smoke the spruce trees in back of the house shimmer like a mirage.

He's in the yard in a moment, I stumble on a tree root and fall behind. He reaches the door before I do—it's locked. She's locked the door, either by accident or on purpose.

I could go through the wall. I could tear away the boards and the insulation, rip through the wallpaper. I run and look for the spare key under the garden table. He pushes me aside, picks up a garden chair and breaks the window with it. Before I have time to yell he's torn the broken glass from the frame and disappeared inside.

ELSA IS BENDING to reach the lowest drawer, searching for a file. She's a little tired. She's fantasizing about soaking her feet in bath salts this evening. She's fantasizing about calling her husband and daughter on the phone. She bends down to grab a folder and sees a hairpin on the floor, a bit of dust next to it, and feels a little annoyed at the mess. And at just that moment, she's called to the phone.

She stands up, turns, and sees the secretary in the doorway. She thinks how the secretary is one of those people who conceal their worry in controlled gestures, who dress in jeans and wear their hair down in their free time, one of those people who just pretend to be secretaries during the day—the kind she was starting to see on the street. She has time to think this before she realizes that the news the secretary is bringing is extremely bad.

Elsa still doesn't know what she knows, but she knows she knows it.

She's shaking all the way home. The trip takes an exasperatingly long time—the taxi, the wait at the airport. She sits in a hall that is alternately abandoned and humming with people, drinks bitter coffee, holds the strap of her purse tight in her sweaty hand and looks at the clock, which has moved forward just one interminable minute, two minutes, finally an hour, two, three.

She's been here this whole time, in this stupid waiting room. She's been here for years. The plane finally takes off into the air, and she squeezes the armrests and bargains with God, although she's not a religious person at all. If her daughter's all right, she won't travel anymore. If her daughter's all right, if she can breathe and run and dream like other children, she promises she'll leave this all behind and be content with teaching beginning courses in a stuffy lecture hall. Heaven is quiet; no one hears her prayer. She leans toward the stewardess and asks, How much longer? Forty minutes, the stewardess says. Too long, Elsa thinks.

When she arrives she rushes to get a taxi.

The thought of her daughter sticks in her throat, she can't get the instructions to the driver out of her mouth in her panic. For a moment she thinks that that's what will keep her daughter alive. She's protecting her life by being silent.

She pays the driver hurriedly and the coins scatter around her like indulgences she's anxious to pay. She doesn't bother to pick them up.

She sees her own reflection in the glass door as she pulls on the door handle. She rushes down the hallway, runs into a nurse. She asks about Ella and the nurse directs her to the room.

When she opens the door, she thinks at first that it's the wrong family, that she's come into the wrong room, because the picture is complete and she doesn't belong in it. A woman is sitting on the edge of her daughter's bed. The little girl's father—the woman's husband, Elsa thinks—puts his hand on the woman's shoulder. The woman reaches up a little. kisses him. He takes her in his arms. The kiss is not a particularly long one, but it's unmistakably the kind of kiss exchanged between people who belong to each other completely.

All of this flashes through Elsa's mind in a brief moment, half a second. Then the little girl looks at her and shouts: Mommy!

Elsa realizes that she hasn't come in the wrong door. She realizes what she already knew.

ELSA STEPS ACROSS the threshold uninvited, pushes past me into my apartment, goes into the kitchen with her coat and shoes on and sits down at the table.

"How is she?" I ask immediately. "How is Ella?"

"She'll be fine," Elsa says. "As long as you stay away from her."

The air goes out of me. Ella's all right. Elsa's eyes drill through me, telling me I have no reason to be relieved.

"Let's straighten this thing out," she says.

"What do you mean?" I ask, although I know how childish it sounds.

"We both know what's going on. I know everything now. I know about what's been going on here for years."

Like an idiot, I ask if she wants some coffee and she says she hasn't come here to chat, so I might as well forget about the coffee. Nevertheless, so that I'll have something to do I go to the cupboard as if I'm looking for something to eat. I don't know how to hide my nakedness in front of her. She looks at me—there's no chink in her. She's beautiful, unbroken. I always thought there would be a chink. I thought that if this confrontation ever happened, this thing that I'd feared and gone over in my mind all these years, I thought that I'd find at least one little chink where I could curl up, where I could go for consolation.

But there isn't one, just a fearless, merciless gaze.

I don't see her hands trembling. I don't see the uncertainty concealed beneath her resoluteness. She's not feeling well; she could throw up right now. She spent the whole morning sitting, lying down. The uncertainty in her is like a disease.

She's surprised at the feeling: it's the same way she's felt the few times that she's been ill. Something has to be done, she thought this morning when she felt the fear welling up in her stomach.

She draped her uncertainty in decisiveness and walked across the city, gathering her anger.

And now she's here, sure of herself, impenetrable.

She looks at my bare legs, my nightgown, which my breasts show through. What a puny thing the girl is, Elsa thinks, and what pitiful breasts she has.

She gets to the point before I do and says it bluntly, without further evasion: "If you think that what you have with my husband and daughter is love, you're wrong."

She snorts. A mere breath, a sound tinged with scorn. It's enough to nullify me.

She looks insolent. I don't know about her uncertainty. I only see that she looks crueler than I've ever seen her. She's not fun anymore—three years have gone by since I first met her, she's become more self-assured since then. She's a tree with roots deep in the earth.

"You don't know anything about us," she says. "You don't know our family and you don't belong in it."

I'm unable to speak.

"Have you ever once in all these years thought about what this would do to that little girl?" And now her voice cracks for the first time. "Did you ever think about that?"

"Yes."

"What am I supposed to say to her when she asks about you? Tell me what I'm supposed to say to her if she asks for you before she'll go to sleep, if she wants you to come and tuck her in."

"I don't know."

"That's not good enough."

Now I start to agree, to say what I believe is right. "You should tell her that I'm not coming anymore."

"And when I've told her that and she starts to cry, what do you think I should do to comfort her?"

"You should take her in your arms and rock her tears away."

"All right," she says, and nods. "That's what I'll do. And I hope you understand that you have to stay away. If you won't do it for my sake—and why would you?—then do it for hers."

After she says this, she gets up. She walks with sure steps over the threshold, the door closes with a slam, and she's gone.

20

YOU KNOW WHAT?" Anna asks.

"Hm?" Matias sounds languid. The sheet is rumpled under his back.

"I met a woman," she begins.

He perks up, the languor is gone. Matias can get into a game if he feels like it. They haven't played this game, although she sometimes tells him stories like this, just like bedtime stories, about strangers passing by.

"On the tram?" he asks.

Anna's heart flutters. It's like she's traveling toward him, through his skin.

Through, through, through.

She just has to continue. She has to give him more clues.

"Not on the tram," she says.

"Where, then?"

"Here. Around here, on this block."

"Why is your heart pounding?" Matias asks.

"I don't know. Stop interrupting." Her irritated words break through the dimness, climb up to the ceiling, and float there.

"Well, go ahead," he says encouragingly. "What kind of woman? Young or old?"

"Young. She has the whole world on her shoulders, though. She has her troubles."

Matias laughs. The laugh is a friendly one, but it's enough to nullify her. "For some reason that makes me think of manure. That fertilizer ad. Like she's carrying her troubles on her shoulder like a bag of manure."

Anna springs upright.

"What's the matter?" Matias asks, amazed.

"Nothing."

"What is it?"

"Nothing! Forget it!"

She goes into the kitchen and runs herself a glass of water. She drinks it in quick gulps. She can hear herself swallowing. She thinks, a person who's drowning can hear herself gulping just before. Matias comes to the door, looks at her, and comes closer.

"I'm sorry," he says gently, gently. "I was just kidding. Just kidding around. Tell me the story."

"Maybe some other time," Anna says.

She lets him hug her. They stand for a long time in the darkness of the kitchen. Then Matias lets go of her and walks with sleepy steps back to the bedroom.

Anna stands in the kitchen. The minutes stretch out. The doorway glows in the darkness.

One step. It's so easy to step through a door. So easy to leave your whole life behind, the whole world. Step over the threshold and close the door. It's so simple.

1967

HE ARRIVES TWO weeks later, at the beginning of September. The little girl is recovering—the only sign of the event is a mark that will fade as the years go by. But he's not recovering. Everything's broken. He doesn't know if he's breathing. He's broken in two.

He doesn't bring much with him, just one suitcase. For the first week we lie in bed and draw familiar maps of each other. I miss the little girl and ask about her. He turns away, his desolation too heavy to dress in words. I go to work in the mornings; I've started a temporary job teaching French at a school on the south side of the city. I walk out the door reluctantly because I know that he'll draw someone else in his mind while I'm away.

And that's what happens—the black settles into his eyes in just one day. When I come home he's smoking at the window and won't look at me. Finally he approaches me, moving his hand along the line of my hip. He lowers his hand onto my rear end. We lean against each other. I'm more angular than he remembers me. I have a scent that he doesn't like, maybe from my day, or maybe it's always been there.

"Shall we make some dinner?" I ask. "Potatoes? Rice?"

"Anything," he says into the pit at the base of my neck.

He can't stand the thought of potatoes, grains of rice that scatter and click against the floor, the red pillowcase, the patter of the rain against the window. He just wants to be inside me, constantly. It's the only thing that makes him forget. Just Eeva from head to toe, Eeva who takes off her skirt and takes a shower, then comes to him. Let me hold you, he says, like in Paris. I take him deep. He forgets his regret while I rock him.

Afterward he rolls onto his back, lights a cigarette, although I've forbidden him to smoke in bed.

"It's grueling being here all day long. Like having nails driven into me. Sawed in half with a blade of acid." He says this as if I were to blame.

I get up from the bed. "Go, then. Why don't you leave?" I say without looking at him. I fasten my bra and snap up my pants.

"I want to be with you."

"Well, bring your daughter here."

"I suppose you think Elsa would let me do that."

"Just for a visit. Why not just for a visit?"

THE NEXT DAY the little girl is standing in the hallway looking uncertain, her doll under her arm, the toes of her shoes shining question marks.

I hug her for a long time. I can't see the scar; it's started to fade. She cries a little.

"Molla was rescued," she says. "She doesn't even have any scars. Daddy saved her."

I whisper the words in her ear that my mother used to whisper to me. We stand there. The hallway doesn't know about fires. The day doesn't know about accidents.

"Do you have any milk?" she asks.

"We sure do," I say.

He pours her a glass. She looks around.

"There's no kids' room here at all. Where do kids sleep?"

"They sleep on the sofa or with the grown-ups, in the same bed," he says.

"They won't fit," she says, and drinks her milk. Then she looks at her father. "Daddy, you can take me to the park now."

TWENTY-FIVE DAYS AND just as many nights. We have nights like cradles, and happy days as well. Sometimes the little girl comes over, other times it's just the two of us. We have walks and meals and talks. He draws a little, it makes him feel better.

I don't know that he goes to see Elsa five times that month. Many of those times they make love and it feels to him amazingly familiar yet new.

We, on the other hand, are separating from each other. To fill up the cracks and corners of longing, we make meals fervently, like communion. We sweep the helplessness from each other's brows with a caress, weaving a trust day by day, night by night. It's not enough.

One night he gets out of bed, dresses as if even that were an obstacle I've placed in his way. He says he's going out. I won't let him.

"You won't let me love you." I'm shouting, pouring the words over his face like a kettle of hot oil.

He convulses under it. He pushes me against the wall. The veins of his neck tighten under his skin. I might have thought, how beautiful, like jewelry, his blood making his veins stand out, if I didn't know that they're gushing with the power of hate.

"What do you want from me?" he says.

"That you let me, allow me."

"Your love is the kind of love that smothers me. It doesn't come from you. It comes from somewhere far away, another world. Who are you, anyway?"

"I'm Eeva," I say.

The name is just soundless syllables shaped by my lips. If you were watching from a distance, you'd think that woman was silently mouthing a prayer, a call for help.

"Eeva is no one," he says. "She's nothing but an image."

He lets go of me. I take a breath. He's already at the door. The door slams. He's gone.

HE COMES BACK two days later. I've waited for him at the window one evening, another, watching the light change. He looks as if he's crossed an ocean to see me. He has his gestures. I've lived in them so much these days that I've lost my own boundaries. It's as if I've gradually flowed into him, or as if I was flowing and somewhere along the way I drained into the sewer, unnoticed.

He sits on the bed without saying anything. I sit on his lap. He lets me hug him, but not kiss him. That's how I know.

"Do you hate me?" he says. "Are you going to hate me?"

"Why would I?"

"Because everything's ending like this."

He says it easily. Drops me like an object from a shelf. Neither of us speaks for a moment. I can hear his heart—it's beating here, although it's elsewhere.

"Your daughter can live with us. It can work."

He's silent. I continue: "We could go to the market on Saturdays. We could go to the seashore sometimes, drive right to the edge of the earth. Look at the waves, scream as they crash against the shore. On ordinary days we could have a dance. And bookshelves, and visitors. We could open jars of jam, build a fort wherever we wanted. No one would get mad if a little paint got smeared in the doorway. There'd be sand in the couch sometimes, but it would be no big deal. Pancakes, forts, jam jars. Nights when we can't tell where one person's skin ends and another's begins. That kind of life."

"Beautiful," he says. "A beautiful story."

"Just a story?"

"Yes, just a story. Like a dream."

I'm silent for a moment, not breathing. "Can I see her again? Just once? Just one more time?"

He doesn't answer right away. "I have to ask Elsa," he says finally. "Elsa can decide."

He gets up. I follow him. He goes to wash his face because he suddenly feels that he can't see properly. But he can see; he sees Elsa. Elsa is in his mind, more clearly delineated than ever.

While he's in the bathroom, I hide his shoes in the oven. I want him to be stuck to the floor. I get some syrup from the kitchen cupboard and pour it over his legs. He grabs the bottle out of my hand and throws it across the room. It hits the wall and spatters a senseless pattern there. I get some milk and pour that; he throws that, too. I get a bottle of red wine, pour it on his feet; the bottle shatters as it hits the wall. Too purple to look like blood; a festive splash like an exclamation mark in celebration of life. He thinks I've lost my senses. What art. Trivial, unpredictable.

We stand facing each other for a minute, five minutes, a whole hour. The sun sets, the night trails in through the window. The buildings crumble around us. I bite him on the collarbone and leave a broken line. He shakes me. The world falls away like a scrim, except that's not true: the trees are there in the yard, the sky is in its place. He pulls me quite close to him again. I don't intend to let him go. He'll have to let me go. I sink to the floor, cling to his legs. He drags me down the hallway. The trip to the door takes three years and four months, as long as this has lasted. It takes forty years because that's how long everything continues even after it's over. Decades later he'll be amazed that he's still on his way down this hallway.

I throw myself in front of the door. He opens the door and steps over me. He closes the door. It's so simple; he just closes the door behind him.

I lie on the floor, unable to get up. I listen to the silence flowing down the walls. I seep into the cracks in the floor.

21

SHE WAS WALKING toward him with brisk steps. Martti could see from far off that she was angry. She had said on the phone that she wanted to meet, preferably out. He had guessed why immediately, but he was still nervous when he saw her. The weather didn't match her anger. No clouds rolling across the sky like an omen. It was amazingly still and bright, as if the sun wanted to record every nuance of her angry face.

He asked her if she wanted to go to a cafe, maybe have a cinnamon roll, or why not some ice cream, although they'd been eating ice cream every day until they were sick of it. He could tell he was talking too much, but her expression was like a wall, and he finally quieted.

Her anger was freshly created. A girl who bore this kind of anger wasn't a girl anymore. It was an ancient anger, hidden away for centuries. Sometimes it would break out in dramas and demonstrations, in disguise. Now it seemed to have found an outlet in Anna's face. This wasn't a harmless threat like the ones he remembered from when she was little, insisting on putting on her own clothes to go outside, stamping her foot at the front door. This was something else.

"Guess what I'm beginning to think."

For a moment he convinced himself that she was going to say something about the birds in the trees or the quality of the light, but he knew what was coming.

"I'm beginning to think that Eeva died because of you. You did something, or left something undone, and she died. If it weren't for you, she'd still be alive."

Anna paused a moment before continuing. Where had she learned this rational, cold way of presenting a chain of deduction, linked together with blame to fill in the blank spots? The worst was still to come. He could see it in her face.

"And if that's the case," she said, her words sifted through with cold anger, "if she would still be alive if not for you, we might as well say it outright. You killed her."

She looked him right in the eye.

The words nearly knocked him down onto the park bench, but he stood fast and didn't look away. This could have been another kind of meeting, one of many—she with a Coca-Cola, he with a coffee. Making believe about strangers' fates, talking about the past. Light and harmless. But the anger made all their fantasies brittle to the point of meaninglessness.

"Don't try to deny it," she said. "You can't get out of it so easily. Eeva's love was beautiful, as big as life, and you cheated her, used her up, crushed her. In other words you killed her, didn't you? Admit it."

He wished they could talk about something else. Where were those passersby, the blossoming young lovers, Rebekka and Aleksi and the others they'd imagined? They had all evaporated into thin air, faint and insignificant. He decided not to flinch under her accusations. He couldn't change the subject now. The early summer day offered up an astounding brightness as if it wanted to be the subject of conversation, but the vastness of the sky had to be set aside. They had to use the heaviest of words.

"I loved her. That doesn't kill a person. It's not killing."

Anna maintained her stony expression. "Sometimes it's the same thing. For men."

She looked uncompromising, defiant. He sketched her expression in his mind, made a mental note of how a grudge is reflected off the one who bears it, takes on accusations stuck in other people's throats. Bitterness gives people's faces an astonished look, he thought. If you wanted to depict it you should open the eyes upward, not narrow them. A narrowed gaze to express anger is a cliché. Real anger is a kind of astonishment. It gives its bearer's cheek a cool red. If he were to try to paint it, he would give the red a milkiness, an opaque quality.

Anna gathered up her accusations.

"Your love was the kind of love that made her disappear. Don't you ever think you might bear some responsibility for that?"

"No one can take responsibility for another person's disintegration."

Anna didn't hesitate in her answer. "Love is an immense responsibility toward another person. So don't try to deny that you killed her."

It was a senseless argument. It shocked him. He saw the scene from the point of view of people passing by: an old man and a young woman harping on overwrought, larger-than-life matters. But all of it had been left unsaid before. Never had he spoken so openly about these things. Never had anyone demanded to know what he thought about it, and he hadn't ever really worked it out for himself, either. But now he was sure what he thought. And he was almost just as sure that it was exactly what Anna needed to know, maybe more than Eeva ever had.

"Eeva was free. She was free to do what she wanted, and she did."

Anna refused to back down, continued to insist, as if she hadn't heard what he said. "You chained her, you locked her up, trapped her in your love, and she never got out."

He heard himself laugh, though he knew at once that it sounded like mockery to her.

"You give me too much credit. As far as I know, I've never chained anyone up. I don't have the power, or the desire. I paint pictures, and I'm not exactly a wizard, even at that."

He wanted to explain, come to some understanding, but what more could he say? Anna had adopted ideas and beliefs about Eeva and was testing their strength. But he still wanted to convince her that there was another way to think about it. Suddenly he felt that convincing her of this was the most important thing he would ever have the power to do.

"I don't believe that love can be a prison for anyone. Do you?"

Anna's stony expression had started to fracture. There was a hint of uncertainty in her voice. "I don't know." She looked for a moment as if she might give in. But she found one more thing to say. "Eeva believed it could. That's all that matters."

He had to continue: "I don't believe in a freedom so fragile that other people can put it in chains."

Anna snorted. "People rot in jail all the time, all over the place."

He took a step back, although he knew it communicated to her that he couldn't hold his own. He glanced at the road. Someone ran to the tram stop, leaping in one nimble stride from one stripe of the crosswalk to another, unaware that here under the oak trees they were having a serious discussion that verged on the ridiculous.

"Chains used in prisons have to be made a bit sturdier than that," he said, speaking more slowly than he intended to.

Anna didn't hesitate. "That's easy for you to say. You're a man. You and people like you have controlled what really goes on for centuries. But that's got to change."

Now he could answer in a firm tone: "If you base your view of women's liberation on the idea that their love for men has chained them then I don't think it's going to be a complete liberation at all."

He didn't say right away what he thought. But finally he had to, he couldn't leave it unsaid. "Eeva was different. She belonged to a different time. Things have changed." Did Anna even want to hear this? Who was he to give advice, a mere picture maker, keeping company with shadows. But he said it, because he wanted her to understand. "You're not Eeva. You have to remember that."

Now she didn't look purely angry. Or maybe Martti was imagining that, believing what he wanted to believe. But what did he know? Maybe there was some other feeling arising in her, something he would never be able to grasp completely. Suddenly he realized—I'll never be able to imagine my granddaughter's reality, not in several lifetimes, no matter how hard I practice at it! This woman is such a stranger to me that everything in her is entirely hers!

He tried to achieve some weight in his words, annoyed at the huskiness in his voice: "Your love is only yours, you have to think about it that way. It's not your prison, and it isn't preventing you from being free. The fact that Eeva didn't know this made her a sad person. Maybe she was always a much sadder person than either of us. But no one can take love away from you, or take the world away. They both belong to you."

He wasn't sure if Anna understood. She was still standing in front of him, ready to state her opposition. But no statement came out. She turned on her heel and walked away under oak branches buoyant with the green light of spring.

Martti stood where he was. In spite of Anna's eruption of anger he felt surprisingly calm. He lifted his gaze to the green leaves above him. The branches shushed a little. The sight was beloved to him. Peace returned to him as an idea strengthened in his mind.

Now everything was said. There was nothing to regret. Not with Eeva, or with Anna.

KERTTU PALOVAARA, ALIAS Katariina Aavamaa, is very different than Anna imagined. Even her voice on the phone sounds wrong, as if she always holds back her answers, wraps them in rigid politeness.

It's Tuesday, the clock reads twelve noon. Katariina opens the door and invites Anna in. Anna is ready to be disappointed as soon as she walks in the door. Kerttu the comical, Kerttu the hilarious, living in real time. Kerttu the comical's days divided into calendar columns.

Katariina Aavamaa suggested they meet at lunchtime and made it clear that Anna should agree, because no other suggestions would be forthcoming.

Maybe Anna expected someone with a twinkle in her eye and a mouth ready to break into laughter, a door that's always open. Long hair, a skirt of Indian fabric, flowers in the window, grandchildren underfoot, an absentminded dog ambling from room to room.

Katariina Aavamaa is a meticulous woman. Her hair is frosted and cut along the line of her jaw. Her apartment is decorated in beige.

"You must be Anna," she says.

She isn't going to offer her a Gauloise or turn up the music or throw her head back and sing Jefferson Airplane's "Somebody to Love."

She has thick, glossy decorator's magazines on her glass coffee table—maybe she leafs through them while drinking a cup of tea. There's a Skanno light fixture on the ceiling. The chairs are covered in cashmere.

"Mineral water or regular?"

"Regular, thanks."

It seems like Katariina Aavamaa doesn't want Anna here. A computer pours an electric gleam into the room. A paperback lies waiting on the sofa.

But still, she's a woman who fulfills her obligations and keeps her promises, so she urges Anna to sit down at the table.

They hold back, thinking about what to say. Katariina offers her some salad from the Stockmann deli. They eat, and Anna doesn't know how to begin. She doesn't dare ask anything about Eeva. On the phone she was able to say the name. Now Eeva's name is stuck in her throat like a fishbone.

Katariina stands up and sighs. She opens a cabinet and, to Anna's surprise, takes out a bottle of whiskey and gives her a questioning look. Anna shrugs and nods.

She takes two glasses out of the cabinet, fills them both with a resinous-looking liquid. If this were a movie, Katariina would be played by Jane Birkin. Jane Birkin would sigh unsteadily, close her eyes and let the air flow out of her lungs so it sounded like a muffled little roar.

Katariina doesn't close her eyes; she stands next to the table and swigs the drink down all at once. Anna has a quick thought: maybe the Kerttu she imagined wasn't completely off the mark. People strip away former selves and find new ways of being.

"Eeva died in August of 1968."

Katariina throws the sentence across the kitchen; it hits Anna like a dagger.

"I know that."

Anna feels like a reporter for a gossip magazine.

"There's really nothing else to tell," Katariina says.

The words would be harsh if Anna didn't notice the slight trembling on the left side of Katariina's mouth. She sighs. She looks just like Jane Birkin again. Or Meryl Streep? Or

Catherine Deneuve? There are so many women who refuse to be at the mercy of careless characterizations.

"I've got a busy workday today. Maybe I'm a little tired," she says.

Anna is relieved at the harmless conversation, which gives her an opening. "What do you do for a living?"

Katariina smiles a little. "I work as an agent. In the theater. That sort of thing. Ours is the only theatrical agency in Finland. It's a fun job. I get to travel, maybe even have some influence—at the grass roots, anyway. It's my own company. I never would have thought that I'd become a business-woman, but I did, a real tycoon!"

She laughs. Then she looks out the window and sighs. For a moment Anna thinks that she's going to burst into tears. She doesn't look at Anna as she says, "You would think that I'd have a lot to tell you. Maybe Liisa thought that I would know things that I haven't told her. But what does it matter how it happened? The only thing that matters is that she didn't survive. That's all."

She opens the window and takes a pack of cigarettes out of a small vase on the windowsill. Not Gauloises but Marl-boro Lights. She lights one and blows out the smoke.

For just a moment Anna can see Kerttu the conqueror in her. She may be wearing Dior powder on her nose, but you can be sure she has Kerttu's freckles tattooed into her skin, the ones she got years ago in San Francisco.

"Look, a squirrel," she says suddenly. "He came! I always wait for him. I've even given him a name. Teppo. At first I thought I'd call him Jorma. We have an agreement. I tell him my troubles in exchange for cardamom rolls."

She gets up and looks for a piece of roll in the cupboard, then holds it out through the window for the squirrel. She looks away, turns serious.

"We were traveling together right before Eeva died," she says. "Something about that trip did her in. All sorts of things happened."

She continues to feed the squirrel.

"It was really stupid, actually. We were just wandering. We just went wherever. She was happy. Happier than she'd been all year."

She takes a drag and blows out the smoke. For the first time, Anna feels like she's without a story. She doesn't try to imagine this woman's regrets, or her wisdom. She was wrong when she thought Katariina Aavamaa was tense and meticulous. Maybe she was wrong about everything else, too. Katariina is one of those people who tell their own stories.

Katariina's gaze sharpens as if she remembers something she'd forgotten.

"Your mother. How is she these days?"

"She's a doctor."

Then Anna thinks that she could just as well have said, she's happy.

"I used to see her now and then. When she was three or four, maybe five. A little button-nosed thing. A doctor. Imagine."

THE PHOTOS ARE mostly of Katariina. Eeva is in a few of them.

"We certainly were childish. It was all about pleasure. Such long parties! We called it a revolution because it suited us. Later on I thought that it was the kind of revolution that's best achieved in a place where the world doesn't get in the way. On a stage, or in a movie."

She laughs.

"But I should be forgiving with myself. If it weren't for idealism everything would stay just the same. Change only happens if someone sees it in a dream first. But I still believe, even now, that true revolutions last a lifetime—they're always quiet, and they happen when no one's looking."

Anna doesn't know what to say. What does she know about revolution? Only what she's read in books and seen on television. On television there's always a revolution going on somewhere, as sure as the latest episode of *Sex in the City*.

Anna suddenly remembers a woman she sat next to on the plane on her way to Paris last fall. "I met an American woman on an airplane once who said that there was a revolution going on in the little Romanian town she was living in."

"Why was an American living in Romania?"

"She was a widow and she decided to travel because she'd always stayed in Alabama to please her husband when he was alive."

"So when he died she left?"

"She went to Bosnia as a U.N. election monitor, and kept traveling."

"What was the name of the place, the town in Romania?"

"I can't remember."

Katariina laughs. "There are revolutions happening all the time in cities with names no one can remember."

For a second Anna can see the woman who painted her eyelashes black and said, Let's go create a world.

In the next few pictures Eeva is in Stockholm. Then a change of channels, to Amsterdam. Eeva sitting at a table in a cafe next to a man—a boy, really.

"Who's he?" Anna asks.

"Eeva knew him from somewhere. She thought she was in love with him for a little while. He came to meet us in Stockholm."

In the next pictures Eeva's sitting at a table in a cafe in the countryside, maybe somewhere in France. She looks thin and exhausted, but she's still smiling.

"I didn't know how to help her," Katariina says.

"Maybe you did everything you could."

Some of the photos are from later years, the seventies. Katariina laughing on the Ku'Damm in Berlin, wading in the sea, looking through a camera, unapologetic. Katariina in a blue shirt among the May Day crowds in Helsinki. And a few years later, judging by the hairstyle, Katariina with a baby.

She looks different in every picture.

She doesn't seem like a family-oriented person, but who's to say, sometimes people like that have the happiest family lives.

When Anna is at the door, leaving, she gets the courage to ask about her husband.

"The same man for thirty years, can you imagine?" Katariina says in the voice long-married people use to talk about their marriages—as if they themselves are surprised that something done on a whim could succeed so well, that they could love the other person for decades.

"He's a banker. I would have laughed myself silly when I was twenty to hear that I would marry the enemy! Or slapped myself silly. What about your grandparents? I've read about them in the paper now and then. They've both had prominent careers. If that's worth anything in this world."

"They've been happy."

She doesn't want to tell her about her grandmother. For some reason it's important to her not to say a word about Elsa's illness.

"I believe it," Katariina says. Then she seems to think of something. "Timisoara."

"What?"

"The town in Romania. Your woman on the airplane must have lived there."

"The 1989 revolution. Of course. That's what she meant. All this time I've been thinking she was talking about the situation in her own life. Too bad. It sort of spoils my story."

Katariina smiles. "Maybe not. What do we know about her? Maybe she wanted to keep the possibility of change alive by living there. I watched the ruckus that was going on there at the time. The television started the revolution in a way; people saw foreign television shows and became aware of the illusion. I wasn't against the destruction of that regime—it was tyrannical. But there was a brief time when I believed in the idea behind it. And when it all started to fall apart I thought it was really too ironic that it all happened because of television. Maybe you should stick to your story. It's a beautiful one. It says something beautiful about you."

The story. Anna wants to stick to her story. That's why she doesn't ask what happened to Eeva, how Eeva finally died.

———

EEVA BELIEVED THAT everything could change. After he walked out the door, she still got to say good-bye to the little girl. She lied to her, told her she would see her tomorrow. She said it even though she knew that it would never happen. She couldn't bring herself to tell the truth. The lie left a hollow in her heart for a year.

But she still wanted to see the world, and she did see it. Then something happened—what was it?—that dashed her to her destruction. It may have been insignificant, a minor event, the kind of thing that can happen on any trip.

Anna thinks about Ella. She even dares to think about Linda. *See you tomorrow.*

Then she looks at her cell phone—accidentally, reflexively— and sees that she has a message.

A premonition.

22

IT ALL STARTED with a harmless phone call.

Eleonoora hung up her coat, closed her locker door, and slipped out of her loose pants and open-necked shirt. She thought she might just *be* for a moment, go for a walk on the beach, look at the seagulls floating in the air as if they were hung there. Then the phone rang.

Her first thought was: Mom.

It was an unknown number. She answered more testily than she meant to. It was Rautalampi from the art supply store calling about a painting Anna had brought in to be framed. Eleonoora let her worry drop away.

"The Ahlqvist that one of you brought in," Rautalampi began.

For some reason he always referred to both Dad and Dad's paintings this way—Ahlqvist. She wasn't always sure if he was talking about the man or the art. Maybe that was intentional.

"It wasn't me," Eleonoora said. "It was my daughter Anna, remember? She wanted to have it framed for herself. I don't have anything to do with it. Is it ready?"

"Well, actually . . ."

"Yes?"

"It's the strangest thing, I'm telling you . . ."

"Did you call Anna? The picture's for her, so I'm sure she'd like to decide about the frame and everything."

"Right," he said. "I hear you. I tried to call her, but I couldn't get hold of her. I thought about calling your father."

"This has nothing to do with him. I don't think he's particularly interested in the picture. He said we could dispose of all the paintings at Tammilehto."

"This one's a bit complicated."

Now she was getting annoyed. When she was stressed she unconsciously took a certain attitude toward people in certain professions—bank tellers, grocery clerks, boys who worked at gas stations and couldn't find blades to fit her windshield wipers. She always got control of her prickliness too late, after she'd already blown up at them. Every time it happened she would remember when she was little and she threw a tantrum because she wasn't allowed to eat a chocolate bar that Rautalampi had given her before dinner. She wondered if Rautalampi saw this as the same childish temper, which annoyed her all the more.

"Well," she demanded. "Can you tell me what this is about? I'm in a hurry."

Not one to be moved by an angry or accusing tone, Rautalampi said firmly, "I think you'd better come see for yourself."

SHE DROVE DOWN the ramp from the hospital and turned left onto the shore road.

Her annoyance was directed at her father, although it was only his painting that had interrupted her day. Sometimes in her younger years she'd been infuriated at him for the very same thing. Who do you think you are? Can't you see that everything here revolves around you? You think you're so big, so all-important, so revered. In reality you're just a joke. You just use your art as an excuse to keep to yourself.

Her father had taken these outbursts surprisingly calmly— It's good that you don't idealize your parents, I guess.

When she opened the door of the art supply store, Rautalampi looked at her over his glasses.

"So."

"So," she replied tersely.

"I was taking the canvas off its stretcher bars," he said.

"I hope you haven't damaged it?"

He gave her a scathing look, a look that said, *I do not damage paintings. What do you think I am, a clumsy child?*

"Just come and look at it."

The frame shop was in the back of the store. Familiar smells of glue and wooden lath filled the room as they always had, as if there were no time.

Rautalampi moved the easel. The painting Eleonoora saw wasn't the one with the oranges.

Rautalampi, who had always eschewed drama of any kind, with his whole being, kept talking, like a grocer discussing an overshipment of coffee.

"There was a little buckle in the canvas. It happens sometimes. I took the top canvas off as well as I could. It's there on the table. It can be restretched, of course. But you'll need to decide what you want to do with this other

one. It's been under here for years, so it's amazingly un-
scathed. That's why I wanted you to come see it. It's actually an unusual work for Ahlqvist. I don't know if he had
any reason for wanting to cover it up. Maybe it was some
kind of experiment. He clearly had a model. You can see it
in the peculiar stylistic fumbling. It's almost like a caricature. It's undoubtedly an adaptation, but I don't know from
what. He seems to be unable to choose a technique—he's
combined several here, not with any great success, if you
don't mind my saying so. Now you have to decide what to
do with it. Shall I call your father or should we leave the
painting here? You can't really call it a completed work,
it's too unfinished. But it's not my place to determine the
worth of the pieces that come in."

The woman in the painting was looking into Eleonoora's
eyes.

Rautalampi coughed at the same moment that the shop
door squeaked. Someone entered, and Rautalampi said he
would be right back.

Eleonoora stood in front of the painting for a moment.
Then she turned, saw a chair in the corner, and sat down.
She actually wished someone would come and cover the
painting up. But no one came.

It was Eeva looking at her, and no matter how hard she
tried, she couldn't stop looking back.

TO BE UNREACHABLE, to be indifferent to everything,
these were the only ways Eleonoora knew to express anger.
She walked without any particular destination. The sea was

a level wall sparkling dazzlingly. The anger came in a wave of nausea, in flashes of memory.

Two hours later she stopped and looked at her phone. Nine calls. Some from her father, some from the phone in the apartment on Sammonkatu, some from an unknown number. The screen blinked. Anna. Maybe it wasn't a coincidence—Anna had tried to call her earlier.

The phone fell out of her hand. She didn't intend to pick it up. Then she changed her mind—perhaps she guessed what Anna was going to tell her—and she picked it up off the ground.

She spoke without asking why Anna was calling, without explaining what she meant: "I saw Eeva. In a picture."

Anna was silent. Anna knew! Anna wasn't denying that she knew!

"Grandma told me about her," Anna said. "And Grandpa. They told me about Eeva."

Eleonoora had just one thing to say to her: "I don't want to talk to you. I can't bear to see you right now."

Anna paid no attention to what she said. "Grandpa has tried to call you several times. He finally called me. Grandma's dead."

1967

THE LITTLE GIRL is sitting on the swing kicking her legs. It's already October.

The little girl's mother wouldn't have allowed it, but she begged, asking again and again, finally crying, lying on the floor and kicking for a long time. Finally her mother asked me to come.

"Half an hour," she said. "In the yard. You can't come inside."

I walk through the gate, her mother looks at me, comes out the door. She leaves the two of us. The little girl doesn't look at me and seems not to care. She's grown, even though it's only been a couple of weeks. She has on a red coat and shoes appropriate to the fall weather. The days have been chilly.

I have to look at her very closely. I have to take in her every gesture, the lines of her face, still only half formed. I go and sit on the swing next to hers.

"Why are you wearing a coat?" she asks.

"Because the weather's getting cooler. You have one on, too."

"Oh, yeah," she says.

She picks up some speed. Her legs bend and straighten and bend again. The swing creaks a little.

"Mommy said that I can swing a little higher because I'm getting to be a big girl."

"That's right," I say.

"Can I come over to your house?" she asks suddenly. "To spend the night?"

"No, not today. You have to stay home today."

"Tomorrow," she says. "Can I come tomorrow?"

"Well, maybe," I lie.

She swings faster. The squeak of the chain sounds frenzied, resolute. Her gaze is focused—she's looking at the door. She swings forward, backward, forward, backward.

"I can come to your house," she says. "I'll ask my mom and dad. We can build a fort."

For a moment I, too, believe that this is possible. She'll come and we'll spend the day the way we often have. I hear myself lie to her, because there's nothing else I can do: "OK. You can come over tomorrow."

"Can I spend the night?" she asks.

"Yes. Maybe you can spend the night."

Ella hops down off the swing. I try to force a smile. "Let's go," I say. "Your mom and dad must be waiting for you."

"It's fall and there's apples in the trees," she says. "We went to the park yesterday and Mommy said that you can make jelly out of them. We're going to make jelly next week. Daddy says jelly is the best thing he knows of. He puts lots of sugar in it. We'll put the jelly on our rolls, and sugar, too. Daddy's going to put as much on as I am. Mommy said that I can't see you anymore, but she doesn't know that I'm coming over to spend the night."

"Mm-hmm."

I nod. I can't cry yet.

"So I'll come over tomorrow," Linda repeats.

"Yeah. See you tomorrow."

Linda's lip trembles. I see a very new expression on her face before she starts to cry. I take her in my arms for the last time. For a moment she doesn't say anything, just sobs.

"We'll build a fort," she says.

"Yes, let's build a fort." I say.

"What if Mommy and Daddy come, too?" she asks. "Can they come too?"

"Maybe," I say.

"And we can sleep with you in the fort," she suggests. She looks at me, thinks of a solution. "Mommy and Daddy can go home and I'll stay at your house and we'll sleep in the fort."

"Let's do that."

"Will you sleep beside me all night long?"

"Yes. I'll be beside you all night long."

She's satisfied with this. We have a plan. She sniffles. I don't let my own tears come yet.

"I'm going to go upstairs now," Linda says.

"Off you go."

She runs to the door. I sit on the swing and watch her go. She pulls on the door handle. She's so short that she can only open it with difficulty. Before she goes in, she turns around again.

"Bye! See you tomorrow!" she shouts.

She's not crying anymore. She's smiling.

Then she's gone. I sit on the swing a little longer before I get up and walk across the yard and out through the gate.

When I get to the street I speed up to a run and for a moment I can't see what's in front of me.

23

ELSA DIED SUDDENLY. The death surprised Martti, even though he knew it was coming. Just that morning she had been in good spirits.

They'd had new potatoes for lunch and Elsa had marveled at how many she could eat. After lunch she wanted to dance, and Martti cranked up the old record player.

Their dancing was just a rocking, Elsa leaning against him and he against her. He remembered how she had felt on their first evening. Lauri had asked her to dance first, and Martti had watched her back. She had a lovely furrow between her shoulder blades. He looked at her neck, at the two dark curls on her forehead, damp from the thick air.

Elsa had seemed assertive, strong, like a country girl who could carry a milk can and herd cows to pasture with an expert hand. He was surprised when she told him she grew up here in Helsinki, in Eira, the daughter of a university instructor and a language teacher.

A broad face, peculiar, thick eyebrows, and dark, wavy hair. Full lips and a little gap between her front teeth. A sweet smile—calm, the kind of smile that made you think there was nothing to be afraid of, not even the sorrows that would inevitably come if you lived long enough.

Elsa was still rocking against him. The record had come to the end. There was the sound of a lawn mower in the yard.

"Summer," she whispered.

The dance changed to an embrace.

"I probably won't be up for strawberry season."

"You never know."

The lawn mower hummed, a breeze blew in the window. The floor creaked a little under their feet. Then the phone rang.

He answered it. Elsa sat down on the sofa and looked like she was listening. It was Rautalampi from the art supply store. Unaware of his role as messenger, he told him about Eleonoora's visit. She left kind of abruptly, Rautalampi said. She just took off. So what should I do with the painting— the sketch? A second passed before Martti understood what Rautalampi was talking about. Then he remembered. Martti said he'd think about it and call back later. He noticed that he sounded calm.

He hung up and looked at Elsa. When he'd told her what it was about—she had already guessed somehow, it seemed—she said, "I have to call Eleonoora. I have to call her right now."

She called six times. She tried calling from their land line, then from her own cell phone, then from his. No answer. She stood for a moment without moving. Then she took several steps, looked around as if she were searching for the door in an unfamiliar room, and sat down.

"Are you feeling bad?"

"A little," she said. "A little bad."

"Are you in pain?" he asked. "Where does it hurt?"

She went to lie down, closed her eyes. Her breathing was a little uneven, as if she were short of breath.

"It's hard to breathe," she managed to say. "A little. A little difficult."

In the ambulance, before they put the mask over her face, she squeezed his hand and said: "I'm not sure exactly what I should ask forgiveness for. The things left unsaid? But I want to have a chance to work this out."

He squeezed her hand and nodded, because he didn't know what to say.

Then she said, "You ask forgiveness, if I don't get the chance."

In the hospital, Elsa was hooked up to a lung and heart monitor. Martti sat beside her. As soon as they'd arrived he had asked the nurse to call Eleonoora again. Elsa reached out her hand and put it over his. Her hand felt light and cold. It was difficult to hear her breathing.

"Are they going to call her?" she said. "Maybe they can try again."

"They tried, she didn't answer."

HE REMEMBERED ANOTHER time when Elsa had held his hand. She had been strong then, obstinate, contradicting him. He'd often thought of her standing in the doorway, preventing him from leaving. He remembered everything about her on that day, every detail. She was wearing a light green shirt, her hair up, her cheeks red with rage and lips tight, not long before she forbade him to leave.

She took his hand. He just wanted to leave. He wanted to push her out of the way. Her resolute gaze opposed him.

He had to push her to get out the door. He shoved her to the side.

A few days after he came back, she got sick. Her fever rose sharply. He tucked Elsa in, put Ella to bed, read her a story, and waited for her to go to sleep. When he came back into the living room to make sure everything was all right, he heard the rhythm of Elsa's breath as she slept, saw the redness of fever in her cheeks, and love flooded him, perhaps stronger than ever, pushing everything else away. He undressed, careful not to disturb her, pulled the blanket aside and settled beside Elsa, held onto Elsa and felt her damp skin under her nightshirt. She bent her knees in her sleep. He wrapped himself around her.

She muttered, Don't leave. Stay here. Maybe she was delirious with fever. But it was a request, not an order. He wanted to be asked.

"**WILL YOU COME** over here?" Elsa said, lightly patting the sheet on the hospital bed.

He looked at the door, as if asking permission. He sat on the bed, moved her over a little—it was difficult but he made a space for himself and lay down.

If you closed your eyes you could think it was any ordinary morning before getting up—the light outside the window, vague plans for the day at the edges of your thoughts.

"Don't go," Elsa said. "Don't go anywhere."

"I won't. I'll stay right here."

Her breathing eased before the collapse. Martti had almost started to get used to its feverish sound. Now the silence felt disturbing. He was afraid to go to sleep.

Maybe he did fall asleep for a moment. Elsa was unmoving. The actual death, the event itself, wasn't peaceful. The doctor said afterward that her organs seemed to have gone into shock, ceasing to function one by one very rapidly.

But it felt to Martti that she had already left by then, a moment before her physical death. Her departure was peaceful. Elsa opened her eyes, and closed them.

He'd seen her do that a thousand times. He held his hand over hers and looked at her. Her form froze, as if taking its last shape, taking its place. It looked as if she was gathering up her weight, her moments, her years, there next to him.

She said very wearily, "You'll stay if I sleep a little?"

"I'll stay. I'll stay right here."

1968

SPRING. I SLOWLY start to breathe again.

The winter was cold and slippery, now and then open and drafty, as if the city were a great hall in an abandoned mansion. The whole first part of the year I felt like my limbs were from a previous century, like my head belonged in a museum, among the fragile objects there, in a glass case.

Sadness had made its porous dwelling inside me. I walked down the streets looking for the little girl, for the man. I never saw them.

I met him in February. We walked—I was on my lunch break and only had half an hour. We went to the park, Kaivopuisto. Then he went on his way and I walked back to the school through the bright day, watching my limbs through the thin air. They felt like they were floating, like they belonged to someone else.

BUT SUDDENLY IT'S spring again and everything is humming. The television in the teachers' room throws images of growing restlessness against the walls, the newspapers start to talk about riots. I teach words to impatient young people from the south part of the city, write the words in French on the blackboard that I could be saying to the people in the streets right now. Why don't I just go? Why am I not already there? What am I waiting for?

Aujourd'hui. Aujourd'hui.

Written there with the screeching chalk, it looks like a prayer.

On the sixteenth of April I get a letter from Marc. He writes to me now and then. He has a lot of ideas, mostly having to do with essential research into the methods of love. In this letter he suggests that I come in the summer and stay with him in Paris.

Katariina would like to go now. Any kind of travel suits her. Of course we'll end up in Paris, she says. Everybody ends up in Paris! She talks about the city as if it were an unavoidable destination for us, the way marriage was for our mothers.

We decide to go by boat because Katariina can't afford to fly. Marc telegrams persistently and says he'll come to meet us. Maybe in Stockholm, maybe even in Finland. What does it matter? He has time. He's even got some money. I telegram back: See you in Stockholm.

Can I love him? Maybe I can. I'm a woman of today, more than I've ever been before. Sometimes a person wants a change so much that she stops being afraid altogether.

KATARIINA'S FRIEND LAYLAH can put us up in Stockholm for a few nights. Laylah's brother Piet has an apartment in Amsterdam where we can stay as long as we like. We have a plan: Laylah—Stockholm, Piet—Amsterdam, then Paris.

I think about Kuhmo, the attic there, the bright nights between cool sheets. The cuckoo calling as I lay down my head.

Kuhmo is just an idea, an idea that I reject.

"Let's do it," I say.

AT THE BEGINNING of June I withdraw all the money from my bank account—my pay for March, April, and May. I've saved a thousand from my years working on Sammonkatu, and another thousand since then. I withdraw that, too. Maybe I have nothing else to show for my years as a nanny, maybe it's left me feeling hollow and forlorn, but at least I have a bank account I can close out. I pay the rent for the apartment on Pengerkatu and change the rest of the money to dollars. I have a thousand francs' worth.

When I get back home, I look at the pile of money. Pieces of paper worth thousands of marks.

I pack pants and bright-colored T-shirts. I leave my skirt at home—thick fabric clumsily sewn by my mother. It doesn't belong in a place where the nightingale sings in another language. It belongs in the closet, collecting dust.

After a moment's thought, I bring along the man's drawing, the one he did at the museum before it all started. I put it between the pages of my diary.

I pack my diary among my clothes. I've let the sadness flow black onto the paper for an entire year, written the little girl's laugh and the way the man curls his toes into its lines. I won't leave that here, I'll bring our story with me to dusty corners and cafes, spill soda or tea or Armagnac on its pages, and it won't matter at all! I'll bring my story to a great city and it will change, become mere ink marks on a page. I'll write other words after these, and little by little they'll become true. *Aujourd'hui, elle va être heureuse.*

WHEN WE REACH the other side of the Gulf of Bothnia, Laylah is there to meet us. She waves to us from a long way off and runs to greet us. She's darker than any person I've ever seen. When she laughs her teeth glow. She lives in a messy flat in Söder with Agneta and Maj-Lis. Mmkemba isn't home—he's from somewhere in Africa. Mmkemba is even blacker than Laylah and I can't stop looking at him.

We're waiting for Marc, he's supposed to meet us at the park at six. He arrives at five after six with a guitar. I had forgotten his eyes—not a trace of seriousness!

He has all the requisites of a dreamer: in addition to the guitar a bright-colored shirt and a vest that looks like it came from a sheep that was only just recently gamboling through the fields.

He smiles. I'd forgotten his smile, too. My doubts, if I had any, melt away right down to my feet.

"Evá," he says.

Yes, I think. Yes, I'll let it come if it's coming.

THAT EVENING LAYLAH makes some kind of risotto out of corn and grains with cinnamon and pepper and spices mixed in that makes my tongue feel grilled. We eat on the floor. I get drunk from the wine, a calm hovers over us, and Mmkemba's eyes look like white pearls.

Marc talks about expanding consciousness. I listen, although I'm suddenly at the edge of a meadow, the meadow of my childhood, the one where my sister Liisa and I gathered seven kinds of flowers to put under our pillows on Midsummer.

A drop of water, plump at the end of a blade of grass, the sun flashing beyond the spruce trees. That's where I am. I've actually never been anywhere else but at the edge of this meadow. It's Midsummer Eve and Liisa and I are guessing the names of boys before we seal our lips because the magic says that you have to be silent when you pick the flowers if you want to see your future husband in your dreams. We have the meadow. The drop of water. The sky that we run through, neither letting go of the other's hand.

Marc persuades me to unbutton my jeans and pull my shirt off over my head. Yes, I remember what it was like with him. His flat nipples like the eyes of violets. I want to throw myself into it, but I've traveled all the way across northern Europe without taking a bath once and first I'd like to take off his sheepskin vest.

"You know what? I want to wash you."

"Why not?" he answers. "The last time I had a bath was in Berlin."

I don't ask when that was, but I lead him into the bathroom. Laylah, Agneta, and Maj-Lis sit cross-legged on the living room floor smoking and talking in low voices, Katariina and Mmkemba are nowhere to be seen. Marc and I tiptoe across the living room.

I pour pine scent into the bathtub.

"All right."

Marc steps into the bath fervently, like he's repenting of his sins. He shows me two scars that he got from a dog bite in the riots in May.

I scrub his back with a sponge.

"You could have kids. You'd be good with kids. You take care of me like you're someone's mother."

"I'm not."

I wash Marc until I find the boy inside. I dry him off. He looks like something just invented as I let him approach.

I look at his nipples again, eyes of violets on his chest, as I sail into and out of him.

Maybe love begins with tender feelings like these. It begins with what the womb knows and reaches out from there to the fingertips, the ends of your toes, to my lips that smile at his words.

"*Je t'aime*," he says.

"We haven't seen each other in years."

"But you're so beautiful."

WE BOARD A train two days later. I haven't yet started to disappear.

The landscape changes, turns to more open fields and farms. Sometimes it's like in the North, then it starts to look like Europe. We go from the train to a ship in Göteborg. Thomas and Paul join the group at the harbor. They offer us a drink. Thomas looks at Katariina's breasts and Katariina looks at Thomas as if she wants to stab him with a knife.

"Finland?" he says.

"In the lap of the Soviet Union," Paul says.

"Or perhaps you're just in its embrace," Thomas adds.

"Neither one," Katariina says. "A friend. It's a question of friendship. There's a difference."

"Whatever," one of them says with a shrug. "What about all this fuss that's going on? Has it reached as far as your latitude yet? Are your students starting a rebellion, too?"

"Even as we speak," Katariina says.

"What about products?" Paul asks. "Do you have to bring your own ballpoint pen when you go to Finland?"

"We've got ballpoint pens coming out of our ears," Katariina says. "And there's no shortage of television or records or orange juice. Everything's just lovely."

"And yet you left," Thomas says. "You're looking for something elsewhere."

He taps his forehead knowingly. Katariina snorts. She leans toward me as the men are ordering drinks.

"What idiots," she says. "They don't know anything about anything."

IT'S FULL SUMMER when we arrive in Amsterdam. We sit next to canals, at kitchen tables, in cafes. Laylah's brother Piet lives in a messy apartment much like Laylah's commune in Söder. Multicolored walls and records everywhere, dirty dishes and mattresses on the floor. I don't leave my things around the house—you never know who might come through the door. I decide to carry everything with me—clothes, the diary that I've written *aujourd'hui* in ten times now, marking off each day, the drawing pressed between its pages. I put part of my money in it, too.

A small part, and a few hundred dollars under the mattress— if it disappears, so be it.

AT NIGHT I make my way toward Marc and he opens me again and again and I start to trust that the whole world is possible for those who say *oui*.

I say it many times in Marc's arms, in a dark room with Catherine Deneuve looking down from the wall. I saw a movie last year where she played a housewife who joins a bordello. Did she learn pleasure in the arms of a stranger among the velvet drapes? I don't know and I don't care because for this moment all I have is yes and a swirling upward spiral.

KATARIINA HAS HEARD that some people are planning to meet at Spui Square. On the third day she disappears and goes her own way for a whole day.

Marc and I can't be bothered with Spui Square until the evening. Marc says true rebellion is enjoying your existence no matter what the circumstances. So we just stroll around and get lost in the red-light district. Marc says that when he was little his mother used to buy flowers and bread from the market on Saturdays. They lived in the Eighth Arrondissement of Paris and walked past the Moulin Rouge every Saturday morning cutting across a little street on their way to the market. His mother would hold his hand when they passed by the whores. The roses were red. The same red in the roses and on the girls' lips, he says. For a long time he thought that was how it should be, that those two reds had something in common that no one had told him about.

And they did, he says. It was the color of beauty, of pleasure. Really the color of love.

Marc and I weave our way between the canals, sit together for a moment in a cafe and then another. We eat roast beef and country bread and salad. We buy wine without asking the price. I pay because Marc doesn't really have any money right now. He watches me as I open my wallet looking for money for the waitress.

"You've become so independent. I wouldn't have recognized you. You act like you own the world."

"I don't own it, I'm just getting to know it."

Marc smiles and kisses me and says *je t'aime*. I already believe him, and answer him. He's playing the guitar and making up a song about me.

"You can compose it while I go to the women's room," I say.

"Maybe I'll start singing and gather a crowd of admirers," he says.

When I get back to the table, Marc has disappeared. The guitar is gone. There's nothing but the dirty dishes on the table. My bag is gone, too. Not just the money, the whole bag. The diary, the drawing of me—gone.

I ask the waitress if she saw Marc leave. Did he say he was going out? Did he say whether he was coming back? She shakes her head.

I find a note on a corner of the table.

Don't think badly of me. I needed the cash. It was beautiful while it lasted.

Love! Peace! M.

I run into the street. Nothing. I run around the corner. I find my bag. It's been ransacked; the money—dollars and francs—was in the diary, he saw me take it out from between the pages in Copenhagen, and in Cologne when I changed crowns to deutschmarks. The book isn't in the bag. Marc has taken it. Not just the money, the whole book, the drawing, the words, everything. Every one of my words has been taken.

I sit down in a slump. The air slumps inside me. The world runs down the storm drain.

I walk up and down bridges all day, asking passersby for money for coffee and a roll. I walk several kilometers to Piet's commune thinking about how to tell Katariina. When I get there I look at Catherine Deneuve's face and ask her advice. But what advice could she give? In the film I saw she was drowning herself in pleasure! I count my money. It's enough to last a little while. I don't have to tell Katariina before Paris.

Katariina comes back late at night. I tell her that Marc won't be coming here anymore. I don't say anything more.

"Why in the world not? You two seemed to be in love."

"It wasn't love. It was something else."

Katariina turns away from me for a moment. I see something in the corner of her eye, an expression I can't interpret.

I think about the diary. About the drawing. Why did I bring them with me? I should have left them at Pengerkatu.

Now there's nothing at Pengerkatu but an old skirt sewn from thick fabric. It's hanging in the closet with no purpose.

WE BOARD THE train. I have money for the ticket, maybe a sandwich, tea or juice. I calculate that I'll have to tell Katariina before we arrive in Paris.

It starts after we go through Brussels. I feel sick, nausea coming in waves. The walls press in on me and the windows lean toward me. Soon I'm lying on the floor, then bent double, heaving over the toilet in the cramped WC. I lie next to a wall. I don't know how much time passes. Katariina gives me some water to drink the way I used to give milk to the calves at home.

My mouth turns to sandpaper, my lips shrivel as if I'm crossing a desert.

We cross the French border. My head feels heavy, my limbs weigh me down. My tongue swells up. My words turn gooey. There's sawdust in my throat and I shiver under my blanket, although the day is hot. I doze and waken. Mumble in my sleep.

Katariina buys me some tea from the restaurant car, but it stings. I try to keep my eyes open but they've swollen shut. I look at my reflection in the mirror behind the counter and see red splotches all over my face. What's wrong with me?

Katariina looks at me with worry and weighs her options. She's distressed. She doesn't want to get off the train and she doesn't want to leave me alone.

"Maybe I should get off here," I say, and every word hurts my mouth. I have to talk slowly, place each word carefully.

"Maybe you should go on without me. I can stay here and try to heal up somewhere, go to a hotel, or a hostel, anywhere."

Katariina thinks for a minute. "No," she says, shaking her head. "Let's both get off."

I nod. "Thanks."

WE GET OFF at a station whose name is difficult to pronounce. People stare at us. Some men who are playing dominos at a table that they've carried out to the street yell after us.

There's no time here. There's country bread, pork chop soup, apple pies baking, a rooster strutting around the yard and a bird jabbering in its tree, bored, with nothing to do.

The hostel is a dump. Cockroaches scuttle into cracks in the corners, a drunken man whose wife has run off with a gypsy fiddler is making a ruckus in the stairway. We're on the border of two countries. Paris is just a rumor here. The revolution is a hundred years away.

Night comes, then day. I lay my head on a pillow that smells of cigarettes and onions and hopes that disappeared into the cracks between the floorboards. I fall, spill off the side of the bed and crash into pieces on the floor. Katariina brings me yogurt that I throw up, potatoes that I can't bear to have near me, cabbage soup, whitefish, finally white bread dipped in juice and fed to me in little pieces so I can swallow it.

I drink water in small sips.

I see him standing in the doorway. I try to get up, but can't. Suddenly he's my father. He says that I left my little sister in the cradle to die, the one who died when she was three months old, when I was five, the one I've always carried with me like a silent twin or a painful wound.

I see my little sister in the corner. Suddenly she's Ella.

Ella walks across the room with Molla in her arms and leans toward me but I can't get hold of her. Then she's my baby sister again. She keeps dying in the cradle again and again and disappearing as if she was made of sugar the whole time.

The sky leans down outside the window. I try to open my eyes but the dream hasn't come to the end yet. I'm far away. A little girl comes up next to me.

"Where's Molla?" I ask.

"I've lost her," she says.

"I'll find her for you."

I can speak to the girl in a silent language. It doesn't hurt to talk to her.

"Who are you talking to?" Katariina asks.

"I don't know."

ON THE FOURTH morning after I got sick, my throat swells shut. I try to say something, but I can't. Katariina looks at me, her brow furrowed.

"I'm calling a doctor."

She pays the doctor with enough francs for a train ticket. I stand chilled in the middle of the floor with my ribs sharp against the cool air. The doctor puts his stethoscope on my back like a stamp. Breathe in, he says and I wheeze. Now out. I wheeze again. Say aah, he says, and I try. No sound comes out.

I can't straighten my knees, I've shrunk ten centimeters. "What is it?" Katariina asks.

The doctor shrugs. "It could be diphtheria. Or even polio. Sometimes it causes a fever. You never know."

"What do you mean you don't know?" Katariina asks. "What do you mean? You're the expert, aren't you?"

The doctor is annoyed. He isn't going to let this little lady give him orders. He leaves without saying another word, but comes back half an hour later. He's mixed a solution for me to take. I have to take it every three hours.

On the fifth morning, I wake up. Katariina brings me some tea and a little cake. She's begged them from the strict woman who runs the hostel, who doesn't want to have anything to do with the shady things of the world, although she seems to take pity on a lot of people in the hostel who have no food. I eat one of the cakes and gulp the tea.

"Feel better?"

I try to say yes. I can't get the word out, but I nod.

Katariina sits on the edge of the bed.

I move my hand, trying to get her to bring me a pen. Finally she understands. She looks for some paper, finds a tissue.

I write with a steady hand: You can go if you want to. I'm feeling better now.

"No. I'm not going to leave," she says decisively.

I write: You should.

"Will you be all right?" she says.

I can see that she wants to leave but she wants to stay. She's pulled in two directions. I write one more time: *Go.*

Finally she nods. "Thanks," she says.

She's relieved, although she doesn't say so. She wants to be where everything's happening, she's restless, feels like the world is someplace else.

I start to feel better. I eat a whole loaf of bread and go out for short walks. How bright it is. The sky is wailing. I think about my diary, my drawing. Where are they?

They're lying in a garbage can in some city whose name no one knows. Marc carried the book with him for a short time until he got tired of its Finnish gibberish and threw it away. That's where my words are—in a trash can. Someone comes and picks up the book and tries to read it. It's in a foreign language, they think, a language nobody speaks. Then this stranger looks at the drawing; what a happy woman in the picture!

Katariina has already packed her things. Her smile makes the air jingle. We order lemon soda from the little restaurant in the courtyard—the only one in the village. Katariina talks about everything she plans to do, all kinds of things that she isn't yet sure about. I answer with nods. I write a few yeses on my napkin, and one no when she asks me if I still feel sick.

Then she leaves. We hug, she kisses me on both cheeks like they do here.

I squeeze her tight.

"You've shrunk to half your size," she says with a worried scowl. "You should go straight to Kuhmo when you get back to Finland. Go eat pancakes made with the first milk. Herrings in cream and potatoes. Your mother can make you Karelian stew, strawberry pie, the kind with whipped cream on top. Cocoa and cinnamon rolls. You'll get your strength back. When I come see you in the fall you'll be your old self again and we'll go to Kosmos and order blinis and vorschmack, spend the whole evening. Everything will be like it used to be."

I would say yes if I could. But my voice hasn't come back, and it never will. I smile.

This is the moment when the future is created, the moment when the past is destroyed and a new world is created. Katariina leaves and I turn.

SHE GETS ON the train, finally makes it to Paris, but the revolution is already somewhere else, in another city, as revolutions always are. She gets bored, wanders for a few days in Montmartre and hangs around the Sorbonne ready to rebel if the rebellion's coming. But no rebellion comes. Tourists come, other people like her. Housewives and professors, pigeons, winos, everyone who inhabits the streets when there's no one making a ruckus. Katariina eats croissants for breakfast and spends the day with a boy she meets named Fabien, who steals her money while she's in the women's room. She's a little upset about it, but she figures these things happen. She lolls in the park behind Notre Dame without any money eating baguettes with nothing on them and writes a few fumbling thoughts in her diary. She doesn't hear from Laylah although they had planned to meet. She sends her two telegrams. Finally she meets Lies at a metro station, holding a newspaper over her head to keep the rain off, and goes with her to West Berlin.

Lies lets Katariina sleep on her sofa and she stays all summer. Their door is always open to anyone who wants to come. And people do come—Hans and Anne and several others. Katariina hears new ideas inside these walls, sings different songs, and memorizes conditional statements—if A then B—statements she's never heard before. She swallows them without choking because she's been looking for something like this. Maybe she's been looking for certainty, the kinds of statements that close off alternatives. The excitement she feels when she recites these statements is akin to the way she felt performing in her high school play. When the lights were lowered and the play began, she felt a strange joy. She felt like anything could happen, and at the same time like she was safe, completely safe.

And in Berlin, inside these walls, making these statements and trying out her raised fist, Katariina feels the same peace and joy.

SHE SENDS ME six postcards. I receive the first two but I don't have the strength to answer them. The last four cards lie on the floor under the mail slot on Pengerkatu, in the dark. Silverfish scurry over them, dust collects on these notes from the wide world until my mother and father and Liisa muster the strength to come and clean out the apartment.

It's at that moment, when they've found the cards, the last one reading, "Why don't you answer?!" that Liisa finally sends Katariina a telegram.

After Katariina receives the telegram, she sits on a park bench in Berlin and feels a strange lightness. There's other news, news about an occupation, tanks headed south out of Berlin, but she doesn't want to think about that. She only has one piece of news in her mind. The sadness hasn't come yet. She's able to get up like it's any other day. She's able to walk down the street, stop at a cafe, smoke a cigarette if she happens to have one.

She lights a cigarette. Actually, she thinks, she knew when they were at the station, talking about pancakes and cinnamon rolls. Maybe that's why she talked in such a carefree way. She wanted to cover up the thought.

Endings aren't desolate and quiet. Endings are ordinary, noisy, a boy running across the street to pick up the evening's bottles of beer at the cafe.

Katariina knows she'll be on Lies's living room floor this evening, compressed to the size of a fist. She'll feel a hint of sadness at the moment when she notices that the labels on the beer are bright green. Amazingly green, as if they were made of acres of rain-drenched grass.

BUT AT THIS moment, as the future is still being created, as the previous world is destroyed and a new one is made, as I'm turning and she's leaving, Katariina still doesn't know, and neither do I. There's still the little village with a name that's impossible to pronounce, still the station in the nameless village.

Katariina gets on the train and I wave. Then I turn and go back to my little room. My train will leave in the evening. I'll go to Hamburg and from there to the harbor to catch a boat home. I buy my boat ticket with the last of my money, writing the name of my destination on a piece of paper. I write the city and then add "home."

It starts again on the boat. I'm floating. The sea is rising up against me. I don't know if I exist anymore.

I've vanished, faded away to invisibility. When I arrive in Helsinki, I'm just a rumor, a story somebody told once.

The smell of herring in the stairwell, echoes from the apartments, all of it cancels me out. I open the door. There's a knee-high pile of mail. I set my bags down on the floor. I close the curtains. Take off my clothes. I'm ancient. I could pull up the floorboards and lie down under them, forgotten.

I lay down my head.

On the seventh day I take the tram to the hospital. I have to lean my head against the tram window. The trees are nodding, the city is a stage set. Is it already August?

The tram route is familiar. I think I see the little girl. Maybe it's not her, just someone who looks like her. She's grown, taken on her mother's features. She has dimples and caterpillar eyebrows. For a moment I think about going and getting her. I could bring her home with me, feed her sweet rolls and milk. Then we could leave, take a boat or a plane somewhere. She would cry for two weeks and ask for her mother and father. On the third week she wouldn't cry anymore.

I feel twinges of pain, a heaviness. I'm made to lie down in a quiet private room because the doctors hear that I've been traveling. They think that I've acquired an unknown infection. They prod my throat with a cardboard stick and shine a little light into the cave of my mouth.

"Nothing out of the ordinary," the doctor says. "Just an infection. It may have spread to the pharynx."

They bring in a specialist. He has a beard, his name is Nylander.

"It's in the vocal cords," Nylander says. His beard is friendlier than the other doctor's. "It's not in the larynx anymore, it's in the vocal cords."

The other doctor nods.

They do more tests on me. My arms are crisscrossed like needlepoint. They weigh me and say I'm lighter than the week before. They measure me and write the figure down. My blood pressure is low, my heart sounds like it's fluttering to the rhythm of a shadowy woman. A dream woman.

The doctor doesn't know about the women of the dream world.

"There's an echo," he says. "A certain echo. It could be the reason for your symptoms."

They take me to a white room. My mother and father have been notified. They come, and so does Liisa. I think it's some kind of interrogation, I'm confused from the medication and desolation, I answer their accusations by blinking my eyes twice for yes. It's always good to say yes, just in case—to agree to anything.

Yes, I say with my eyes. Yes. Yes.

It's good to become affirmative, when all other means are lost.

My mother says, "There must be something you can do. She was always such a vigorous girl. She was strong, working in the barn morning and night."

"That doesn't matter," the doctor says. "A lot depends on the way she's been living the last few years."

My mother looks at me. She doesn't know a thing about how I've been living. She doesn't give up.

"We'll bring her home once she's well enough. The fresh air will help her heal. Lake water, steam from the sauna stove, milk from a new-calved cow."

"All right," the doctor says. "If that's what you want."

THE DAYS CRAWL by, sometimes whiz by, outside the window. The linden tree casts a shadow on the wall, I can see from the light that summer is full-grown.

I manage to walk around in the day room. I see tanks in the corner, in black and white. There's spiderwort at the window and flower print curtains and an invasion on the television. A person is lying on the ground, being run over. He looks like he's just stopped for a moment to look at the sky, fallen asleep, and then been changed into a bundle on some mysterious whim. Like he wanted for just a moment to be something other than skin and muscle and platelets and plans and fears. Like he wanted to be a still, quiet pile of cloth in the middle of a riot.

That's when it occurs to me for the first time.

"Gone crazy," an old man says. He has black gaps where his teeth should be. He smiles as if he were talking about doves. "This whole world is nuts," he says.

I nod. I would say it sure is if I had a voice to say it with. I would say, maybe we're the ones who are crazy, the ones who don't understand.

The sadness comes at night. I lie awake, although the white capsules should put me in a deep sleep. The ink flows into the room from the corners toward me. I imagine a meadow, Liisa and I at the edge of the meadow. I imagine a drop of water at the tip of a blade of grass, a sky, Liisa's hand reaching toward me. She won't let go of my hand. She turns into Ella, reaching toward me, and I won't let go of her hand, I won't.

MY SHOULDERS HUNCH over more and more each day. My hair falls out like I'm shedding dead leaves. The sadness grows dense as I grow thin. The medicine can't take hold in me.

They murmur among themselves at the end of the hallway, express their uncertainties about the diagnosis. After a week they decide to send me home.

I sit in the cool room and hear their final judgment.

"We can't find what your illness is. We don't know what's wrong with you. It's best that you go home since you aren't getting any better here. Get outdoors, eat, add cream to all your food. Drink milk. Keep working and try to get a grip on the world."

I get a glimpse of my chart; it has a word on it that I once heard a gossipy neighbor use to describe the Rahikainens' maidservant, who went around the village naked. Her daughter had died at birth, and she carried around a bag of potatoes wrapped in swaddling. They used that word for her, a word that sounded like a rare variety of plant, a whispered word, a word that counseled silence.

Hysss.

And I keep quiet. Absolutely silent. I don't say a word.

24

MARTTI SAT NEXT to Elsa for a long time. The sadness hadn't yet rubbed him into the cracks between the floorboards.

Elsa still had her ring on her finger. He thought for a minute about leaving it on, but then it occurred to him that it would be good to have it that evening when he went to sleep.

He reached out his hand and eased the ring from her finger. There was a pale stripe where the ring had been.

In the hallway, he saw Eleonoora. She looked like she'd been crying—she'd heard the news. He didn't dare to make a move to approach his daughter. He also could see that Eleonoora had heard about the thing they'd never spoken about. Anger, hatred, disappointment? He tried to find traces of her feelings in her eyes.

But what was he feeling? Regret? No. He remembered what the woman like a wise clown had told him in the hospital cafeteria: you should never regret your life, none of it.

He didn't take a step toward Eleonoora or reach out to touch her, he just held the ring tight in his right hand.

Eleonoora came closer. She didn't hug him.

"I'm too late," she said.

She said it with a sputter, like a child.

"She died. She just collapsed and died."

"I'm going to go look at her now," Eleonoora said.

They decided that she would come in the morning to dress Elsa for burial. He asked her if she wanted him to come, too. She shook her head. He agreed.

Eleonoora was shaking. It was all between them: betrayal, anger, love, all the accusations. Every memory was folded up between them so that even when they were standing face to face the decades separated them.

"I'll call the funeral parlor," she said.

"Good," he said.

When he got to the door he turned to her again. She looked small and frightened. He remembered how she was as a child when she was frightened or sad—her posture was somewhat like that now. Ella when she was six, her back a little bent, her head to one side, her eyes cast downward. As if she'd just discovered the existence of sadness, just sensed that she would have to bear it alone. That there was no one who could come and tell her how long it would last or what its limits were.

Should he have asked for forgiveness?

He wanted to ask for forgiveness for the pain he had caused his daughter, but did that mean that he regretted everything that had happened?

Then he remembered a fight that Eleonoora and Elsa once had. He couldn't remember the reasons for it. Eleonoora was fifteen—headstrong, ungovernable, impossible to control. Maybe Elsa had done something wrong, slapped the girl to make her come to her senses, and then apologized for her quick temper. Eleonoora would have none of it: *You can't say you're sorry if you don't mean that you were wrong. If you say you're sorry, you have to admit that I'm right, that I can live the way I want to.*

Elsa had looked at her calmly, and then said what she believed in: *No. An apology is a request to be seen as you are, in spite of what you've done. Responding to one is the deepest love a person is capable of.*

"I'm sorry," he said.

Eleonoora turned to look at him. His words bounced around the empty room.

"Please forgive me, for everything," he said.

Eleonoora looked at him, through him, opened the door and went inside, disappearing from view.

HE WALKED UNDER the linden trees, heard seagulls, cars, the shrill beep of the traffic signal. The door opened just like it always had. An early summer evening. It was the time of the year when the magic hadn't yet been shattered, when the light was limpid and time seemed to float.

He still held Elsa's ring in his fist.

He was having trouble seeing objects, went straight to the bedroom without looking around. He didn't want to see the bureau in the living room, the plate on the kitchen counter that Elsa had eaten from yesterday.

The air in the bedroom was a little stuffy. He tried not to look at the water glass on the night table. Elsa had drunk from it this morning.

He opened the window and sat on the bed. He looked at his own ring; should he take it off? He didn't want to. He wouldn't.

And now he allowed himself to really think about Elsa for the first time. Elsa on the evening they first met. He had been so nervous that he'd felt ill.

He had wanted to put it off, still wasn't sure about anything. He had fiddled with his cap and walked along beside her pointing out the birds he had learned from his father as a boy. He even said, I learned that one from my father before he died.

He had walked half a meter away from her, not daring to get any closer. He couldn't make any mistakes. He had to do everything right, he couldn't afford to lose this girl because their love was just beginning, he knew it when he noticed himself feeling calm and terrified at the same time, clumsier than he'd ever felt, shivering like a newborn.

Martti looked at the glass on the night table. The open window swung a bit on its hinges, a bird sang outside in the park. He didn't dare to make a move. He still had Elsa's face. If he made the slightest careless gesture, she would disappear.

The water glass, the wall, the window, the package of pills on the table, the pain pump, the bird in the tree.

He had wanted to be a gentleman and had walked her home. A bright moment at the end of spring with the city all around them, dozing quietly but nevertheless awake, as if in a daydream or a peculiar, alert sort of narcosis.

I want to marry this girl, he had thought. When they got to her house she surprised him by inviting him in.

She invited him into her room and showed him the collection of poems they'd been talking about. And suddenly, without fanfare, Elsa took off her dress in front of the window, in the dozing light, dropped it at her feet, and looked at him. A fluffy mound at the base of her abdomen, her breasts with their dark nipples visible under her cotton bra, heavier breasts than the ones he'd sometimes touched after slowly easing his hand under a synthetic dress at the end of a smoky evening. He stepped closer, Elsa took his hand in hers and pressed it first against her breast and then between her legs. Coarse, moist, firm; he let his forefinger linger there, too afraid to pull his hand away, too afraid to move. And then they kissed for the first time.

Now that you've touched me there, you have to marry me, she had said with a smile.

All right, he said, stupidly, besottedly, before he realized that she was teasing him.

Well, maybe not yet, she said laughing. Maybe we should get to know each other a little better.

They had gone out in the wee hours and walked to the seashore and looked at the water, thinking, This is happiness, there could be no greater happiness than this overwhelming feeling, the feeling that it was all you could do to contain yourself within your own boundaries.

He hadn't been sure at all about what was to come, what would happen to him, whether he would get this girl and all the other things he aspired to, but something was coming, and it was the very fact that it was unknown, stubbornly remained hidden, that gave the experience its overwhelming eagerness, that gave him an inexhaustible belief that all his endeavors would succeed, no matter what they were.

It wasn't the only kind of happiness, just one kind. Others came later.

HE THOUGHT ABOUT the shed at Tammilehto, the paintings there. He thought about the one in Rautalampi's back room, left straggling, half-formed, clumsy, forever lacking something, forever failing.

The picture of Elsa he'd made in the past few weeks—should he leave it as it was or should he finish it? All his paintings were silent now. The reality they carried didn't mean anything right now.

He had everything right here. Eleonoora as a child, six years old, maybe younger. Eeva laughing, her hair damp. Eeva after a sauna at Tammilehto in one of those summers. And earlier memories—toys, his mother's face, taking hold of his father's warm hand. A slice of cardamom bread that a vendor at the market square gave him when he was a child. His child's hand reaching out right now toward the warm piece of bread, his father saying, Careful, don't drop it.

Elsa whole and complete.

He looked at the water glass again. There was a faint trace of her lips on it, it was still half-full of water. If he made a move it would all slide into the past, slip into the imperfect tense.

He sits there for another moment holding it all together. Elsa's face, Eleonoor, Eeva, this day. He won't get up yet.

1968

KUHMO, AUGUST. EVERYTHING'S old, ripe, and heavy, like it used to be. I can't help my mother and father with the milking, but my mother ties Assi to a tether in the yard and asks me to brush her. The barn door is open, she shouts orders at the calf, throws a bucket of water down the walkway and starts scrubbing the floor. A familiar sound, a wet rasping. It's existed here for all time. I had just forgotten it for a while. Maybe I've never been anywhere else, maybe I just thought I was. The things that happened in a room high up in a building with a chestnut tree in the yard were someone else's life. It was a dream.

Assi says thank you in the way that cows do, by swinging her tail back and forth.

My mother comes out into the yard. She doesn't say that my strokes are too light, although she thinks it. She chats about all kinds of things, although she knows I won't answer.

She sighs, pats Assi's back. I see her as an old woman. Many decades will go by before she dies. She'll die between white sheets, when her skin has turned thin, but I don't know that.

She leans on her broom, her gaze trailing along the lumpy length of the cow's back, a little low-spirited but still good-natured, as if the broom is a diligently collected but cheap stamp collection whose triviality she has only just noticed. She sighs, slaps Assi's rear end.

"That's that, then. Let's go make some coffee. Your dad's probably done with his chores."

I walk across the yard behind her. The damp grass is flattened under our feet, Riepu twitches on his chain, barking briskly. All this has been here the whole time, but I was gone, believing I was something else, and now it's turned into a museum where my mother and father wander, weary but dutiful attendants. It's a completely different country, where a dew drop condensed on the tip of a blade of grass and we ran to class when the bell rang with our braids slapping in rhythm against our backs, urging us out to take the measure of that world we heard on the radio, a world someplace far from here.

My father is sitting in front of the television, very close to the screen.

"Ahti Karjalainen's gone up to speak now."

"Oh, what about?" my mother asks, but he doesn't answer.

My father looks nervous. The television is still on when we put the evening coffee on the table and cut thick slices of cardamom bread. My mother spreads it with her own butter and pours the coffee. The world is a rectangle flashing in the corner.

Someone with a band tied around her head is saying slogans like a student in an eagerly anticipated school play. We can't hear her, the words don't reach us here, where we sit with the oilcloth and the flowered curtains and the geraniums, because Riepu is barking in the yard, and my father opens the window and yells, "Shut up out there."

My mother says, "Would you still like to take a sauna? You could put some tar and birch branches in the steam water, some marsh tea in the washtub. It might help get rid of your illness, if your voice came back."

I nod.

"Do you want to go by yourself?"

I nod.

"But don't go swimming yet, or you might take a turn for the worse," she says.

I shake my head: no.

EVENING. THE SKY is pink, slanting. I throw the first steam on the stove. The steam wraps around my legs and I'm happy the way I was as a child.

I step down off the high bench and open the door. I walk down the narrow path to the shore.

I think about the bundle I saw on television in the middle of the riot. How peaceful it was. I think about Assi and her calf. I think about the man, who at this moment lifts his eyes from the newspaper and says to Elsa: Well, this is going to change everything. They think they can stifle change by showing up in tanks, but it's already started. Elsa kisses him. If you say so, she says, and there's no sarcasm in her voice, just tenderness.

I think about the little girl, who has already forgotten me, the way a child forgets an old wound. I think about Katariina. She's in Berlin, and at this moment she is laughing with Lies, they're frying eggs for dinner because it's all they have, and thinking about what to do this evening. But I don't know that.

I think about my mother and father and Liisa. And, again, about the little girl, the man, and Elsa, too.

I wade into the water.

It's a beautiful day, my love—in dreams, in words, in death.

Soon the water is up to my knees, then my thighs. Under the surface is silence, the world of the fish, where there is no sound.

Just the words that echo in the little girl's ears years later. They echo in these underwater rooms and in rooms far away, when I'm not here anymore, when I've joined the family of fish.

25

MOM LOOKED SMALL.

What had been in her, her personality or spirit, had taken up a large space, because now she looked like a doll. Eleonoora would have liked to take her in her arms again. She came closer, stroked her hand a little.

She looked at all the familiar features, the mole on her neck, the scar on her arm that she got long ago when she was reaching for a vase on the top cupboard shelf. Eleonoora remembered coming into the kitchen when she heard the crash and the tinkle of glass. Her mother had been standing there, dumbstruck, and laughed at first until she noticed the blood flowing. She'd needed ten stitches.

The scar was still there. A pale line from the wrist to the fold of the elbow.

Eleonoora had often followed the scar with her finger, taken her mother's arm onto her lap and stroked it, thinking how strong her mother was, and yet still fragile. She had realized that even her mother's skin was thin, just like her own, that her mother could easily be broken. And she had made her mother whole again with her caresses. She did it again now, drew her mother back to her with her finger. She was the same, but already a little different.

Slowly, barely touching her, Eleonoora ran her finger from her wrist to her elbow. I'll never do this again, she thought.

She had knit her mother a sweater.

Eleonoora watched Anna and Maria from the side and nodded. They could begin now. Eleonoora would have liked to wash her mother, to dry her feet, scrub her cuticles and spread lavender-scented lotion on her elbows. Her mother had washed her hundreds of times and dried her off with a rough towel. After she dried her off she would wrap her up in a quilt and call it her swuddle. It was their own word, the safest word she knew. Then she would carry Eleonoora across the yard, her skin damp from the sauna as she felt her mother's neck against her cheek. She stopped to listen to the nightingale. It was almost like in a dream, smelling the lavender on her mother's neck.

Or maybe that was Eeva. Maybe it was Eeva, after all.

Anna took the white smock in her arms and stepped closer with an uncertain look. They put the smock on her. For a moment she looked like a child at confirmation.

Next they put on her stockings. Eleonoora got out the sweater. Thin, pale blue angora, with silk ribbons to close it. They carefully lifted her head—it was as heavy as before. They put her arms in the sleeves. Eleonoora was still thinking about the scar. She would never see it again now.

There were still the wool socks to put on. Eleonoora had knit those, too, from the same yarn as the sweater. They were thin, but Mom would be all right. Anna put one on, Maria the other.

"Grandma has little feet," Anna said.

"Yes, she does," Eleonoora said. "She always has."

It felt good to say it like that: she has. When they left here, went home and started to think about the flower arrangements and the cake for the memorial service, they would already be saying: she had. They would say, "Mom liked lemon cake," they'd say, "she liked lilies, but I think she liked roses most of all."

The three of them put the blanket over her, lifted her hands and crossed them. Her ring had been taken off. Had Dad taken it?

There was still a line from the ring pressed into her finger. Dad had seen the same thing. He had taken the ring off and seen the imprint of it.

"Do you want to be alone?" Maria asked.

"No," Eleonoora said. "We can be here together."

They stood quietly and let the time pass. Maria came near her and took her hand. Anna took the other hand.

"Bye, Grandma," Anna said finally. Maria repeated it.

Eleonoora said it, too: "Bye, Mom."

They waited another moment.

"Should we put the lid on now?" Anna asked.

"Yes."

They put the lid on the coffin. It didn't feel bad anymore. Anna and Maria looked at their mother. She was quiet for a moment.

"We can go now," she said finally. "Everything's done."

There was a little wind as they stepped outside. Summer had come. Anna and Maria didn't dare to speak; Eleonoora didn't need to. Maria took her hand again.

Anna asked, "What now?"

"I'm going to go talk to Dad now," Eleonoora said.

26

I'M BOARDING THE tram, riding it across town. I saw Grandma before the coffin was closed, saw her at peace, quiet on the white sheets. I cried a little.

Yesterday Mom didn't look me in the eye—not when Dad came to get us in the car and not when we were drinking tea in the garden after it was all over.

The evening darkened slowly. Pink, lavender, peach.

My dad hugged my mom, I watched them and envied the simplicity of it, the comfort they had always been to each other. Maria hugged her, too, wrapped her arms around her. Mom stroked her back distractedly.

I didn't even try to hug her. She didn't look at me all evening. It felt like I'd ruined everything. I'd ruined it by knowing, by imagining, by bringing her the message.

I spent the night at home, made my old bed in crisply folded sheets that Mom had put through the wringer.

Later that night, when I'd already gone to sleep and woken again, I lay awake, then crept down the stairs and saw her in a corner of the sofa and asked if she was crying and she finally looked at me. I was still in the doorway. I was afraid to come any closer.

"Are you crying about Grandma?"

She slowly turned toward me, and I saw that I couldn't reach her grief.

"I'm crying about my mother," she said.

Then I went to her and hugged her. She didn't try to stop me. I comforted her the way children are comforted. I had the words and the strength for it now, and my arms went around her.

She said she was going to talk to Grandpa. I won't hear what they said, and I don't want to. The things that happen between parents and their children, the accusations and the apologies made perhaps clumsily—no one else can understand them.

My job is to be here, to ride the tram across town. This time I won't pluck anyone's story to take with me, I have other stories to tell.

Eeva stepped into the water, intending to swim, and she did swim, as if she'd always been part of the family of the fish. Grandma was put in a coffin. Mom talked with Grandpa.

I ride across town and get off the tram.

MATIAS IS HOME. He's on his way to play tennis, his racket leaning against the door, his bag packed. He's been eating bread and reading the paper. I see the crumbs on the paper that's lying open on the kitchen table.

"Well?" he says.

He comes and gives me a hug. I let him come. He opens me like this, little by little. Over and over he opens me, even though I thought I had closed myself forever.

———

IT'S A BEAUTIFUL day, my love—a beautiful day in life.

NOW I CAN tell him what I've been keeping to myself all this time.

It all begins at the moment the man walks out the door. It all begins at the moment the child asks, Will we see each other again? and I say I'll see her tomorrow, even though I know it's not true. It all begins when I lie on the floor for eleven days.

I start in a whisper. Once I've started, the words come easily. I haven't told him this story. But I'm telling it now.

Tell me where the trouble comes from.
Tell me what has caused this curse.
Was it a stone? Was it a stump?
A twisted twig in an old stone wall?
Honey bee, our little bird,
Bring us honey, bring us honey,
Six full cups of golden honey,
Far across the seven seas.

. . .

All better?

RIIKKA PULKKINEN studied literature and philosophy at the University of Helsinki. Her debut novel, *Raja* [The Border], sparked international interest when it was published in 2006. Her second novel, *True*, will mark her English-language debut. Riikka Pulkkinen received the Kaarle Prize and the Laila Hirvisaari Prize in 2007.

———

LOLA ROGERS is a freelance translator of Finnish literature living in Seattle. Her published translations include selected poems of Eeva Liisa Manner in the anthology *Female Voices of the North*, published by Praesens of Vienna; the graphic novel *The Sands of Sarasvati*, based on Risto Isomäki's novel of the same name, translated with Owen Witesman for Tammi of Helsinki; and *Purge*, by Sofi Oksanen, for Grove/Atlantic.